Chocolates

for

Breakfast

Also by Pamela Moore

FICTION

Pigeons of St. Mark's Place

The Exile of Suzy-Q

The Horsy Set

Kathy on the Rocks

Chocolates
for Breakfast

PAMELA MOORE

HARPER ● PERENNIAL

NEW YORK ● LONDON ● TORONTO ● SYDNEY ● NEW DELHI ● AUCKLAND

HARPER PERENNIAL

HarperCollins books may be purchased for educational, business, or sales promotional use. For information please e-mail the Special Markets Department at SPsales@harpercollins.com.

First published in hardcover in 1956 by Rinehart and Company.

FIRST HARPER PERENNIAL EDITION PUBLISHED 2013.

Title page art by Carter Kegelman.
Designed by Michael Correy.

Library of Congress Cataloging-in-Publication Data is available upon request.

ISBN 978-0-06-224691-2 (pbk.)

13 14 15 16 17 OV/RRD 10 9 8 7 6 5 4 3 2 1

Foreword

This is the very best kind of story—a tale of imagined sophisti-cation, of New York City apartments, of Hollywood has-beens, of family tragedy, of beatnik intellectuals, of private school crushes, of time traversed through fiction. *Chocolates for Breakfast* is an incredible novel, but the story of how it comes to exist in this form, to be held in your hands, is equally noteworthy. I'll start at the point when the novel entered my world, fifty-plus years after its initial publication in 1956, and then we'll work our way forward and backward as necessary.

A few years ago, a small press crowd-funded a story of mine by promising readers that I would write them a love letter if they bought the story in advance. The love letters were my idea—who doesn't en-joy getting mail, after all?—and I happily wrote hundreds of them. The letters to strangers were the easiest: I just made something up based on their home address, something along the lines of "You are the most beautiful girl in Virginia Beach." Letters to people I knew were more straightforward thank-you notes, with a few exceptions. What does one say, for example, to the very nice French and Latin

teacher from seventh grade, the one with a pack of contraband cigarettes in his shirt pocket and gorgeous wavy hair? I decided to tell
this teacher, whom I refused to call by his first name, exactly how
dreamy he'd always been. When the teacher (fine, fine—Kevin,
I can call him Kevin) showed up at a reading of mine some time
later, I was surprised and flattered. That night he mentioned that
his mother had also been a writer, and did I know that? I didn't. He
gave me a copy of her first novel, *Chocolates for Breakfast*, and I
slipped it into my bag, not thinking too much about it.

The book was written when Kevin's mother, Pamela Moore, was
only eighteen years old. It proudly said so on the cover. And that
she was to be our American answer to Françoise Sagan: sexy and
bold and teenaged! The novel had been out of print for years, and
Kevin had been buying up pulpy paperbacks wherever he could.
The book he gave me had yellowed pages and an illustrated cover.
Kevin hadn't told me anything about his mother, and so I went into
the book blind. All I knew was that the title was electric—what
could be more delicious than chocolates for breakfast?

The novel is catnip—delicious and intoxicating. It opens in a
boarding-school dorm room, with fifteen-year-old Courtney Farrell and her roommate, Janet Parker, lazing around teasing each
other about whether Courtney has gotten too close to her English
tutor, Miss Rosen. We also learn in that first scene about Courtney's family: the girls are just back from vacation, during which
Courtney spent a few days marooned at school because each of her
parents (her publisher father off on an island, her actress mother
off in California) thought the other one was taking care of her.

Written in the kind of voice that an older writer would have
needed a medium to channel, *Chocolates for Breakfast* still feels fresh
and current—Moore's narrative is often hilarious with a soupçon of
melancholy, the exact recipe for a teenage girl of any era. While things

were very different for a teenage girl in the 1950s, some things never change. Her scenes of prep-school boys and grand, empty apartments are precursers to *Gossip Girl*, complete with morning martinis and endless cigarettes. Once Courtney is summoned to Los Angeles to live with her mother, the action moves to the hazy apartments at the Garden of Allah, F. Scott Fitzgerald's former home. Characters are in and out of sanitariums. At sixteen, Courtney loses her virginity to a homosexual actor who can't be bothered even to buy her breakfast. She drinks Cokes at the counter at Schwab's drugstore.

I fell in love with the book immediately. I felt, as I do about only half a dozen other novels on the planet, that it had been delivered to me at precisely the right moment. I was writing a book about a Hollywood star, and in went he Garden of Allah. I grew up on Manhattan's Upper West Side (a far cry across the park from the Upper East Side, the only New York neighborhood that matters in *Chocolates for Breakfast*, but much has changed in the last few decades) and recognized the way my friends and I played at being sophisticated until it became habit, until it became an actual part of our personalities. I quickly passed my copy of the book onto my agent, telling her what I am telling you now: it was a crime for this wonderful book to be out of print. I also told my agent we were going to change that.

What delights me most about *Chocolates for Breakfast* being back in print is the idea of seeing girls—teenage girls, former teenage girls, teenage girls hidden deep inside the bodies of grown-up people of either gender—clutching copies of the book on the subway, rapt. All readers, regardless of gender, will pass it on to each other, having underlined passages of note. (One of my underlined passages is this: "Courtney was like her mother. If she were drowning, she would wave off the rescuers, in a last gesture of defiance, because they were fisherman in a rowboat and she wanted to be saved by a yacht.") I now have a 1964 edition of the book, and the largest blurb on the back calls it "appallingly frank," which I'm not sure is a compliment. Even so, *Chocolates for Breakfast* stands out for being ahead of the curve and for its witty, knife-sharp tone. Readers who love *The Bell Jar, Perks of Being a Wallflower, The Catcher in the Rye,* and *The Dud Avocado* will swoon. The book is as refreshing as a tall glass of vodka and grapefruit juice, like an early morning swim when everyone else is still sleeping off last night's party.

As I mentioned, I read the novel without knowing the whole story, without knowing how Moore's own story ended. There is more material about her in the back of this edition, so I won't include much of it here except to say that Pamela Moore killed herself in 1964, at twenty-six years old, some eight years after this book was published. There are several suicide attempts in the book, and as in *The Bell Jar,* the real-life struggles of its author cast a pall over the proceedings. It's hard to read the novel now and not diagnose Courtney, fearing for Pamela's life, but the book is a novel, and Courtney survives.

I spoke to Kevin recently, both of us giddy with excitement over the book's re-release. We started talking about the wonderful lightning-bolt title, and how no one actually eats chocolate for breakfast in the book. There are eggs, there are Bloody Marys, there are cigarettes and Champagne, but never so much as a pain au chocolat. Kevin said that he thought the word "chocolates" stood in for everything else, for the drinking, the sex, and the perfect teenage misery that would have had the book censored left and right. It sounds like a confection, *Chocolates for Breakfast,* like a treat given to an adolescent on her birthday. Let's hope it is, over and over again, with all of life's complicated magnificence tucked safely inside.

—Emma Straub

1

Spring at Scaisbrooke Hall was clearly the most beautiful time of year. All the alumnae said so as they remembered the apple blossoms in the quadrangle, and the grass growing long and fresh beside the brook, where illegal Cokes were placed to keep them cool for clandestine drinks before the evening study hall. In spring the sweaters that were always too big and the matching blue skirts and the sturdy Oxfords were shipped home, to be replaced by the blue dresses and the saddle shoes of the spring uniform. Scaisbrooke had been founded sixty years ago on the pattern of English public schools, and its high-beamed halls were dark and heavy with tradition. This was the time of year when the students exchanged the winter pallor of studies and indoor basketball for early sun tans, and they looked scrubbed and healthy as they walked about the grounds and laughed in groups in the shadowed courtyards.

The windows of Courtney Farrell's room were opened to the lush Connecticut spring, and her roommate, Janet Parker, was lying with her clothes off in a patch of sun across her bed. Courtney was a slim, dark-haired girl of fifteen, with the pale skin and high coloring of the Irish. Her eyes were almost green, and deepened under the sunlight. They were large, rebellious eyes, with a coldness that a girl of fifteen should not have known. Her face had already lost most of its childish roundness, and as she puzzled over her translation of Caesar her strongly molded chin was thrust forward in characteristic defiance and determination.

The soft afternoon crept in through the window and curled about her on the bed, and she sighed deeply as the season got the better of her studies. Courtney put down the textbook and closed the Latin dictionary. She took a banana from the tin box beside her bed and threw it to Janet, and peeled herself another.

"I feel so relaxed," Courtney said. "I never appreciate school so much as after a vacation."

"I don't appreciate school any time," Janet said. "Especially after a vacation. I really had a ball this spring," she said reflectively. She turned to her roommate. "You had a pretty good vacation too, didn't you? I mean, staying with your mother at the Plaza and all?" She grinned. "Even though the vacation was delayed a couple of days."

"Oh, I didn't mind that," Courtney said with a mouthful of banana. "Mummy was awfully upset, and blamed the whole thing on Daddy—she said she assumed Daddy was coming back from the Virgin Islands in time for my vacation. Of course, Daddy wrote me a long letter saying that he had assumed Mummy knew he still had a week of his vacation to go—you know, all about how he was up to his ears in his publishing work even on vacation, and how he needed the rest. But Mummy wasn't working on any picture, so the studio let her come in from the Coast right away. She was awfully upset that I had to stay at school two days of the vacation, but I didn't mind."

"I don't know what you're complaining about, then. You seemed to be living well when I saw you—the Plaza is certainly an improvement over Scaisbrooke."

"Well," said Courtney, "it's just such a strain. You know, Mummy and I used to be so close, and now we aren't, of course, but I have to pretend we are." She turned suddenly to Janet. "Tell me—why do we have to pretend to the parents?"

"Hell, I don't know. Self-defense, I guess. I know if my father knew that I made out with boys and occasionally got tight and all he'd kill me. I guess that we just get into the habit of pretending so that we don't upset them. I don't know. You ask the damndest questions."

Courtney let the answer suffice and they were quiet again.

"Oh, by the way," Janet broke in, "I forgot to tell you that Miss Rosen came by while you were sun-bathing. She wanted to see you about something."

Courtney looked up, suddenly interested.

"Did she say what it was?"

"I didn't ask her."

Janet threw the banana peel across the room into the wastebasket. She picked up a mirror and began to pluck her eyebrows. Janet was sixteen, spontaneous, gay, attractive if usually too heavily made up, and loathed by women of any age. At Scaisbrooke, where lipstick and fur coats were prohibited, she made a fetish of looking unattractive, in a wrinkled uniform and shoes barely clean enough to pass morning inspection. She had just come from New York and a round of sub-deb parties and night clubs, however, and she plucked her eyebrows by inadvertence.

"I don't dig this *thing* that you two have," she went on. "You know, I was up in Alberts and Clarke's room before lunch, and they were talking about you and Miss Rosen. I've been meaning

3

to talk to you for a long time about her. I've gotta stretch first, though. Arm yourself with another banana or something."

Courtney looked over at her roommate as she stretched languorously in the spring sun, wrapping her arms around the pillow behind her, twisting her legs and contracting and releasing her body, deriving a relaxation that only the very young can get from such a simple action. She had a lovely young woman's body, athletic and lightly tanned around the bathing-suit marks.

"Put a cover over yourself or something," Courtney said.

Janet grinned. "What's the matter, do I get you oversexed?"

"All right, all right. Go ahead and talk."

"Well, granted everybody in these psycho boarding schools has a crush on some older girl or staff member. It's a kind of idolizing, okay. But you've gone overboard, so that you've cut yourself off from the rest of the girls and bound most of your life here up in Miss Rosen. The girls resent it, you know. They feel that you're snubbing them."

"I am."

"But, sweetie, if you were like me and had men and social life separate from school, it would be okay. But all you have is your mother and her friends. You ought to try to make a life here, because whether you admit it to yourself or not, offices and all that crap and acceptance by the clique mean a lot to you, because you haven't anything outside of school. I know that you want to be editor of the *Lit Review*, and you ought to be because you can write circles around everybody here. But you know that offices aren't awarded by merit. They're kind of badges of social approval. So you ought to admit to yourself that you want to be accepted and stop escaping into this relationship with Miss Rosen. If you don't watch out, sweetie, you're going to find yourself kind of queer. Alberts says that you're in love with Rosen."

4

"What business is this of theirs, anyway? Sure, she has even told me that she loves me, but she loves all her friends. I mean, she uses the word in the Biblical sense."

"Oh, sweetie, don't pay any attention to this social-worker crap that she picked up in the University of Chicago. From all you've told me, she sounds queer as hell to me. All this bit about you going over there every night to talk about literature or something."

"What do you think we do!"

"You don't need to get so mad. I don't think you make love or anything. I don't even think you know how."

"You're making something grubby out of this." Courtney lay back and put her arms around her head. "She's a tutor. She knows that the English bores the hell out of me, so she gives me books like *Finnegan's Wake* and T. S. Eliot poetry and stimulating reading that I don't get ordinarily, and in the evenings we discuss them in a kind of a bull-session, that's all."

"She's more than an English teacher, and you know it. I've never seen such a change as what's happened to you this year. In the beginning of the year you were moody and selfish and bitchy once in a while like everybody else, but now you've got some idea that you've got to be the modern saint, and love the masses and all that University of Chicago crap that she's filled you with. You've become all drawn into yourself so you don't get mad any more, but bury it somewhere, and you've become critical and superior as hell. You know, you're not like that, and you can't possibly escape into her world, absorb her nature. You are two entirely different people, from different social and intellectual backgrounds."

"Oh, dammit, Parker, you don't understand at all. I didn't like myself, do you get that? And then I met this new teacher, who had a kind of calmness and seemed to like herself, and I had never known many people like that. So one day at lunch we got to talking about some book, and she offered to lend me another book that she figured I'd like. So we talked about that book then, and I got to know her, and I started to talk to her about some things in my own life, because she had a good mind and I could somehow talk to her."

"Look, Court, you don't need to get so belligerent. I'm only trying to help you because I am a year older than you, even though we're in the same class, and I can see that you're throwing away your life here, to invest it in this escape. That's all it is. Remember, there are a couple of things I've learned in a year that you don't know."

Courtney took an orange from the box and threw it across the room. It splattered on the wall with a very satisfying effect.

"Court," said Janet patiently, "sometimes I remember that you're only fifteen. That was my orange, too."

"Here we go with the Mama Parker routine. I'm going for a walk. Save me a seat at dinner."

Janet sighed and resumed plucking her eyebrows.

In the hall, Courtney passed the headmistress.

"Hello, Farrell."

"Hello, Mrs. Reese."

"I heard that you got another conduct for having an unpermissioned book," she remarked.

"Yes, Mrs. Reese. It was a James Joyce book, *Finnegan's Wake*, and I assumed that Joyce was on the list of permissioned authors, so I didn't bother to get it okayed by anyone."

"You can't assume," she said coldly, "you should know."

"I realize that, Mrs. Reese." How she hated to be polite and prostrate herself before staff members! "I realize that I was wrong."

"Well, you'll be more careful next time," she said more warmly. Self-abnegation always made staff members warmer. "For a bright girl, Farrell, you get too many penalties. I had hoped that you would help straighten out your roommate this year, but instead the two of you get into trouble."

"Yes, Mrs. Reese."

With relief Courtney walked out to the quadrangle, and as soon as she was outside she began to run because she was fifteen and it was a wonderful spring day. She ran across the hockey field and jumped across the little brook on the far side, where hockey balls always landed. As she cleared the brook, she fell into the long grass from her effort, and she laughed at herself and got up. She ran up the little hill onto the cinder track that skirted the tennis courts, the track that she ran around before breakfast as a part of hockey training. When she got to the second hockey field she stopped, because that was as far as she could go without entering Mrs. Reese's grounds, which were out of bounds except for seniors when they went to her house for tea. She was out of breath and she fell on the grass, which had just been cut and smelled very fresh and young. Grass smelled hot and wet in the summer, but in the spring it smelled properly young, which was a relief from the old and dead smell of Scaisbrooke's corridors.

She turned on her back and smiled at herself and looked up at the sky. The sky was terribly vast. In the summer she sometimes floated on her back in the Pacific and tried to convince herself that the sky was really shapeless and she was on the edge of a round world. The *Rubaiyat* said that it was a "great inverted bowl," and secretly she agreed with it. Scientists try awfully hard, she mused, to convince us that things which are obviously so really aren't, and try to convince us of the minuteness of marvelously big things like the sky and mountains by breaking them down into little atoms. She had never seen an atom and never wanted to, because the idea of mountains and people being just different arrangements of things of the same shape was disagreeable to her.

The sound of the warning bell for dinner carried very softly across the hockey fields and interrupted her thoughts. She had to hurry because she had to change into her dinner uniform and there was a penalty for every minute of lateness.

All through dinner Courtney looked forward to seeing Miss Rosen. Courtney always felt comfortable and secure when she was in Miss Rosen's room, and it was a nice walk through the courtyards to get to the faculty house. After she passed through the two courtyards she went along a walk beside the chapel, a walk that was flanked by tall trees in spring green and some which had blossoms on them. The evening was early yet, and the chapel was silhouetted against the light sky. Sometimes she would go into the chapel, and though she was Catholic and it held little religious significance for her, it was a quiet and shadowy place where she could think, and pretend that she was in Hollywood.

But tonight she passed the chapel, because she was looking forward to talking to Miss Rosen. Under her arm was the copy of *Finnegan's Wake*, which she really didn't understand although she puzzled over every abstruse paragraph, and whose possession had cost her three hours' work and two weeks of being campused. She climbed the dingy stairs and at the top of the second flight turned left. The door was a little open, and she could hear that Miss Rosen had her Bach records on. Somehow Bach was always playing in her room, and the solidity and sureness of his music was as closely connected in her mind with Miss Rosen as her shelves of wonderful books. Years later, when Courtney heard that music, the picture of that room and the warm feeling that she had when she was in it would come back as strongly as though she were again climbing those stairs which she knew so well.

Miss Rosen was a tall woman in her early twenties, short-waisted and somewhat round-shouldered. Her eyes were large and brown and intense. She was not an attractive woman, yet she had an intensity and a warmth which caused people to overlook the defects in her face and body when they had spent a few minutes with her. She was engaged to a scholarly young man whom she had met at the University of Chicago and who was now an instructor in philosophy at Harvard.

She smiled when Courtney came in, and motioned to a chair. Courtney sat down and took off her blazer while Miss Rosen made a notation on an English paper that she was correcting. She put the paper down on her cluttered desk.

"How are you coming with James Joyce?" she asked pleasantly.

"Not awfully well," Courtney confessed. "What is he trying to say with all this stream-of-consciousness gibberish?"

Miss Rosen picked up the book from the table beside Courtney and thumbed through the pages Courtney had been reading.

"What he is talking about in *Finnegan's Wake*," explained the English teacher in her precise, analytical manner, "is the eternal conflict between parents and children. He presents the parent as the figure who must be conquered if the child is to gain independence and identity."

"How simply and clearly she puts it," Courtney thought as Miss Rosen went on, quoting from the book and analyzing the selections to prove her thesis, "when the subject is so terribly complex. Teachers are a little like scientists in their way of breaking down the magnificent vastness of life into small particles that can be analyzed, and thereby robbing it of its emotion." She remembered the scene when her mother had said she could not spend that weekend with her father because she had too much schoolwork to do.

"You're trying to possess me," Courtney had accused her over the long-distance telephone. "You know that I have to have your permission for school because you're listed as my guardian. You don't want to give it to me, you want me to stay at school when I have a free weekend, because you're so afraid that I might find one of these days that I really like Daddy."

"Now Courtney, don't be unreasonable. Your father is a very fine man and I should hope that you like him. You just wrote me that you have a term paper due next Monday and you didn't see how you could get it in in time, and now you call me to see if you can spend the weekend in New York."

"I'll get the paper in late. It's all right, because I have an A in medieval history anyway, and it won't make so much difference. I don't want to stay here when I have a free weekend. You're trying to possess me, that's all, and you're using the paper as an excuse."

"I couldn't want less to possess you, and you're always accusing me of it. My life would be a great deal simpler if I didn't have you to worry about and take care of," she said angrily. "I could run it the way I want to. I'd still be married to Nick now if it weren't for you. I had to choose between my second husband and my child, so of course I chose you. You bitch up my life because I have a sense of responsibility for you, and now you accuse me of wanting to possess you. Go ahead and stay with your father, spend your life with him for all I care!"

Courtney had thanked her mother and hung up before she could change her mind.

"He outlines the overthrowing of the parent by the child who has come of age," Miss Rosen was saying.

Courtney thought of Janet's father when they had double dated with a beau of Janet's and his roommate at Andover. Janet went out with the boy a great deal, and his roommate had driven them back from Jones Beach with Courtney in the front seat so that his roommate and Janet could "make out" in the back seat. When they went into Janet's apartment on Park Avenue, her father had been sitting with a glass of Irish whiskey and had seen that Janet's lipstick was smeared, and had been terribly rude to the boy, saying to him, "I suppose you have been *necking* with my daughter all the way back from Jones Beach!" Of course he had, but Mr. Parker made everyone feel so embarrassed that they left very soon and went to the Plaza instead. Janet apologized for her father. "Daddy was a little bombed," she laughed, "and he always thinks that I'm being led into dissipation or something." Janet even necked with boys that she did not like, and her father knew it and always blew up at her, cutting her allowance whenever she was even a little late.

"He completes the cycle," Miss Rosen continued, "by showing how the child of that child will overthrow him in turn, in a primitive ritual which civilization has only disguised but not altered."

"The cycle?" Courtney said stupidly.

"You haven't been listening," Miss Rosen chided. "You remember how I showed you that the very last sentence in the book is the beginning of the very first sentence, how they run together?"

Courtney nodded.

"Well, his book runs around in a circle, so to speak, because he is using even the form of the novel to indicate the parent-child-parent cycle of successive revolutions."

"I guess I see now, but I certainly never would have by myself. Gee, I have a pretty good vocabulary, but every fifth word is something I've never even heard of."

"He invents a lot of words, like the famous sound of the thunder, and he also uses words in German, Gaelic and God knows what all."

She smiled and handed the book back to Courtney.

"Try the next ten pages for tomorrow, and if you get discouraged, I have a *Key to Finnegan's Wake* that you can borrow. It explains some of the references. I'd rather that you tried to get something out of it yourself, though."

She got up and turned the stack of records over in the victrola, and then sat down and lit a cigarette.

"I haven't had a chance to talk to you since spring vacation," Miss Rosen said. "How did you and your mother get along?"

"We got on fairly well," Courtney said. For a moment she resented the presumed familiarity of the older woman's question. She always withdrew instinctively when she sensed that someone had slipped through her defenses. But then she remembered that Miss Rosen was a friend. "We always do." She was still guarded. Both Miss Rosen and she knew that this was not true, but Miss Rosen waited patiently for the familiar flow of words from the girl, for when they were alone she spoke freely as she had never been able to speak to a woman. Courtney was a girl who had a whole string of what she termed "adopted fathers," usually friends of her mother, to whom she told the worries and fears that a child can never relate to her own parents. Miss Rosen was the first woman whom she had trusted since she lost confidence in her mother at the age of six.

"We can't communicate, that's all. She doesn't know me very well, and she knows me less every time she sees me on a vacation. I'd talk to her if I could," she went on, "but you know, you can't talk to women. Their minds don't run straight the way even yours does; I try to talk about something and prove a point and their minds have skittered off to some minor but vaguely related subject. Drives me crazy."

"Don't you think of yourself as a woman?" Miss Rosen said, amused.

"No, not really," Courtney said thoughtfully. "I don't think the way they do. Men always tell me that I think like a man. It would be a lot simpler if I were a man. I guess. But maybe it wouldn't be. I probably would still dislike women, and it would be an awful mess to be a faggot."

Miss Rosen laughed at her simplicity. "Would you really like to be a man?"

"Well, you know, since I can remember I've dreamt that I am a man. I hardly even notice now that in all my dreams I'm myself, but a man. I wonder why that is," she mused.

"You said that your parents always wished you were a boy, and that your mother has you make drinks for her and take care of her the way a son would. Perhaps that's why."

"Perhaps." She thought about that for a moment, but not long, because it wasn't very important for her.

"You know," she went on, "Mummy was awfully upset about my vacation being screwed up."

"Don't use that expression," Miss Rosen said.

"Why not? I have used it since I was a little girl. What's wrong with it?"

Miss Rosen did not pursue the matter further, but instead said, "You're always a little hostile and defensive after you have been with your mother."

"She's a bitch," Courtney blurted out.

"You know you don't mean that," Miss Rosen said gently.

"I know," she answered petulantly.

"Then why did you say it?"

"I wanted to."

"You're too intelligent to talk like a little girl."

"Dammit, I *am* a little girl," Courtney said suddenly. "And that's what I hate about being with Mummy. It's as though *I'm* the mother. I have to soothe her when she's npset about having blown up at me, and I have to reassure her that she's a good actress—you know, I've only seen four of her movies in my whole life, it's enough to live with the parts—I wouldn't know if she's any good or not, but I tell her she is because I like to make people feel good. And I have to hold her hand when Nick periodically leaves her—or *did* leave her," she said remembering, "and I have to fix her lousy drinks because she doesn't like to feel she's drinking alone, and all that. I'm *awfully* sick of it!"

"Now, although I've never met your mother," Miss Rosen said, "I know that she's a very immature woman, but you have to put up with that and try to help her. She's also a very lonely woman, and you're really all that she's got—particularly now that she's divorced again."

"You're so damned holy," Courtney said bitterly. "I mean, you're just like my father. You say all these things and it's easy for you because you don't have to live them. This is all a lot of crap."

Miss Rosen flinched. She got up and put her hand on Courtney's shoulder.

"You don't have to talk that way with me," the woman said gently. "You can relax when you're here. You don't need to strike out in self-defense, through a fear of getting close to me."

Courtney stared moodily ahead. She knew that if she looked up at Miss Rosen while that hand was on her shoulder, she would get that funny feeling that she sometimes had when she was taking a bath or about to put on her pajamas, as though a whole crowd of people were looking at her body.

"You told me once," she said searching, "that you loved me."

Miss Rosen took her hand away and sat on the bed facing Courtney.

"Yes, you poor child, I do. Why do you ask me again—don't you believe that anyone can love you?"

"Not unless they want something from me."

She saw the expression on Miss Rosen's face and said, "Yes, honestly, that's the way I feel. And don't call me a 'poor child'! I'm not to be pitied, not by anyone. Nobody needs to feel sorry for me, because I can take care of myself, and I always have. I don't even need anyone to love me, because people don't mean that much to me. I'm a cold person, and kind of selfish."

Miss Rosen sighed. "No you're not. Haven't I taught you *anything*? I don't know who or what gave you that idea, but you're a very warm, impulsive girl, with the potential to be a fine woman if you give yourself a chance to love and to be a mature person."

Courtney looked up at Miss Rosen, the defiance gone for the moment from her face, so that she looked almost like a child.

"Maybe I can be all that if you help me. When I'm here I feel that you have something I can hold on to. Since I've been with you I've seen that people can tell other people that they love them, and trust other people, without being afraid of being rebuffed or taken advantage of."

Miss Rosen lit another cigarette from the one she was smoking because she did not like to say what she knew she eventually must say.

"Mummy said I was like a different person when I came to

15

Hollywood last Christmas," she said proudly. "She said I was like somebody she didn't know. I wasn't so afraid of her, and I didn't jump so much when she called my name. You did that for me," she said, trying to draw a response from the older woman.

"You know, Courtney," she said painfully, "I did have something I wanted to say to you. After all that you've been saying it's going to be very difficult for me, because I do love you, but I feel it's for your own good. Would you like a cigarette?"

"No, thank you, I don't smoke. Gee, it must be something grim," she smiled. "Staff members only offer cigarettes to girls who have tried to commit suicide, or whose engagements have been broken or something."

The girl was trying to be flippant because she sensed that what Miss Rosen had to say would hurt her.

"I enjoy your coming over here very much. I like to talk to you, because you have a good mind and I'm very fond of you."

Oh God, thought Courtney, don't say what I am afraid you are about to say.

"But you know, you should spend more time with people your own age. There is a lot that you can learn from them, and there are girls here with fine minds who have read quite as much as you have."

"I'm bored with people my own age," she said desperately. "I've always grown up with Mummy's friends, and I find it easier to talk to them. I find older people more interesting." She searched the woman's face for understanding. "You know that."

"That's just the point," Miss Rosen said. "You've never learned to get along with your contemporaries, and Scaisbrooke gives you a fine chance to learn. That's a more important lesson than you'll ever get from me."

Courtney stood up. She felt the way she had when she learned, through the *New York Times*, of her mother's marriage to Nick Russell in Hollywood. Courtney had the same half-comprehending feeling now, a vague realization that she was losing someone whom she loved.

"You mean that you don't want me to come over here in the evenings any more, and that you don't want me to sit at your table or talk to you after class."

"Yes, that's what I mean," the woman said helplessly.

"Then why don't you say it? I can take it." She threw the copy of *Finnegan's Wake* on the bed. "I guess I'd better return this," she said, and turned to walk out.

Miss Rosen stood up.

"Courtney . . ."

Courtney stopped and turned back suddenly by the door. Perhaps she had changed her mind. Miss Rosen walked over to her and looked down at the girl with a sadness in her eyes. She leaned down and kissed Courtney on the forehead.

"Please don't be angry with me," she said. "I had no choice." Courtney was never to understand what Miss Rosen meant.

Courtney did not know yet how much she had lost, she only felt the pain of her loss and a numb sense that somehow her life would be different now. She ran past the chapel and through the courtyards because she had started to cry and she never liked anyone to see her cry. When she got to the main building she stopped and rubbed her face dry on the sleeve of her blazer, and she smiled to a committeeman on the stairs although she did not trust herself to speak.

Janet saw that Courtney did not want to talk, and so she wrote letters and did not intrude upon her roommate's privacy. After lights out she heard Courtney crying into her pillow. For half an hour she lay in the darkness and listened, and then she reached over and turned a light on.

"It's after lights out," her roommate murmured.

"The hell with that," Janet answered. "I'd offer you one of my illegal cigarettes but I know you don't smoke. But I have another illegal commodity that is exactly what you need."

She got out of bed and picked up her silver perfume bottle.

"This has escaped every committee inspection," she said proudly, and handed Courtney the perfume bottle that was filled with a very excellent Scotch.

"Goddammit, Farrell, you drink every drop, and appreciate it. There's just about a shot in there. I don't care if you don't like Scotch," she said in the harsh tones reserved for a roommate's tenderness, "I plan to get some sleep tonight, and this will calm you down. You can tell me in the morning what that bitch said to you." She turned off the light and rolled over.

2

There was only one light on in Courtney's room, because Janet was studying her history and Courtney was doing nothing, only lying on her bed and looking up at the ceiling where a whimsical predecessor had painted black footprints leading to the door. Janet was playing her records of Stan Kenton, which Courtney did not like very much, but she was too lethargic to protest as the moody dissonance filled the room. It was raining, a cold spring rain that was very depressing after the week of fine weather. Janet was smoking a cigarette which she held in the hollow that her knees made under the comforter. When she took a drag she would lift up the comforter and blow the smoke in with her legs. After lights out she would fumigate her bed before she went to sleep, but it was too dangerous to have smoke in the room when committeemen were prowling about.

It seemed strange to Courtney to have so much time to herself, now that she could not see Miss Rosen any more. Kenton took a riff and Courtney jumped at the sudden and strange volume. Crazy music, so intensely personal and almost neurotic. Bizet was so agreeable and gregarious. He was nicer to listen to but tonight Kenton's music seemed to fit in with the lonely rain and the rolling bursts of sudden thunder. It had been a week since Courtney was condemned to this solitude. She often lay in her room now and looked up at the ceiling. She felt that it was even too much of an effort to go outdoors, and Courtney loved the outdoors.

"Take a drag," Janet commanded her.

"I don't want to. I don't know how to smoke."

"You've gotta learn sometime, and you might as well learn *well.*"

Courtney didn't bother to protest.

"Jesus, you don't hold a cigarette like a pencil. Look."

"That's better. Now when you take a drag, inhale *beyond* the point where it catches in your throat."

Courtney tried and coughed like any neophyte.

"I said inhale *beyond* the point where it hurts. Otherwise you'll cough like an idiot. Pretend it's air."

Courtney steeled herself and this time it was all right.

"*That's* it," Janet said with pleasure. "I'll teach you to look sophisticated yet."

Courtney handed Janet back the cigarette and Janet waved away the smoke. She put on another Kenton record, "Abstraction," and then she went back to her history. Within a few pages the medieval history had bored her again and she looked resentfully at Courtney.

"Haven't you got any studying to do?"

"Sure," Courtney answered unconcernedly. "But I don't feel like doing it. I can bull through French class and I've done my Latin—those are the only two that I worry about."

"Going to hell fast, sweetie."

"I feel kind of lazy. . . . It's a lousy night and it's been a lousy week and I don't want to do anything but lie here and pretend I'm out of this hellhole."

"You're going to get a jolt when finals come around."

"What the hell."

"Oh, cut this crap with me," Janet said angrily. "Stop feeling sorry for yourself and damning the world because you got hurt. I won't put up with moods like this. Shape up, sweetie."

"That's easy for you to say," Courtney answered gloomily.

"Look, Court, do you think you're the first person who's ever been cut out of something that meant a lot to her? Do you think you're unique or something?"

"No. No, I guess not. I'm sorry, Jan, I really am. I've been a bitch, I know."

"Now don't start talking to me as though I were a staff member or something. This self-abnegation bit is no good, either. We've gotta shape up Courtney, that's all. I think we'll begin with studying. You're still in this lousy place for another three weeks, you know, whether you want to be or not."

"You sound like a parent."

"What's the matter, haven't you got anything to live for but that Miss Rosen?"

Janet had struck on a vulnerable point.

"Sure, I've got a lot to live for. I've got myself, and that's the most worth living for. I don't die when somebody leaves me. I go on."

"You talk all right but you live like a coward."

"What the hell are you trying to do to me? Make me mad at you?"

"Yes, I'm trying to make you mad enough to come back to life."

"Okay, go on. What do you mean, 'come back to life'?" Courtney said soberly.

"I mean do your schoolwork, for one thing. No one is a bigger goof-off than I am, but there are some things that have to be done. And make some sort of effort to talk to people. You can't talk to Miss Rosen any more, so talk to other people. Alberts and Clarke, for example. They're all right, really they are. *I* enjoy talking to them. You've cut yourself off and that would be all right if you were happy that way, but you're not."

"Okay, I'll try. I'll go up there tomorrow afternoon. But are you sure that they want to talk to me?"

"Of course, sweetie. They like you, I know that they do because we've talked about you. They would have been good friends of yours if you had given them half a chance, if you hadn't run to Miss Rosen instead."

"Okay, I'll do that, then. Because I'd really like to."

"Maybe this will be a good thing for you, this Miss Rosen thing. That was the kind of un-Regsman behavior that kept you out of the clique, you know. Everyone's got to be regular and conform. Maybe if you let these kids know that you'd really like them for friends, you'd have a chance to be editor of the *Lit* next year."

"I don't have much chance for that. Mlle. de Labry is the faculty advisor and has to pass on the editor, and she hates my guts ever since she was trying to pump me on some gossip column bit about Mummy and Nick's divorce, and I told her to go to hell. In those words," she mused. "I'm amazed she didn't give me a conduct for disrespect."

"If the board really wanted you, you could get on. She couldn't veto it if you really got a good vote."

"Oh, that cruddy publication is only a mechanism of social approval."

"Sour grapes."

"I know. I'd love to get on. Do you really think I could?"

"I don't know the criteria for social success in the clique that runs this school," Janet said. "But becoming friendly with Alberts and Clarke would help. You know, they're great buddies of Fairchild, and since she's this year's editor she has a lot to say about next year's."

"Actually I'd love to get in with that group because there are a lot of kids in it that I like. But I'm not used to talking to people my own age much."

"I know, you never even see any boys. That's too bad, because if you did this Miss Rosen wouldn't mean so much to you."

"Maybe."

"Tell me," Janet said, "has a boy ever really kissed you?"

Courtney grinned.

"This New Year's Eve, at that party they gave for Mummy, this crazy actor kissed me. Really kissed me. He was kind of tight."

Janet laughed. "What do you mean, 'really kissed you'?"

"You know, with the tongue and all that bit. I really flipped."

"Sweetie, that's great!" Janet grinned. "Your first French kiss. Oh, that's really funny. I mean, I can see you flip."

"He was this male-lead type, and he was really drunk out of his head." Courtney was beginning to enjoy herself as she talked about it.

"Has anybody ever made a pass at you?"

"Oh, you know, all the remarks about the beautiful young body and the Hollywood greeting of an embrace."

"What do you do?"

"I just kind of stand there."

"With your arms hanging down?"

"Well, yes."

"Oh, Court, you've got a lot to learn. You put your arms around a man's neck because then your bodies kind of fit together. Otherwise you're like a stick of wood, and it's not comfortable and natural."

"I always did feel kind of awkward."

"Well, sure. But you'll learn."

"Do you really know a lot about sex, Jan?"

"I'm still a virgin, if that's what you mean—rumor to the contrary."

"But have you ever really made out?"

"When you say 'really,' I never know what you mean. I've slept with boys when neither of us had any clothes on, if that's what you mean."

"Honestly? But doesn't that—"

"Doesn't that bother me? Court, everybody does. I mean, all the girls I know. It doesn't mean much, and it's nice. I kind of enjoy it," she mused, "going to sleep with a boy's arms around me."

"But when do you get a chance to do that?"

"Oh, on weekends at prep schools and colleges, and in New York when the parents are out of somebody's apartment for a while. You've missed a lot by being brought up in Scarsdale. You don't even drink, and you're fifteen. Most of the girls I know and certainly the boys start to drink a little bit when they're thirteen."

"Mummy lets me have Daiquiris. And a couple of times I've had as many as four when she's been a little bombed and hasn't realized it. I've drunk Daiquiris since I was fourteen."

"Yes, but how long ago was that—November, only."

"I'm not so out of it. I know pretty much about sex and what goes into it and bodies and all, and I even know about homosexuality so I can recognize it in actors a lot of times, and I know how they make love."

"Really? How?"

"Well, you see, one of them—oh, hell, sweetie, I don't like to talk about things like this. I wondered and I asked Mummy one time when she and Nick had been talking about some actor and another actor, and Nick said, 'You tell her,' and Mummy did."

"Oh, I don't mean to say that you're naive or anything. I just think you ought to make out with boys a little."

"But prep school boys are so grubby. They have bad skin, and they press your hand and their palms are all wet, and they are so *awkward!* I mean, I like these actors who are so charming and put their arms around you with a Martini in one hand and all that. I like men who are older."

"Yes, but here you go again. They're not for you; there's no future in *that*. I mean, none of them has ever kissed you or anything."

"No, of course not, because I'm still a kid. But they will, when I get older. I'll have some older man teach me all these things, just as you said about smoking, because they'll teach me to be smooth the way they are. I don't want to find out by trial and error with some awkward prep school boy what is the lovely way to put my arms around a boy. That's grubby. I want to be charming, to live in a charming way and to love in a lovely way."

The lights-out bell rang in the pause and they listened to it and it rang twice. They had not heard the warning ten minutes before, and now the committeeman would come around to see that they were in bed and that their polo coats and galoshes were at the foot of their beds, in case of a fire. You got a penalty if you weren't ready. The polo coat was to put over your pajamas and the galoshes were to stamp out ashes or something like that. At any rate it had worked very well when Scaisbrooke had the big fire in 1923. Courtney and Janet were always late for lights out, so they had a system worked out. Courtney tumbled out of bed and threw out Janet's polo coat and galoshes from the closet and Janet arranged them at the foot of Courtney's bed. Then Courtney ran to the other closet and threw out her own, and Janet jumped onto Courtney's bed and arranged them while Courtney ran around the beds and turned out the light. Then they both rolled into their own beds laughing, and pulled the covers over themselves to hide the fact that they had not changed into their pajamas yet. The entire operation had taken less than a minute.

The next day couldn't make up its mind between rain and clear weather, but the two athletic periods had been held outdoors. Sue Alberts and Brookie Clarke were both on the Junior hockey team of which Courtney was a member, so they all had first-period athletics together. As the other two girls put their pinnies in the basket after the practice, Courtney lingered on the pretext that she had to be sure all the pinnies were in, because she had been on the non-pinnie scrub team. As they walked back to the main building Sue announced that she was going to get a piece of cake in the tearoom, but Brooks Clarke, a lovely, tall girl with lank blonde hair and a little Boston in her speech, had reminded the slightly plump Sue that she was on a diet, so they had passed the tearoom by. Courtney hung with them and the other girls were hardly aware of her presence, although Courtney was going through agonies of unsureness and watching them closely to see if they resented her presence. They had all climbed the stairs, hot from their two hours of hockey, and gone into Alberts and Clarke's room.

Their room was antiseptically neat, unlike Courtney and Janet's with its casual disorder. It looked as though they were expecting inspection any minute. But then, Alberts and Clarke wanted the ten-bar honor of having served ten months on the committee, and they wanted to hold the important offices and be esteemed by the faculty. By this, their fourth-form year, they were both on the *Lit Review* and had been on the committee for one term. By their senior years, the personable and popular Brookie was to be head-committeeman and editor of the *Lit*, while her roommate was business manager and a committee member, controlling the school through her influence over Brookie and her in with the faculty. They were to carry their successful combination into Vassar as well, and were always well liked. Janet was right that they would make powerful friends.

"Want an orange, Court?" Brookie asked pleasantly.

"Oh, thanks."

"Split one with you, Brookie," said Sue. Courtney noticed that they were splitting an orange while they offered her a whole one, as a guest and an outsider.

"Gee, we haven't seen much of you lately," Brookie said, trying to put Courtney at her ease.

"I've been doing a lot of studying," Courtney lied.

"Oh, that's right, you're a brain," Sue said.

Courtney didn't answer and Brookie said hastily, "How was your spring vacation—did you go to Hollywood?"

"No, I stayed in New York."

"If *I* lived in Hollywood," said Sue wistfully, "you'd never get me out of there. Tell me, what's it like?"

"Oh, it's all right. There are a lot of parties and there's a lot of drinking and all that, and people work terribly hard for spurts of time."

"I'll bet there are a lot of stars sleeping with their directors, and a lot of fairies and all that."

"No, not really. Not any more than on Broadway and not many more than in a business like writing or art," she said. She hated people to make statements like that, but she didn't let Sue know it.

"I'll bet you know a lot of gossip," Brookie said.

"I guess so."

"Tell us about people like Gregory Peck and Tyrone Power and Susan Hayward and all," she said. "What are they really like?"

"I don't really know those people very well. I'm not out in Hollywood much. Mummy knows them, and she likes them."

"That isn't what we mean," said Brookie. "We mean, what are they like to talk to and do they drink a lot or throw temperament or anything, and is there any gossip you know about them?"

"In the first place I don't know, because my mother talks about their ability and their work and things like that, and in the second place even if I did know I wouldn't mutter cheap gossip about them."

The two girls were silent, and Courtney saw that she had not started out very well.

"You needn't get so superior," Sue said.

"Well, anyhow . . ." Brookie said.

"Hey, it's four o'clock, and I've got to wash my hair before study hall," Sue said.

"You're lucky to be on the honor roll so you can study in your room," Brookie said weakly to Courtney.

"I've . . . I'm sorry I can't stay," said Courtney, "but I've got a lot of studying and I'd better get at it."

"Come up more often," said Brooks. It was a remark that is never made to a friend.

"Yes, don't hide in that room of yours so much studying," Sue said.

"Thanks for the orange," Courtney said, and left.

When she got to her own room she flopped on the bed.

"Did you see Alberts and Clarke the way I suggested?"

"Yes, I saw them."

"How did it go?"

"It was a fiasco!" Courtney laughed at herself. "The first thing they did was ask me about all this crappy gossip, and I blew up the way I always do when people ask me that. And then I left. They gave me an orange."

Janet sighed. "Have a banana."

"Janet, sweetie, you're an idiot."

They laughed and split a banana and when Janet left for study hall, Courtney stared at the ceiling again and fell asleep, although she wasn't tired.

D r. Reismann's office was heavy and pine-paneled, and its manliness made Courtney immediately comfortable. The idea that she was there to talk about herself pleased her, despite the fact that Mrs. Forrest had insisted on being present. House-mothers were so zealous in their intrusion of their students' privacy. The doctor, a short and scholarly-looking German, who, Sondra Farrell had told Mrs. Forrest, was one of the best diagnosticians in the New York area, leaned back in his upholstered chair and looked at Courtney.

"Well, Courtney, you are a very healthy young woman. I can find nothing wrong with you but a very slight anemia, which is common at your age. Let me see, you're fifteen, aren't you?"

"Yes. You mean that you don't know why I'm tired all the time, either?"

"There is nothing physically wrong with you. Tell me, you're on the hockey team at Scaisbrooke, aren't you?"

"Yes, I'm on the junior team."

"You must have to train a great deal. Does that tire you?"

"No more than it tires the other girls. I'm most tired in the mornings when I wake up."

"How much sleep do you get?"

"About ten hours a night."

"I see. What do you do right after you wake up?"

"I make my bed and straighten the room for inspection, then I have breakfast, then we have to walk around the quadrangle after breakfast, then we have inspection of our uniforms, then we go to chapel, then there are about ten minutes before the first class."

"You're busy in the mornings."

"Mmm-hmm." This was dull. "I get awfully tired in the afternoons, when we have some free time," she added.

The doctor was looking over his sheet of paper.

"Your parents are divorced," he commented.

"Yes, when I was about ten," she said. This was more interesting.

"Do you see much of them?"

"Of Mummy, yes."

He was making notations so steadily that Courtney hardly noticed.

"Being so far away from your mother," he said, "I suppose you get homesick—think about California."

"No," Courtney answered. "I'm never homesick." She looked out the window. "I daydream a lot though," she said. "When it's nice weather like now, I go out to the hockey field and lie in the grass and daydream, and in the evenings I used to go into the chapel." She leaned forward. "You know, in a corner of the quadrangle there's a big rabbit's burrow. Used by whole generations of rabbits, I suppose. Anyhow, it's very big and I can fit in there under the brush, and it's as though there's no one around but me in that rabbit's burrow, as though the school buildings and all the people weren't there at all."

It sounded kind of silly to talk about a rabbit's burrow, she thought. She would have told him about the place on Mrs. Reese's grounds where the boxwoods were all around, and there was a little path that she had discovered one day that seemed as though nobody had used it in about fifty years, it was that faint. She followed it in and pushed aside the boxwood, and inside she found a little cracked marble bench, that also looked as though it hadn't been used in about fifty years. So she went in and sat on the little marble bench in that secret place all hidden by the boxwoods, and liked the thought that probably nobody around Scaisbrooke now even knew it was there. When she left her secret place, she brushed the snow over her footprints, so that the gardeners wouldn't follow them and find the cracked marble bench. That place was her favorite in the winter, but in the spring and fall she liked the rabbit's burrow best. Crazy, a rabbit's burrow. She ought to talk about more adult things to this man. She couldn't tell him about the boxwood place anyway, because it was off bounds and Mrs. Forrest was there.

"What are your daydreams like?" he asked casually.

That one made her stop and think. What were they like? What ran through her mind when she sat in a secret place and imagined? She thought a lot of silly things about Miss Rosen, like having dinner with her in New York and wild things like that, but she couldn't tell him that because Mrs. Forrest was there. Anyway, she didn't think about that much any more, because she only thought about things that might conceivably happen. Courtney was a very practical girl.

She put her hand up to the lapel of her blazer and pulled at it while she tried to remember, then she stopped that because it was an ill-at-ease gesture and she had to be charming.

"Well," she said uncomfortably. "I guess I think about people I know, as though I were with them and talking to them." She thought about the way she pretended she was talking to Al Leone when she was confused, and how the matter-of-fact answers that he would give helped her to think clearer.

"Do you just think these conversations, or do they seem real?"

"Oh, they seem awfully real," she said intensely. "Sure, the people talk just as they always do, with the inflections and all that. They don't just talk like me or something," she said scornfully.

"So it's almost as though they were there?"

"Yes, it's really as though they were there, except I know they aren't, although I have a picture of them in my mind so I can see their faces and their expressions."

Mrs. Forrest sat forward incredulously, and then remembered that she should show no reaction, like the doctor, and sat back.

"Well, we all have daydreams," the doctor said absently as he wrote. "Yours are very vivid."

Courtney nodded. This was an accepted fact, and there was nothing remarkable about her having a better imagination than most people.

"Tell me, Courtney, do you ever get depressed?"

Courtney thought about looking out her window at the ground two stories below it, and thinking what it would be like to fall there. That frightened her, but she liked to do it all the same. Heights had always terrified her, even when she was a little girl in Westchester and had climbed trees like all the other little boys, even though she was terrified when they swayed in the wind and she was very high up. She liked to climb high all the same, although she always thought about falling down. That's how she felt when she was very depressed, as though she were looking down from a height and thinking what it would be like if she should fall down.

"*Yes*," she said. "I get depressed sometimes."

"Mmm-hmm. For very long, or just for a couple of hours?"

"For periods of time," she said thoughtfully. "And then there are times," she said with pleasure, "when I feel just terrific and as though I can do a whole lot of things better than most people."

She stopped herself there, because Mrs. Forrest was listening and she sounded awfully conceited when she said things like that. They were always accusing her of being conceited, because when she felt that she wasn't such a good person after all, when she felt that she wasn't even as good as everybody else, she didn't let anyone know it.

But the doctor was standing up now, and she knew that the appointment was over. There were a lot of things that she would have liked to say to this man who seemed so interested in what she thought, but she hadn't had time and she never got around to them. She felt that she hadn't said anything that would have helped him very much in finding out why she was so tired, but she didn't know what she could have said anyway.

"I very much enjoyed talking to you, Courtney."

"Thank you," she murmured automatically. She said thank you as a reflex, answering almost any statement, instead of just uuh or something.

"You take these iron pills and see if they help you at all. I can't suggest anything else, except possibly cold weather instead of this lovely spring," he smiled.

"Thank you, Dr. Reismann, and goodbye," she said and extended her hand. She didn't so much mind leaving, although his office was very manly and comfortable, because the day outside was lovely and it was a nice walk from town to Scaisbrooke. Even

Mrs. Forrest was easier to take on a day like this. It was Saturday and the dinner was foul, but there was no study hall, so she didn't mind going back after her brief sortie into the world outside. On the walk back she wanted to run, but she stayed with the plump steps of Mrs. Forrest, like a polite Scaisbrooke girl, although it was difficult not to respond to the sun like any other young girl in the springtime.

"Oh, Jan, you haven't any clothes on again," she said in exasperation when she came into the room.

Janet stretched and said, "No. I feel *terribly* sensual, I feel as though I ought to be out making love with somebody. Anybody," she said thoughtfully, "so long as he wasn't overweight."

Courtney eyed her suspiciously.

"Have you been reading my Christopher Isherwood?"

"Isherwood? Never even heard of him."

"He heard of you," she smiled. "Read it some time. You'd like Sally Bowles."

"What's she like?"

"Oh, she's out of her head. Really game, but out of her head."

"Like that Zelda that you were telling me about, F. Scott Fitzgerald's wife?"

"Yeah," said Courtney. "Like that Zelda, when she jumped into the fountain near the Plaza because it was a hot night."

"I'm like that," Janet said proudly. "Like a Fitzgerald person."

"Kind of," Courtney said.

"I'm glad I have a literary roommate," Janet said. "Did you get any bananas while you were out?"

"No, I was with Fo-bitch, and she wouldn't let me. Ran into some little second-former, Sommers, and she said she'd get them."

"How did you and Fo-bitch get along?"

"Oh, it was all right, because I didn't have to talk to her or anything. This doctor was great. Asked me all sorts of questions, about daydreaming and being tired and feeling depressed and all. It was kind of interesting, but didn't prove anything."

The iron pills did not help Courtney at all, and her excessive sleeping got worse as the weeks passed and summer vacation drew near. Dr. Reismann knew that they would not help her. As he said to his wife at dinner that night, "Why shouldn't the child sleep when she has nothing that she wants to be awake for?"

4

The Garden of Allah was conveniently located on "The Strip," a block from Schwab's Drugstore where a whole afternoon of black coffee was provided for the price of the first cup. Across the way was a reducing salon which advertised itself by a bicycling mannequin in the window and pictures of broad-shouldered 1940 stars on similar machines, and nearby was a Chinese restaurant where a cheap and filling meal could be found. The Garden shouted its identity to the passers-by on Sunset Boulevard by a glaring, blinking, shifting neon sign of generally neurotic behavior. The palm trees, of course, were lit by floodlights because it is man's business to improve upon actuality. The general impression given to the uninitiated by the sign and the bizarre name was one of a particularly brazen house of ill repute, but the prices of the villas were equal to those of the bungalows of the more sedate Beverly Hills Hotel, and any behavior of ill repute indulged in by the inhabitants was generally not on a professional basis.

The villas surrounded a pool whimsically built in the shape of a lotus leaf, but of course the pool wasn't meant to be practical, only symbolic, and in that it succeeded admirably. The lotus-eaters gathered daily around the pool to play gin rummy, talk about the work that they hoped to get or that they had recently completed, and drink vodka in various guises. Beside the pool was the main building of the hotel, if it may be called that—actually the Garden was only symbolic and symptomatic as well—and in the hotel was a bar, which was very definitely practical.

The bar was papered in an unobtrusive green, and the seats were of green leather. A later and more flagrant management papered the bar in candy-stripes in an attempt to make even that room into a symbol, but their reign was short-lived anyway, and at this time the green that had solaced F. Scott Fitzgerald in his brief and tragic stay in Hollywood still remained.

This was the interim time of day, the hour that was once, in an earlier and less uprooted time, referred to as the children's hour, but which today is called the cocktail hour. This was the time when working Hollywood showered and changed, and when out-of-work Hollywood looked out of its window at the evening sky and put on its corduroy jacket.

This was the hour that Sondra Farrell hated with a hatred bred of solitude, and which she passed in the bar of the Garden of Allah because it was one of the few places where a woman could go alone without having overly determined passes made at her. Marty, the bartender, saw to that for her.

"How are you this evening, Miss Farrell?" he said pleasantly. He expected no information but few remarks are made in that expectation, being used only to fill space and cover gestures like the clearing of glasses.

"As well as usual, Marty. Make that a Barry Cabot martini," she added, meaning nearly pure vodka and a great deal of that.

"Mr. Cabot was in late last evening," Marty said as he mixed the vodka martini.

Barry Cabot was a juvenile, boy-next-door actor in his late twenties, conscious of the fact that he would soon be very much out of work. For his type, the working years were as short as a boxer's, and the wait until he could go into character roles would be long and hungry. He was often "in between roles" now, and almost any bar in Hollywood knew what was meant by a "Cabot martini."

"Did he behave himself?" Sondra smiled.

"Oh, you know Mr. Cabot," Marty answered. "But he was all right. Just kind of moody, that's all. Didn't throw any martinis in anybody's face or anything like that."

Cabot was a young man who had particular appeal to older women, but since Sondra was never more than briefly interested in weak young men, they had a comfortable, working relationship. He was a good drinking companion when he was sober, but that was less and less of the time now, so Sondra seldom bothered to speak to him when he sat sullenly at the bar. Barry Cabot's chief contribution was his amusement value.

"How is your little girl?" Marty asked, because he could see that Sondra was very lonely this evening.

"She's all right," Sondra lied. "She'll be coming home soon," she added.

Marty digested this piece of information and moved to the other end of the bar to serve some people who had just come in. One of them nodded to Sondra Farrell, and she raised her hand in a slight gesture of greeting. She couldn't remember where she had met him, probably on some picture.

Suddenly someone slapped her on the back very hard, so that her martini splattered a little way from her lips. The man next to her chuckled and said, "Friend of yours?"

"Hiya, Sondra, you bitch, where have you *been*?" Barry Cabot had an ingratiating way about him.

"Available," Sondra smiled. "Who's been buying you the martinis?"

Barry smiled that white, boyish smile.

"That doesn't matter at all, darling, because you're buying them for me now." He was almost as famous for his beautiful and deep voice as his martinis, and he realized this and spoke slowly as though he were stretching in bed and hadn't gotten up yet. Yes, thought Sondra, he had a bed voice.

"Only if you're charming, Barry. I can't *bear* moody gigolos."

"I don't know that I shall be charming now that you put it that way," he said petulantly. "Tell me"—and he smiled again, that totally insincere but effective smile—"how is your daughter?" He knew that Sondra hated to be reminded that she had a daughter fifteen.

"Oh, a problem, as usual."

"I should like to meet her," Barry said to annoy her.

"She'll be out here soon, dammit. She's my duenna, you know."

"She's lovely, of course."

"Oh, yes. Very."

"With all the charm of youth," he said.

"Yes, of course."

"Youth appeals to me, you know," he said.

"I hadn't noticed."

"Don't be bitchy," he said.

"But I always am."

"Margaret's only your age," he said.

"She looks ten years older."

"She's convenient," he said. "Where the hell is my drink?"

"How delightful it is to be with you."

"You don't have to be, you know," he said.

"Would you rather I left?"

"You're paying," he said.

"God, you're a spoiled child."

Barry picked up his drink, and then slowly and deliberately turned his back on the woman. Everyone who knew Barry Cabot was accustomed to this. Sondra did not take the trouble of leaving. The best way to treat a difficult child was to ignore him. She looked at Barry's classic profile reflected in the mirror behind the bar, a face too weak to play male leads. His expression was one of practiced arrogance and did not change. He was posing now. In the mirror Sondra saw with relief that Al Leone had entered, and she waited for him to see her and come over. When he came up to the bar Al looked at Barry, shrugged to Sondra and ignored him. Al, like most men, intensely disliked Barry Cabot.

"Drinking alone, I see."

"Yes, Al, that's the usual now."

"Don't go into *that* again, doll."

Sondra smiled. "All right," she said in the childlike, intimate voice that made men think that she was flirting with them, which she was. "I promise not to be depressed if you have a drink with me."

"Sure, baby. Can I buy you another?"

"I *like* you, Al."

"I'll tell you what, let's move to a table." He felt that he was in Barry Cabot's lap, standing between him and Sondra.

"How's your kid?" Al asked.

"Darling, if one more person asks me that this evening, I'll scream."

"Oh, shut up. You ought to be proud of having such a great kid."

"Courtney doesn't make me seem any younger."

"Who the hell do you want to be young for, anyway? A fag like Barry Cabot?"

"No, no. He couldn't interest me less. I want to be young for myself. I was never meant to be someone's mother."

"You got a point there."

"Look, if you're going to be difficult too . . ."

"I asked you how your kid was. She's the only worthwhile one in your goddamn family, you know. That weak first husband of yours, and that bastard Russell—"

"Let's leave him out of this. You have no sensitivity."

"Sensitivity. I leave that for the screwballs like you. I'm a business manager, sweetie."

"Frankly, Al, I'm a little worried about Courtney. She doesn't seem at all happy at school. Her housemother wrote me a long letter, and she told me how Courtney wishes she were here, and how she neglects her studies and has no friends to speak of."

"I told you at Christmas that that kid needs a home. Now that Russell is out of the picture—I know, I know, I have no sensitivity—I think you ought to let her stay here, with you."

"Al, do you know what you're asking?"

"Yeah, that you act like a mother to the kid for a change. That you face up to your responsibilities."

"Look, you know as well as I do what kind of a life I'd give her."

"I'm afraid I do. Propping that kid up at a bar on her Christmas vacation."

"Propping her up at a bar! Really, darling! Courtney loves to feel like an adult, drinking a daiquiri with all of us."

"Crap. A kid likes to feel like a kid."

"Nonetheless. I don't like to be alone, you know. I'm a woman who was meant to be surrounded by men dancing attendance on me."

"So let them. But take that kid out of boarding school."

"But she has security there."

"The hell she does. How can she have security when she has no home?"

"Are you trying to tell me how to raise my child?"

"Yes. You know, the kid talks to me like I was her father. I know what goes on inside of her."

"Then you know more than her father or I."

Al nodded.

"Where do you suggest we send her to school?"

"Hollywood High School."

"Good God, no."

"What's wrong with it? *I* went there when I was a kid."

"That's just what I mean. No, she wouldn't get along there at all. Courtney has been sent to all the best schools and camps in the East. I can't ask her to change her way of living and face an entirely different group."

"Then send her to Beverly Hills High School with all the little rich bastards."

"You know," she said toying with her drink, "that might not be a bad idea."

"It might not be a bad idea either if you moved outta here and got a house in Beverly Hills."

"Well, I don't know about that. We'll see. You might have something in what you say, though."

"I'll leave you with that, doll. I gotta go. I have a date with that cute little broad I had in here the other night. She wants me to

45

pick her up at her *apartment*, for Chrissake. She's got real class, this broad."

"Have a good time," Sondra smiled.

"So long, screwball," he said fondly.

Sondra Farrell was frightened by the thought of having Courtney live with her, of having to make a home for the child. She had been able to live as a young woman for the four years that she had been in Hollywood. Now suddenly she would be the mother of a child who was almost a woman. The idea appalled her. But she knew that Al was right, Al was always right, damn him, in that coarse, direct way of his. Courtney did need a home, and Sondra had realized it for several years now. It took time, but Sondra Farrell always faced her responsibilities eventually, and she prided herself on the fact. Of course, she always did it reluctantly, conscious that she was making a sacrifice, so that the good that she might have done was lessened. She gave Courtney the best schools, the best camps, lovely clothes, as she often told herself. Giving of herself was something else again. She had never been able to do that, not even with her husbands. She knew, however, that it must be done, and so she left the bar of the Garden of Allah and wrote Courtney a letter.

5

Courtney was glad that she could tell Scaisbrooke to go to hell. Although she experienced a pang of remorse when Mrs. Reese told her that she was being seriously considered for editor of the *Lit Review* for next year, she felt good about finally leaving. She didn't like to be a malcontent, and she felt that it was only fair if you didn't like a place to get out of it. Besides, Janet was being kicked out, and Courtney wouldn't have had anyone to room with.

She felt even more excited than usual when she got on the plane at LaGuardia, because she knew that this time she was leaving boarding school for good. Although Courtney had been flying since she was a year and a half old, and flying alone since she was seven, she still got a feeling of exhilaration when the motors revved before the take-off. When they had been out of New York for about an hour, and that view of the city that she loved so much had given way to the confining denseness of night clouds, she took out her mother's letter to read it again.

Courtney Darling,

The other day I received a letter from your housemother which upset me a great deal, but I hesitated to answer it until I could offer a solution for the problems so clearly indicated. Your housemother told me about the session with Dr. Reismann. The school is very worried about you. I don't know what stories you made up to give the doctor the idea that you had suicidal tendencies—although we know that is nonsense, the school does not, and you mustn't play games with this sort of thing. But enough of chastisement.

I was very glad to hear that you ended your dependence on that English teacher. I know how difficult it is for you to make friends of your own age, but you make life even lonelier for yourself by forming an attachment to an older person—such things can't help but alienate you from your contemporaries. Your housemother said that you seemed to be seeing more of the other girls, and she mentioned a couple—Alberts and somebody—that you seemed to have struck up a friendship with, which I was happy about.

I gathered, reading between the lines of Mrs. Forrest's letter, that you are even more dissatisfied with Scaisbrooke since spring vacation. At any rate, it is clear that your excessive sleeping means something is bothering you. I don't know what you want to escape from, but it seems to me that it is about time I gave you a real home. For one thing, you should be having dates and parties, and you should be free to raid the icebox at night if you want to—the things that most children take for granted. I know I can never be the little gray-haired mother, nor can I give you the stability that you find at boarding school. But you know all this. The choice is up to you.

*I talked this over with your father on the telephone yes-
terday, and he thinks that you should come out here—that
is, if you want to. He is, of course, always delighted to have
his responsibilities on the other coast. If you do decide to
leave, tell me as soon as possible so that I can enroll you in
Beverly Hills High School, and let your father know so that
he can talk to Mrs. Reese. Don't feel we are putting pres-
sure on you, though—if you want to stay at school we will
understand that, too.*

*By the way, Al Leone sends his love and the entire
Garden is alerted for your arrival. Do well in your exams,
darling, and I look forward anxiously to seeing you. We'll
have champagne for breakfast and I promise you'll have a
ball this summer.*

I love you,
Mummy

There hadn't been much question in Courtney's mind, and as
she got off the plane in Burbank she was even more confirmed
in her decision. The Garden had been alerted; Al Leone and assorted actors were waiting in the bar, and they did have Champagne for breakfast. There was an actor there that Courtney had
not met before, Barry Cabot. He was a little loaded but rather
charming, and he greeted her with the expected embrace and
the expected comment on her eyes, which were very dark in the
dimness of the bar. He had an arrogance that interested her; it
seemed like her own. As he turned his head, he posed as though
he did not want the camera to record the fullness under his chin
which, despite his lean body and his twenty-eight years, was the
inevitable result of countless martinis. In this pose he reminded
Courtney of the picture of Rupert Brooke in the front of her

well-worn copy of Brooke's poetry. Barry Cabot stayed in her mind as she fell asleep that night.

The next morning Courtney awoke with a vague sense that she was late, and had missed breakfast and chapel. The soft morning sunlight fell on her bed and she looked around her. She saw a palm tree brushing against the window and lay back in bed, reassured. Scaisbrooke was far behind her. Courtney dressed and went into the living room, which was cluttered with empty glasses and full ash trays. This reassured her further; cocktail parties were one of the few constants in her life. All her life she would associate liquor with her childhood. When she was alone and did not wish to be, a drink would reassure her as the smell of dinner cooking or the sound of a hose spraying a summer lawn would another.

On the couch, wrapped in a blanket against the cold California night, Barry Cabot slept soundly as a small boy. She looked at Barry, his head buried in his arms and his face relaxed and boyish in sleep. She sat across from him. She did not know why she liked to watch him in sleep. His skin was pale and clear, like a woman's or a child's, and a shock of reddish brown hair fell across his high forehead. His mouth was finely and delicately formed, with a petulant fullness to the lower lip.

She looked up as her mother came into the living room, very tan in her white satin bathrobe.

"Good morning, darling, did you sleep well?"

"Very well, thank you, Mummy." She looked over at the couch. "Our guest is sleeping well, too."

"Oh, yes. The party broke up late last night— I made the mistake of having a ham sent in, and I don't think they had eaten in days. Barry was afraid to go home—you know these Peter Pans who are frightened to be alone with themselves in the dark—so

I told him he could sleep on the couch."

There was a sudden and demanding knock on the door. Courtney got up to answer it. Framed against the late morning brightness stood Patrick Cavanaugh, a *New Yorker* writer and one of the guests of the evening before. In his hands was a silver tray with four Bloody Marys. Courtney grinned and took the tray.

"Patrick, you *darling!*" Sondra Farrell rushed to him and threw her arms about him.

"Wake up that freeloader Cabot," he said.

Barry put his face into the couch and muttered something incoherent.

"We've got a Bloody Mary for you, Cabot," said Patrick.

Reluctantly awake, he sat up.

"May I have one, too, Mummy?"

"I brought one for you," said Patrick.

"No, Courtney, not vodka at eleven in the morning. If your father knew, he would have an asthma attack."

"Let the kid have a drink," said Barry.

"Well, you may have a quarter of a glass," her mother relented.

Patrick raised his glass solemnly.

"To Courtney," he said. "May she always rise late to find a drink awaiting her."

"And amusing men around her," her mother added.

"Daddy would flip," Courtney said, but she liked the toast, and she was pleased to find that the Bloody Mary tasted like tomato juice with tabasco.

Her mother ordered breakfast brought for all of them in the villa, with more Bloody Marys and a great deal of black coffee. Courtney wasn't allowed to have another Bloody Mary, but she was hungry anyway and she wanted to finish breakfast and go for a swim.

She put on her black strapless bathing suit, and looked at her-self in the mirror while they talked in the living room. She had a good body, and she was very aware of it. Her legs were firmly muscled, like a dancer's from years of athletics. She was slim and athletic, her shoulders were broad and the collarbone and the molding of her upper body was smoothly distinct beneath her warmly tanned skin. Her breasts were firm and full, even at fif-teen. She had a woman's body, curved, firm and sensual, and this did not pass without notice. The ease and assurance with which she used her body even in such simple actions as walking, her perpetual consciousness of her body, the vitality and challenge in her green eyes—all these things spoke clearly of passion. She was not yet sixteen, but she was ready for love. Men were aware of it, although her mother could not be and Courtney sensed it only vaguely. She had never kissed a man, she had never indulged in any of the byplay of love-making as Janet had, but her passions ran high and her need for love was great.

When she came to the pool, she was surprised to see three young boys there, about her age. Somehow the couples that lived at the Garden seemed incapable of breeding children, and the youthful laughter as the boys ducked one another in the pool seemed to startle the sun bathers and disturb the haze of fantasy and self-delusion that hung about the lotus-shaped pool. She was not pleased to see the boys there; they were intruders from the harshly bright, barbarian world of youth invading the soft un-trodden sands of disappointment.

Al Leone, mahogany-tanned, had come over from his apart-ment across the street and was doing push-ups on his deck chair.

"Hi, doll," he greeted her amiably. "What time did you go to bed?"

"About two, I guess."

"Where's your mother?"

"Some people came by the villa and they're all drinking Bloody Marys. So I left, because I wanted to swim."

"Barry Cabot there?"

"Yes, he slept on the couch."

"I thought so. What do you think of him?"

"I like him. He kind of interests me."

"Christ, I was afraid of that. Look, baby doll, watch out for that faggot. He is worth exactly nothing."

"What do you mean, watch out for him?"

"He is the sort of guy you would like, being an artist type with intellectual pretensions and also having some charm for women. Also, he is around your villa a great deal as your mother provides him with occasional drinks and dinners and finds him amusing. So don't you start to get interested, because he is a real shit-heel guy."

"Al, I'm not interested in anybody—and not anybody of Barry Cabot's age," she said patiently. "I'm just a kid, you know."

"I don't know. You are a woman, and an attractive one. There are some guys around here who would take advantage of that."

"Who are these kids in the pool?" she said, changing the subject.

"Two of them are the sons of a television producer, and the third is the son of a director. They're here for the summer. Want to meet them?"

"Not particularly. They're making a lot of noise."

"I'll introduce you to them. They're kind of young for you, but they're nice kids. A couple of years older than you."

"I'll meet them when they get out of the pool," she said without enthusiasm.

Al lay for a few minutes in the sun.

"Sweetie, I want to talk to you about your mother," Al said in a confidential tone. He looked around him, but no one was nearby. "She would be the last one to tell you this, but I figure you ought to know," he said in a low tone. "She is about to go into bankruptcy, unless some break comes along awfully fast."

Courtney frowned, puzzled. "But her contract . . ."

"The studio is not taking up her option. There's a chance that she might get the lead in Nick Russell's new picture, and that's about the only hope she has. You know, she isn't the draw that she was a year ago. They've been tightening up, as you probably know, and actors are being let out of their contracts by carloads. She's very much in debt, and unless she gets this assignment I don't see anything for her to do but declare bankruptcy. Those last two pictures were really bombs, and everybody's so frightened they're not able to take a chance on her now."

"But what about the Plaza, and the Garden, and the house she's going to get in Beverly Hills this fall?"

"Baby, you know your mother as well as I do. She's a screwball, and she thinks that money will always be provided for her by some invisible power. She can't believe that she is broke, so she just goes more and more in debt, figuring that at the last minute something will come along."

"Mr. Micawber," Courtney mused.

"Huh?"

"Nothing."

"So, kid, that's how things stand. I thought I'd better tell you, because you're the only sensible member of the family, and maybe you can keep her from crazy shopping binges and all that. Also, I didn't want all this to hit you like a bomb. I wanted you to be prepared, because you're old enough to handle these things."

Courtney was reminded of what had been said to her all her

childhood as she was handed responsibility that a child should never have, and as she was made aware of realities that a child should ignore until the child himself chooses to step down from his tower of fantasies to the plain of Babel. She sighed inaudibly.

"I'm glad you told me, Al. Maybe you and I together can make her act a little sensibly, but I doubt it. Anyhow, I'll try, and I'll try not to ask for money or clothes or things, so she won't be tempted to go more into debt."

She saw the house in the hills above Beverly Hills become indistinct in the sunlight, merging with the pastels of this most unreal of real worlds. What the hell, she thought, I didn't base my decision to come out here on money. Though money always helps, she added. How grubby! she thought suddenly, angrily. How grubby and obscene to be facing bankruptcy! But then, that was the price that had to be paid for living in a world of fantasy and illusion, a charming world. Maybe. She didn't know.

As Courtney lay in the sun beside Al Leone, she found herself thinking about Barry Cabot. She would like to know him, she would like to talk with him. It would be nice to sit beside him in the evening, during the hour that she usually walked along The Strip by herself. She was sick of solitude, she was a little frightened of it, though she did not know why. Suddenly, irrelevantly, she wondered what it would be like to kiss Barry Cabot. But that was a foolish thought; she was still a kid, and a man like Barry Cabot wouldn't pay any attention to her. She dismissed the thought.

"Court," said Al, "how would you like to come over to the apartment for a drink?"

He felt sorry for the kid, sitting there so alone and thoughtful. What he said must have upset her. He should have waited until she was settled here before he sprung the bankruptcy business on her. But he was always speaking without thinking. When he had something to say, he simply said it.

Courtney was delighted at the invitation. No one had ever asked her to have a drink with him before.

"I'd love to, Al."

They walked across the street to Al's apartment. As they entered, it suddenly occurred to Courtney that maybe she shouldn't be going into a man's apartment. Her mother had always told her not to. But then she laughed at herself because this wasn't a man, this was Al, and she was only a kid anyway.

When the "drink" turned out to be grapefruit juice, she felt even more foolish at her moment of hesitation. She sat across from him on the couch in the dim living room.

"I hope what I said didn't upset you, sweetie," he said as he sipped his grapefruit juice.

"No, Al, not really. I always expect everything to be perfect, I guess, and it kind of spoiled my illusion to think that we were going to be broke, and to face a reality like that."

"Christ, kid, I thought you were the sensible member of the family. You're sounding like your mother."

"You know, we're a lot more alike than you think we are." She leaned back against the couch and stared at the ceiling with its indirect lighting. "Sometimes I wish I could leave it all—this sophistication—and be different from what I see around me."

"You can try, Court."

"No, it just doesn't work. Last night, when I got back here, I realized that I couldn't ever be different from what I had been brought up to be. Maybe if I'd been farmed out to somebody like you when I was six or so, I could have been different. Now, I'm just stuck with cocktails at eleven and breakfast at noon."

"You sound as though you were my age."

"I'm nearly a woman, Al. If I ever had a childhood, it's behind me now, and the kind of person I'm going to be is established whether I like it or not. I can fight it, but I'll just wear myself out and confuse myself." She sat up and rubbed her neck. "I'm stiff from sleeping on that plane."

"Want me to rub your neck?"

"Yes, I'd like that."

Al took his grapefruit juice and sat beside her. He put his square, brown hands on her neck and manipulated the smooth young muscles under his fingers. He could feel the tightness and concentrated on it, trying to ignore the firm, tanned body beneath his fingers. After all, Courtney was only a kid, and she trusted him.

Courtney liked the feeling of a man rubbing her neck. She leaned against him and smiled. She liked men, and she was fond of Al. She felt a warmth, leaning against him, and she was conscious of a new feeling. This was an alive, communicated sensation, a sensation of warmth with a growing tension. She was not that young: she knew that she was attracted to Al and liked the nearness of his body.

Al leaned down and kissed the back of her neck. Courtney was no longer Courtney, she was a vibrant young woman leaning against him. Gently, he put her head down on the couch and moved her legs until she was lying down beside him. He kissed her shoulder softly and ran his hands along her arms. He put his head against her, and the vibrancy that the young body gave out became intense.

Courtney, too, had lost her identity in emotion. She had never known a sensation like this. Her mind, the mind that had always ruled her, became shadowy and inconsequential in the passion of her release, and she had no time to regret its passing sovereignty. Her body was suddenly alive, with an awareness she had not known it was capable of. She was wanted, and she was happy in being wanted.

"Relax," he said softly. "Put your arms around me."

As she heard his voice it became real to her, and she was shocked and turned her head away.

Al sat up and looked at her, young, untouched and somehow defenseless. She lay there, saying nothing, not moving.

"You're like a doll," he said. "A wooden doll."

She didn't answer.

"You're a very decent kid," he said. "I'm glad to see that. You're all right, Courtney. Stay that way. Don't let some bastard like me make you."

"No, not very decent," she murmured, for she felt very unclean and sweaty, and she was disgusted at herself. She sat up. Al moved to the couch across from her, taking his grapefruit juice with him.

"I'm sorry kid. I didn't know—I wasn't sure. You seemed to know so much more than you do know. I'm sorry if I hurt you, because I'm real fond of you, and I wouldn't want to hurt you. But I never do think."

"No, Al." She grinned to make him feel better. "Hell, no. I was to blame, too, because I wanted you to make love to me. I wanted somebody to—and then I was afraid and I knew I didn't want it. Have you got a cigarette?"

She had never asked for a cigarette; she didn't really want to smoke, she had learned so recently and was unused to it. But somehow it seemed appropriate to have a cigarette, and she smoked it with concentration, being very careful not to look like a neophyte.

Al was surprised that she should ask for a cigarette. She had never smoked before, and he didn't like the idea. But he had lost his right to guide her by becoming merely a man before her. He had lost his place of honor, and he said nothing as she smoked the cigarette and stared into space. He felt awkward in the silence. He had made passes and been rebuffed before, and girls had been embarrassed, but none of them had ever sat silently looking at the opposite wall. He felt like a real heel.

"For Chrissake," he said finally.

Courtney looked up.

"Can I take you to dinner tonight?"

Courtney didn't want to. She didn't want to see him; she wanted to erase what had just happened. But she didn't want Al to be upset, for after all, a woman should expect to have passes made at her and shouldn't blame the man. Besides, she knew she couldn't run away and if she said no she would be running away again.

"Okay, Al."

"I'll come by the villa at six."

"Okay, Al."

"All those people should have left the villa by now," she said. "I think I'll go back."

"Want me to introduce you to those kids?" He felt he should do something to restore her to being a kid. He had lectured her mother so much about that, and now he had gone and violated his own purpose.

"No." She had no desire to meet them, the young intruders. She was not one with them and never could be. She got up.

"See you, Al."

"I'm sorry," he said again.

"For what?" she said. "What the hell, Al."

She shrugged and walked casually into the California afternoon to her mother's villa, and seeing that no one was there, flung herself on the bed and cried.

6

The late afternoon was quiet and thoughtful. Courtney was wearing those Levi's which her mother disliked, the tight ones, and she was sitting beside the window reading Baudelaire's *Les Fleurs du Mal*.

As she watched Courtney, Sondra wondered what had depressed the child. She had been pleased that Al asked her to dinner. Courtney was so fond of Al, and she trusted in him so. Yet after dinner Courtney seemed even more upset. She was silent and withdrawn. But then Courtney had become more withdrawn than Sondra had ever seen her during this last year. Possibly that only meant that she was growing up and away from her.

"Courtney—"

"Yes, Mummy."

"Courtney, I wish you would tell me what's bothering you. Maybe I could do something about it."

"Nothing's bothering me, Mummy."

"I suppose you wouldn't tell me anyway," Sondra said wearily.

"Probably not."

"Would you like me to have someone in for dinner? Would that cheer you up?"

"Mummy, I'm not depressed."

"Of course you are. Aren't you having a good time? You have those nice boys to swim with, for a change."

"Yes, they're nice kids. They're awfully young."

"You're not that old," Sondra smiled.

"Mmm-hmm." Courtney was trying to read.

"Well, you can't wallow in this mood," Sondra said finally. "You're an awfully dull person to have around."

"I'm sorry, Mummy, if I bore you."

"We'll have a marvelous dinner at Scandia, and I'll ask someone along." Sondra thought a moment. "Barry Cabot, or Patrick Cavanaugh. They're always amusing."

"Mummy, that's awfully expensive."

"Not really." She looked sharply at her daughter. "What is this sudden concern for money? Last night you told me that you didn't want a new winter coat, you said that your old polo coat would do. You're getting to sound like your father."

"We ought to—well, we're kind of broke, aren't we?"

"Did your father tell you that?"

"He kind of mentioned it, but—"

"For God's sake, what is he worrying you with money for?"

"Well, Daddy wasn't the only—"

"What?"

"Nothing."

"Nick is going to star me in that next picture, so we don't have to worry, even though the studio didn't pick up my option. I think I'll make more freelancing, anyway, so it's just as well."

"Crap."

"I beg your pardon."

"I said, crap."

"Don't talk to me that way."

"Sorry."

"What's gotten into you, anyway?"

Courtney shrugged. What could she say? There was so much to say.

"I'm asking Barry to dinner. Why don't you go over to the Thespian and ask him? The walk will do you good."

It was easy to predict that at four o'clock Barry would be at the Thespian, a bar a block away from the Garden. He didn't come over to the Garden until he had managed to have someone buy him a Caesar salad ("Oh, no, I've eaten. But I'll have a salad to keep you company while you have dinner, darling.") to sustain him until breakfast at two the next afternoon.

Courtney saw his car outside, a snub-nosed and defiant little '41 convertible. She waited outside a few minutes, looking at the car. She was as nervous as though she were going in to see the headmistress. Finally she took as deep a breath as her tight Levi's, worn low on her hips, would allow, summoned up her fifteen (nearly sixteen) years of sophistication, and walked in. She looked falteringly around the dim and almost empty bar. The white-haired bartender looked up—disapprovingly, Courtney thought.

"I . . . was looking for someone," she said in a clear and defiant voice. "Is Barry Cabot here?"

"Hel-*lo*, sweetie." He got the full value of the words, speaking in a soft and rich voice. "Come have a Coke with me, Court."

"Barry—I didn't see you." She was intensely self-conscious. "I came over to ask you to dinner with Mummy and me. She sent me over." She was regaining her poise, and was very excited that she was in a bar with Barry Cabot; she felt terribly adult.

"I would love to have dinner with you and Mummy," he smiled. "But have a Coke while I finish my drink."

Courtney paused, but only for a moment. It wasn't as though the Thespian was a *bar*, for Chrissake, it was a quiet little place where everyone went. Families and all that. And her mother would know where she was, and she would only be a few minutes drinking her Coke, anyway.

"Okay," she said. "Thank you." And she sat beside him at the bar.

"A Coke for the young lady, Pete. And another of the same for me."

"I have to get back to tell Mummy you can come," she said.

"It will take me about three minutes to drink that martini."

Courtney nodded reluctantly.

"Cigarette, Courtney?"

"Yes, please." She was going to hell fast, as Janet would say. But no, Janet would be pleased.

He lit her cigarette, solemnly holding the match until she finally took a long enough drag to get it lit. He quickly blew the match out because it was burning his finger. There was no reaction on his face as she took a long and obviously determined drag and exhaled it immediately.

"I've heard a great deal about you," he said. "I've been anxious to meet you for quite a while."

"Mummy's told me about you, too." Yes, her mother had told her that Barry was a near-alcoholic and a homosexual. She had also told her that Barry was very charming. The rest meant nothing to Courtney.

"Your mother is quite a woman."

"Yes, she's a fabulous person."

There was a silence. The bartender brought the martini and the Coke. Barry lit a cigarette. He started to hum.

"Bored?" Courtney said coolly. It was a line her mother used.

"No, no, sweetie. Not at all."

He shifted in his chair.

There was a sudden burst of laughter from one of the tables in the corner.

"And of course," said a woman's throaty voice, "the part that Marilyn had in that last picture she could have phoned in. *Phoned* it in, for God's sake." The two men at the table laughed.

"Pete," Barry said, "another martini."

"A Coke for you, Miss?"

"No thanks, I haven't finished this one."

There was another silence.

"And the scene that George made when he found out," said an effeminate man's voice. "Christ, you could hear him for blocks. As though it hadn't happened before."

"Besides," said the other man, "everyone knows that he screws all his clients."

So that's what screw means, thought Courtney. No wonder Miss Rosen objected to my using it. Conservative little woman. She smiled.

"What are you thinking about?" asked Barry.

"Nothing in particular," Courtney said.

"How do you like it out here?" Barry said finally.

"Oh, I adore it!" Her green eyes were intense. "It's a marvelous fairylike town. Unreal. Of course, its unreality is kind of frightening after a while. It's the only town I've ever been in where I would wake up in the morning and look out the window to be sure it hadn't disappeared in the night."

"Yes, that's the way I feel, too. It's a town of waiting. Waiting by the phone for a call, waiting in the morning for the mail, to see if you can eat for the next few months. And then the escapes.

Having a stiff drink, or calling some broad—excuse me—because the call or the letter never came. It's a lousy town. I wish I could get out of it. I wish to hell I could leave. I've been here for eleven years."

"Why don't you leave? Go to New York, for example?"

"Well, there's always the chance that a break might come. I guess that's the reason I stay."

"You're afraid to go," she said. "You're afraid to build a life and work in another town."

"No, I'm not afraid," he said angrily. "I've put in a lot of work here, and it's bound to pay off."

"The way it's paid off for the actors who sit around the Garden and drink themselves into unreality?"

"Why are you talking to me like this?"[7]

"Because I think it's true."

"Jesus, you're a funny kid. Nobody's ever said anything like this to me. You're real frank. I like that. It's refreshing."

"Pete," he said, "another martini. Would you like a drink, doll?"

"Yes," she said. "I would like a daiquiri."

"And a daiquiri for the lady."

"Is she of age, Mr. Cabot?"

"I'll vouch for it, Pete."

"I'll have nothing to lose by speaking frankly," Courtney went on. "No job at stake, no future contacts, and as for losing friends by frankness, I stopped worrying about that a long time ago."

"A long time ago. How old are you, Court?"

"Fifteen. Almost sixteen," she added hastily. "Sixteen at the end of June."

"Sixteen. God. You know, I'm twenty-eight. I must seem like an old man to you."

"No," she grinned. "Not at all."

"What marvelous eyes you have," he said. "What color are they—gray?"

"They're kind of green."

The bar had filled up, the people at the corner table were still talking and laughing, but they were now shut out and their voices an obbligato.

He leaned toward her, his hand on her shoulder. Her body tensed, as it had yesterday, and that communicated sensation was there again. What was happening to her lately? Why was she suddenly so receptive and so conscious of men? Was it boarding school, and being unused to seeing men, or was it something else?

"Yes," he said. "They are green. Green, very big, and intense. They're marvelous eyes, like the eyes of an actress."

She was a little embarrassed. He leaned back and raised his glass. She took her daiquiri and they touched glasses.

My God, she thought, this is wonderful. Barry Cabot.

"Glad to be out of boarding school?"

"Oh, yes," she said. "Awfully glad. I hated boarding school. For one thing, I hated being with all those women all the time. I don't like women."

"You like men?" he said.

"Oh, yes," she said. "I adore men."

"Really?"

"Per se. Indiscriminately." She grinned.

He raised his eyebrows. "Drink up," he said.

"People had told me that you were a very lovely girl," he said. "They were right. Ever consider going into the movies?"

She grinned, "Could you get me a part, Mr. Cabot?"

"Oh, call me Barry," he smiled, continuing the play. "Yeah, baby doll, I can get you a part."

"Oh, that would be wonderful, Barry. Do you know directors and producers?"

"Do I! Baby, I been in this business a long time. What about—coming up to my place for dinner and we could—talk about your career?"

"Barry, I don't know what to say! This is the first break I've had since I've been out here!"

They both laughed and he put his arms around her.

"Sweetie, you're all right. Pete—another round."

As they talked, Courtney forgot her depression and her solitude, and she was very happy. More people came into the Thespian as the evening came, and they looked at Courtney and Barry leaning close together at the bar, engrossed in their conversation.

"Look at the new broad Cabot has with him," said one man to his companion. "She's young, but she's real good-looking. That sonavabitch does all right."

They didn't see the people who came in, and they didn't see the windows darken and the lights go on.

"Barry." A husky young man came up to them.

"Oh, hi, George." Barry was embarrassed.

"You said you'd call me at seven," George said petulantly. "I waited and you never called, so I came to get you."

"My God, I'm sorry, George." Suddenly he was resentful. "Why did you come to get me, anyway? You could have called me, you know. You have no right to come after me." He turned to Courtney. "I'm awfully sorry, darling. I can't have dinner with you. I have another engagement. . . . George," he said, "this is Courtney—Sondra Farrell's daughter."

"How do you do." Courtney held out her hand.

George ignored it, nodding briefly.

"I didn't realize it was so late. Mummy will be furious!"

"Can you get dinner all right?"

"Mummy has probably gone on by now, knowing Mummy."

"Isn't there anything you can have at the villa?"

You weak bastard, Courtney thought angrily. You know you ought to buy me dinner, even a hamburger, and you know Mummy will be angry with me, but you really don't care.

"I guess so," she said. She wasn't going to make him feel obligated.

"I don't need to walk you home, do I? It's dark, but it's only a block."

"No," she said wearily. "You don't have to walk me home. I often walk alone at this hour. Good night, Barry."

"Good night, sweetie."

"Very glad to have met you," she said to George.

He nodded and sat beside Barry in the seat Courtney had just vacated.

"I'm really sorry, George," she heard Barry say as she went out. "But for Christ's sake, she's only a kid—"

7

Her mother was furious. She had gone on to dinner, assuming angrily that Courtney was having dinner with Barry. She had said little to her that evening, and Courtney had gone to bed in disgrace. The next morning she got up before her mother was awake and slipped out of the house. She went to the pool. Al Leone was there, and Courtney was pleased to find a friend. The incident of three days ago was unimportant in her present ostracism.

"Hi, Al," she greeted him brightly.

"Hello, Courtney."

That was odd. He never called her Courtney.

"Did you ever get home last night?"

"What do you mean, Al?"

"I saw you, propped up at a bar with Barry Cabot. I thought I warned you about him. If you knew what you looked like sitting at a bar in your blue jeans with a guy like Cabot, *drinking*!"

"Christ, you can't do anything in this town," she said angrily.

"You looked real cheap," Al said curtly.

"Cheap! I've never looked cheap in my life!"

"Then this was the first time. Look, what kind of a reputation do you want to get?"

"That's what Mummy said last night, for Chrissake. Only she said, 'How do you think it makes me look?' That made me mad."

"I don't care about your mother. I care about you."

"Oh, Al, shut up! Stop criticizing me! First I'm criticized for being a prude and sounding like a social worker or something, then I'm criticized for looking like a cheap broad. How am I supposed to live? Under the water or something, coming up only to say, 'I beg your pardon if I disturb you by coming up for air. I'll do my best to remain submerged.'"

"Stop being silly. I'm serious."

"Oh, go to hell," she said angrily, and left.

I shouldn't have said that to Al, she thought as she walked to the villa. But I meant it.

"Well, well, Courtney," her mother greeted her as she came in. "I'm pleased to see you're spending the morning here, and not having breakfast with some indigent actor."

"Mummy, please."

"How do you think people will feel about me when they see you drinking until all hours of the night with some actor in a bar?"

"Only until about eight o'clock, Mummy."

"Only until about eight o'clock," she mimicked. "Think of me, and how it looks!"

"Think of you, think of you! That's all you care about, what people will think of you! I'm sick of that, sick of it, and I'm sick of your criticism!"

"You may like to think of yourself as an adult, Courtney, but you're still a child, and as long as you are, you will obey me and behave in good taste."

"I'm not a child," she said angrily, thinking of the other morning with Al Leone. "I'm nearly a woman." Suddenly she was glad that Al had made a pass at her, glad because it proved to her that she was a woman and that she was wanted by men. She almost wished her mother knew; that would shut her up!

"Almost a woman," she scoffed. "You overestimate yourself, my dear."

"Someday you'll see! Someday you'll know!"

She ran from the house. She couldn't stay in the house, and she couldn't go to the pool because she would receive more criticism from Al. There was nothing for her to do but walk along The Strip.

She walked north, away from the stores and the people who stood outside Schwab's and Googie's, the restaurant next door. She walked feeling somehow unrelated to the trees and the cars and the sidewalk. She felt detached, as she had at school, with that strange, dizziness that was not exhaustion but was very like it. As she walked, her anger changed to imagining. She quieted herself by pretending that she was talking to Miss Rosen, and telling her what had happened.

"You must understand your mother," Miss Rosen was saying gently. "She was only thinking of what people would think of her, and she wasn't really so angry with you."

"But what about Al?" Courtney said.

"Maybe he was a little jealous," Miss Rosen smiled.

"Maybe," Courtney grinned. "Maybe that's it. Maybe that's why he called me cheap, after my rejecting him and then sitting with Barry Cabot."

She was pleased with those thoughts, and she rejected Miss

Rosen because she did not need her any longer. She had satisfied her hurt, explained it away, and then she was able to notice the trees and the sunshine and the pastel houses with the swimming pools. She was almost in Beverly Hills! She must have been walking over half an hour. There was the Beverly Hills Hotel, and above it were the hills in which her mother said they would live. But she knew that they wouldn't live there, she knew that it was just another promise that would be defeated by reality. A role in Nick Russell's picture. She knew these promises that her mother had built into realities.

Beverly Hills was a lovely town, totally discrete from The Strip area, and different again from downtown Hollywood where the studios were. The Strip area was a compromise between working Hollywood and the purely residential Beverly Hills. There were apartment houses instead of homes, but they had lawns and most of them had pools. It was quiet off The Strip, and there was a relaxed air that she did not find in Beverly Hills. Beverly Hills seemed self-consciously pompous and wealthy, like a Wall Street broker who had worked up from office boy.

She wandered through the palm-lined, broad streets until the sun was high in the sky and harsh on the pastel houses. Then she turned and walked back to The Strip, past the expensive stores and the broad lawns, toward the Hollywood that she knew, the Hollywood of Schwab's and Googie's and the Thespian.

She had seventy-five cents in her pocket—she didn't want to ask her mother for money—so she went into Schwab's for breakfast. She walked down to the end of the counter. Dick, a young actor who had come from Ohio a year ago, was behind the counter. He looked up as she came in.

"Hiya, Court. Home for vacation?"

"Home for good," she smiled.

"Your usual breakfast?"

"Please."

She got up and went to the newsstand. She looked through the racks and picked up a *Hollywood Reporter* and a *New Yorker*, and sat down again. It was understood that as long as they did not soil the magazines, the regular patrons could read them without paying, returning them as they left.

Dick brought her two eggs, ham, whole wheat toast, orange juice, a side order of French fries, and black coffee, and set the check for fifty cents beside her.

She read through the casting in the *Reporter,* looking for people that she knew, looked at the gossip columns, skipped the news about unions and box-office receipts, and drank her coffee. Dick refilled the cup. She began breakfast.

"Dick," a young man beside her said, "give this note to Walter."

Dick took the note and gave it to a slight young man at the other end of the counter. Then he came back.

"He broke up. What did the note say?" Dick asked the man.

The young man giggled. "It was dirty," he said.

Courtney picked up *The New Yorker* and thumbed through the fiction.

"Well, Charlie," said a man a few stools down from her to his companion, "how did the audition go?"

"Pretty well, I think. You know West, he never gives any reaction. I kind of sensed that he liked me. It's a real good part. He asked me if I'd dye my hair red for the Technicolor, and of course I told him I would. I think that's a pretty good indication that he wants me for the part."

"Well, I'm on Kraft next week, you know."

"That's *great!* With Marilyn Patten?"

"I'm afraid so. She's a bitch."

"Helluva good actress, though."

"Mmm-hmm."

Courtney looked up absently from her magazine. In the mirror that ran the full length of the counter she saw Barry Cabot walk in. She tensed, and then her whole body began to tremble. She dropped her fork, and, very embarrassed, she picked it up and resumed eating.

What's happening to me? she thought. What's wrong with me?

She could not control the trembling of her body, the inner tension that took possession of every muscle. She didn't look up.

"Hiya, Court," Barry said pleasantly, and sat at the other end of the counter.

Dick filled her cup again. She wanted to talk to Barry, but she knew that she had no right to. She knew that she must not presume on him. All these men were so terrified of possessive, chasing women. Her mother had told her that. He didn't talk to her, he read his *Hollywood Reporter* and ignored her. She finished her coffee, paid her check, returned the magazines, and left. She was confused.

She walked out into the street. She didn't want to go to the pool or to the villa. Yet she didn't dare go back into Schwab's. She stood undecided outside Schwab's for a moment; she had twenty-five cents. She went into Googie's next door.

As she walked into Googie's, most of the men who sat with their backs to the door swung around on their stools. There was no mirror at Googie's. Seeing that it was no one of moment, they turned back to their breakfasts.

"Cup of coffee, please," she said to the waitress. "Black."

They didn't know her very well.

She was perplexed, and upset. She had gotten in trouble with her mother, Al Leone was disappointed in her, and she thought that it all would be worthwhile because she had made contact with Barry Cabot. Now Barry ignored her, was even rude to her, and she found herself more alone than before. She couldn't figure it out. She always made the wrong move, because she never thought.

Another group came in the door, and Courtney found herself looking, too. It was George, wearing Levi's and a leather jacket, with two other men.

"Hello," she said automatically as he passed her. He simply looked at her, giving no sign of recognition.

I can't handle *this!* she thought. I don't know where I am!

She drank her coffee and went back to the pool. There was no one around that she knew very well, and she was thankful. Patrick Cavanaugh greeted her, and then resumed reading *The New Yorker*. The three boys were in the pool. They were racing each other. When they finished they got out of the pool, laughing, and stretched out along the rim in the sun. She envied them. She wished that she could join them, and leave this strange world of adults and emotional intrigues. But she was afraid to go over to them. She had been rejected by her own too often.

Instead she went up to the roof of the double villa, locking the door behind her. The roof smelled of sun-tan oil. There were no buildings nearby, and it was used as a solarium. She took off her clothes and lay down. She sun-warmed and spread her body. She ran her hands down her ribs and along her hips. She liked her body. She could trust her body. It was strong and beautiful and it never disappointed her. It would swim as many laps as she asked it to; it would play many hours of hockey; it moved with grace; it relaxed when she wanted to sleep. She certainly couldn't trust in her mind that way. Her mind slept when her body wanted to live. Her mind would lose her in daydreams and force her to sleep when she wasn't tired. At times she hated her mind.

"This body," she said to herself. "This body should be loved and admired. This body wasn't made for me to hold to myself, to secrete in the damp corners of solitude." But then, she didn't really feel that way. She didn't want to make love. She knew how foolish it was for a woman to make love, how a woman hurt herself. She knew these things as she knew most things of life, from what her mother had told her and what she had seen. Besides, it was sinful to think sensual thoughts. She would have to confess that in church tomorrow, along with the dreadful thing she had done three days ago. She was becoming very sinful. The way her body had trembled when Barry Cabot came in. She was afraid when that happened. She didn't know why it had happened, but she knew it had something to do with sex, and it frightened her that her body should act that way without her control. She was a little afraid of herself these days. And as she lay there thinking these thoughts, as she had one day on the hockey field, she knew that she must leave again and go someplace where people were.

There was no one at the villa when Courtney entered. It was dim. She hated dimness. All the houses her mother had ever lived in were dim. At Scaisbrooke and at camp she had insisted on keeping the shades up all the time, even though the sun woke her up often at dawn.

For some reason—she had no idea why—she went to the kitchen and took out the bottle of vodka. She took a swallow from the bottle. It tasted ghastly, and she cupped her hands under the faucet and drank some water. But she liked the idea of having a drink, and she took another swallow. She didn't take any more, because her mother would notice it was gone and she didn't like the taste anyway. She went into the living room, pleased by the gesture. She didn't try to explain it to herself. She picked up her Baudelaire.

Youth, she thought irrelevantly, is a ghastly time.

8

The harsh, sudden August rain closed in the living room and made it dim and solitary. Courtney got up and turned on some lamps. She put on the radio. The news was on. Korea. Something depressing about Korea. She wondered what her mother and Nick were saying. Her mother had left in high spirits, wearing the black suit she got in New York and the French perfume Courtney's father had brought from the Virgin Islands. They were going to Chasen's to talk about Nick's new picture. "We'll have champagne when I get back, darling—champagne and lots of money." This rain was depressing as hell.

Courtney got up, put a shot of vodka in some tomato juice, and lit a cigarette. Now that she was sixteen by two months, her mother allowed her to drink and smoke. The news was off and they were playing records. It was a jazz station. "Abstraction!" They were playing Stan Kenton's "Abstraction." She wondered what Janet was doing now. Some house party on the Island, no doubt. Courtney had written Janet all about Barry Cabot and then when he ignored her more and more pointedly, being casually sociable when they met at a party of her mother's—which was even more insulting than ignoring her—she didn't write Janet for a while because she was embarrassed at having to say that she had built something in her mind which was implausible and nonexistent.

She went to the movies once with one of the boys who swam, and after the movies they had coffee. That was that. She decided to confine herself to her mother's parties, where too, she had a chance of seeing Barry. It was nice that she could smoke and drink. It made her feel older and more a part of the parties.

She wondered what it was like for her mother and Nick, who had been married and had slept together and all, to see each other. She thought that, sometimes, about her mother and father, but they had been divorced so long ago that their present relationship was of longer duration than their married life. Anyhow, Courtney gathered that the sleeping together part wasn't as important with her parents as it had been with her mother and Nick, because her mother and Nick hadn't been able to—hadn't wanted to—establish any other sort of relationship. What the hell, she didn't know anything about that. It was a whole sphere of life that she couldn't know anything about—the only one, she thought, that she couldn't even guess at.

Her mother should be home soon. They had gone to dinner and that was at seven. She had an idea. She went to the phone and called the liquor store.

"This is Miss Farrell, at the Garden?"

They would probably think it was her mother.

"Yes, Miss Farrell."

"I'd like a bottle of Piper Heidseck, 'forty-seven."

That was what her father always bought.

"Anything else, Miss Farrell?"

"Some potato chips."

"Villa nine, isn't it?"

"Mmm-hmm."

"We'll send it right over."

She was pleased by the idea. Her mother would like coming home to find that Courtney had bought the champagne, and they would eat potato chips and wouldn't have to go out in the rain. That would mean more to her mother than if they went out someplace. It was the kind of thing her father would have done.

After the champagne came she decided against having another Bloody Mary, because she was a little afraid of the idea of sitting and drinking all by herself, so she had a cup of coffee and picked up a novel by Evelyn Waugh.

When she heard her mother come in, she was pleased; and excited. The champagne was iced and the potato chips were in a bowl on the cocktail table. Everything was ready.

When Courtney saw her mother as she opened the door, she knew something was wrong. Sondra looked older and tired as she always did when she was upset. Courtney could tell that she had been crying. Immediately she decided against the champagne. She took her mother's coat.

"May I get you a drink, Mummy?" That was all she said.

"Yes, please, dear."

Courtney made a Scotch and water, putting in two full jiggers of Scotch and only enough water to disguise the liquor. Then she looked at the color and decided it was safe to put in another splash of Scotch. She muddled the drink with her fingers and sucked the finger, checked the color again and brought her mother the drink.

Then she went back to the kitchen and made herself a Scotch on the rocks because her mother didn't like to drink alone. She came back to the living room and sat down, not saying anything.

"Courtney," Sondra said finally.

"Whom did he give the part to?" Courtney asked.

"The studio is about to drop him. Because of those two flops, the ones that I was in—and the TV scare, it's the same at every studio. So they gave him this one picture, with a very powerful book, as a final test. He can't take another chance."

"Stop excusing him."

"No, really, Courtney. He needs a star with a big following, box-office insurance. He can't take a chance."

"Did he give it to that bitch he's been sleeping with?"

"Courtney! Don't say things like that!"

"Well, did he?"

"That doesn't make any difference. The point is, I didn't get it."

"The son of a bitch."

"Courtney," she said, "Hollywood is a tough town. Nick said that to me when I came out here the first time. He was right. It's a struggle for survival, and everyone must look out for himself. There's no room for sentiment. You can't ask a man whose own career is in jeopardy to destroy himself to help an actress who is hitting the skids."

"You're not, Mummy!"

"I can't fool myself any longer," she said wearily. "I didn't tell you this before, because I thought I would get this part and everything would be all right. We're in debt to the Garden for over a thousand dollars. We've got to move out."

Courtney didn't say anything, because she didn't want to upset her mother any more. Move out of the Garden! She wouldn't see Al any more around the pool, she wouldn't be able to swim and sun-bathe on the roof . . . there wouldn't be any chance of her seeing Barry Cabot even at Schwab's or on the street.

"Where are we going to go, Mummy?"

"There's an apartment building on the outskirts of Beverly Hills that a girl of Al's used to live in. He told me about it. It's very cheap, and rather nice. We can get a studio apartment there. It's near the Fox lot."

Near the Fox lot. On that great, cold, broad street with all the gas stations! How horrible.

"When are we going," Courtney said quietly.

"Our week at the Garden ends this Wednesday."

"Wednesday." Wednesday! Only two more days!

"We'll still be near Beverly Hills," her mother said hurriedly, "near enough so that you can go to Beverly Hills High. And we won't have to stay there long, only until I get some TV work, you know, there's such a demand in TV, only I didn't want to get committed before, thinking I'd be going into Nick's picture, but now I'll really look into it. I have some good connections with NBC, you know—"

And she stopped short because she saw Courtney staring at her.

"I promise you, darling. And as soon as we can we'll move into a house in Beverly Hills, with a swimming pool—"

"I don't want to live in Beverly Hills," Courtney said miserably. "I want to live right here."

And then she was sorry she said that.

"Look, Courtney, we can't live here. Don't you think I'd like to, too? If it weren't for you, with just a little television work I could have a room here by myself, but I brought you out here because you refused to go back to boarding school. Don't make things harder for me than they are."

"I'm sorry, Mummy. Really." That had been a childish thing to say. She should have thought before she said that. Of course her mother wanted to stay in the Garden.

"May I fix you another drink?" she said.

"Yes."

Courtney made her mother another drink and then excused herself.

She knew she shouldn't have gone to bed when her mother was upset; she knew she should have stayed with her. But she didn't want to. She wanted to be by herself, to be in bed. She was sick of thinking of other people. She was terribly tired of assuming part of other people's unhappiness. She wanted to nurse her own disappointment. She cried herself to sleep, leaving her mother alone in the living room.

When she got up in the morning it was still raining, that miserable rain. She went into the kitchen and cooked herself a couple of eggs. When she got the eggs she shoved the bottle of champagne behind some milk, so her mother wouldn't see it when she got up. She noted that the bottle of Scotch, new the night before, was nearly empty. She didn't want to be around when her mother got up. A hangover added to everything else would be too much to face. It was already eleven o'clock. Some of the men in the Garden would be playing gin rummy in the room with the fireplace, but she didn't want to go there and watch them play and feel like a nuisance.

Then she knew where she would go. She would go to see Al. Only she would have to call him first, of course, because he might not be alone. It was still kind of early.

"Hello?"

"Hi, Al, this is Courtney Farrell." She always gave her full name on the phone; she liked the sound of it.

"Oh, hi, Court."

"I hope I didn't wake you up—"

"No, sweetie, I've been up about fifteen minutes."

"Oh, good. Al . . . I wondered if I could come by and talk to you."

"Sure, Court. Something wrong, baby?"

"Not really. I just wanted to talk to somebody. I hope I'm not intruding or bothering you or anything."

"If you were, babe, I'd tell you. No, come on over and have some coffee while I have breakfast."

Al had an idea of what Courtney wanted to talk to him about. Yesterday the manager of the Garden had come to him and told him that Sondra would have to leave security or pay at least half of the bill before she left. Knowing that the Garden bill was not the only one that Sondra owed, Al had made the arrangements. That was yesterday, and Sondra was perfectly willing to leave security, sure that the arrangement would never have to be put into practice.

Courtney took her cup of coffee and put it on the table beside the couch. She set some pillows under her head and lay down.

"Get to bed late?" said Al as he brought his breakfast in.

"No," Courtney said. "I'm just awfully tired, for some reason. I got to bed kind of early, but I could hardly get up this morning."

"Mmm. Rainy morning," Al suggested. "Want some toast?"

"No, thanks, I'm not very hungry."

"Al," Courtney said suddenly, "we've got to move out of the Garden."

"I know, sweetie."

"Nick gave somebody else the part."

"The bastard. I knew he would. He's that kind of a guy. I kind of think that's one of the reasons your mother fell in love with him. She never did know how to handle kindness."

"No," Courtney said, looking at Al. "She's always been a little afraid of people who were kind to her, like Daddy. Al—what's this place like that we're moving to?"

"Not bad, baby. Not bad at all for the money. A room with a couple of studio couches, and a legitimate kitchen. Of course, it's no Garden of Allah, but you ought to be just as glad that you're getting out of there. Don't think I haven't noticed the way you follow Cabot around. And when you go to confession you go down Havenhurst, so that you'll pass his apartment house. Don't think I miss that, sweetie, when I see you pass here. And you never eat breakfast in the second shift at Schwab's any more, because you know he always eats at two. Everything here is in about a three-block area, so nobody misses a thing."

"Nobody who's looking for it."

"Well, you're knocking your brains out, kid, and making a fool of yourself. He doesn't want to get involved with a young girl. And if he did go out with you, it would be for only one thing. That's no good. I admit I looked at you that way, too—once. But then I realized that you were just a kid. That's what Cabot realizes, and you ought to be glad."

"Well, I'm not glad, Al. Honestly, I get so lonely sometimes. And now we're going to move out by Beverly Hills, and I'll never see anybody but Mummy."

"You'll be starting school pretty soon, and you'll have dates and friends your own age."

"No, I won't, Al," she said soberly. "You don't know what it was like at school. I don't have anything in common with people my own age. I had one real friend at school, my roommate. For all the years I was at Scaisbrooke, only one friendship grew out of it. I don't know what's wrong with me, Al, why I don't fit in. But it's no use telling myself that when I move to a new school I'll suddenly have a group of friends, because all I have to do is look at the record."

Al shook his head.

"Crazy mixed-up kid. In a few years you'll find some guy, and you won't be lonely any more. There's a helluva potential there, and some guy is gonna see it."

"Yes, in a few years. The rest of the time I just go on like this. And, Al, I'm frightened. I don't know if you'll understand this, but this morning I couldn't get up, even though I'd had a lot of sleep. And last night I just wanted to get to bed, even though I wasn't really sleepy. It was an effort for me to walk over here, as though I'd had about three hours' sleep. That hasn't happened since I left Scaisbrooke, and it means something is wrong. Something is happening to me, and I don't understand it, and it frightens me because I can't control it."

Al didn't understand what Courtney meant, but he understood when she suddenly rushed to him like a small child and buried her head in his chest.

"I'm afraid of it, Al," she said, her words muffled. "And I'm afraid of being so alone with it."

He ran his hand gently through her hair, mussing it as he would a child's.

"What you need, kid, is a couple of parents. Even one would do."

"I have one, Al. But I won't let her be a parent. She wants to be. But I won't tell her the things that are bothering me, the way I'll tell you. I feel kind of—well, protected—with you, because you're a man and I just feel resentful with her, because she's Mummy and she's a woman. Does that make any sense?"

"Sure it makes sense, sweetie. But you won't find what you want with Barry Cabot, because he's not man enough. Don't deposit your need there, because you'll only get hurt."

"But Al, I don't plan to—"

"Now listen to what I say, baby doll, because I know you damned well. I've known you since your mother first came out here and I took her account, and that was five years ago. I've seen you grow from a skinny, frightened kid to a real attractive young woman—still frightened. And I can tell you what you're going to do better than you can tell yourself. So all I can do is warn you, the way I did last spring, to stay away from Barry Cabot, to forget about him. Things happen to a woman when she wants a man, and follows him around, and is rejected. He becomes more important to her than he has any right to be."

He looked down at the girl, her head buried in his chest.

"But we'll be leaving here. So I won't see Barry."

Al smiled.

"I said I know you pretty well, Court. What you want, you get. Remember what I told you." He ran his hand fondly along her neck. "Though you won't pay any attention to me, you crazy kid."

9

Beverly Hills High School looked as though it were designed for a Technicolor musical comedy. The front grounds were spacious and terraced, there were many sterile, carefully balanced buildings, including a gymnasium whose floor rolled back to reveal a large swimming pool. As Courtney sat in the November sun on the carefully cut lawn, she thought a little wistfully of Scaisbrooke, whose hockey fields had been trimmed for over half a century by a herd of goats, owned by the Italian groundskeeper. While the team played on the fields, the goats would graze quietly in the tall grass behind the field. The power mower was used only occasionally as a supplement. She thought of her favorite places, the rabbit's burrow in an overgrown corner of the quadrangle, and the cracked marble bench in the boxwoods. There could be no special, private places at this school; it was too carefully planned, too recently man-made.

For the first two weeks Courtney ate her lunch in the cafeteria, but then she gathered that the élite brought their lunches and ate them on the lawn. She was eating on the lawn among the school élite, the football players and the sons and daughters of men prominent in the Industry, and she was terribly alone. She knew a few of them by name and face, and she knew whose father was the head of what studio, and whose most recent stepmother was that rather notorious actress, but none of them knew her. Soon after she arrived, she established herself as a "brain," which was the way she began at every school. They also knew, from her accent, that she had gone to Eastern private schools. These two things were enough to exclude her from their society.

She wished that the school day would end, so that she could go home. Home! That awful little room where her mother sat all day and waited for phone calls that never came. But she wished the day would end, anyway. She was terribly, terribly tired, and she wanted to take a nap or something. She had never been as exhausted as she was now, as she had been ever since she entered Beverly. She hesitated to call the school by that familiar name.

She didn't know how she would get through the next two hours. Not that the classes made any demands on her; Scaisbrooke was too far ahead of even the best public school. It was just that she hated it so, and she was so tired. At least the next class was a study hall, so she could sleep. That would be good; then maybe she could stay alert through French. French class was a bore; she had read more demanding books in her second-form year. The fact that the teacher realized that didn't make the class any more enjoyable for Courtney, who had the secret—and justified—conviction that her accent was better than the instructor's. An American teaching French! She had never heard of that.

She took the bus home. Ordinarily she would have walked; it was less than a mile, but she knew she would be too tired if she tried to walk. When she passed the Fox lot and came to the apartment building, low and floral, with little plants on the terraces, she looked up at their door, indistinguishable from the others. She knew she would go in the door, set down her books, greet her mother—carefully avoiding asking if she had had any calls from her agent—and lie on the bed until her mother made dinner. They had eggs or lettuce-and-tomato salads for dinner, which was all right with Courtney, because she never was very hungry these days.

Then she knew that she would not go home today. She would not go home and sleep. She knew, somehow, that it was very wrong for her to sleep so much. There was something immoral about it, like eating or drinking too much. Today she would fight it. She had a dollar in her pocket. She would take the bus and go down to Hollywood, and maybe she would have a cup of coffee in Schwab's. She knew her mother didn't want her to go to Schwab's, or even be in that neighborhood, because people would ask her what had happened to Sondra, where she was living and what she was doing. But Courtney would find something to say to them. She had to see people, people that she knew. She had to talk to somebody or she would sleep again. She put her schoolbooks at a corner of the building and turned back to the road.

When she walked into Schwab's she was suddenly a little afraid. Barry Cabot was there. She knew that he would be, and she knew that that was one of the reasons she had come down here. She wanted to see him; she had wanted to see him for almost two months, two months spent in awful solitude. But she had lain in bed so many nights and thought of seeing him, and had built little pictures of his talking to her, warmly, and even of his kissing her. In her total abstinence from contact with any individual but her mother, a situation almost impossible for Courtney to endure, she had built her brief contact with this young man into a fantasy which pervaded her solitary hours.

"Courtney! Courtney Farrell!"

"Hi, Barry." She went over to him. She had no choice.

"Christ, I haven't seen you in two months. Here, have a cup of coffee."

Barry was a difficult man to predict. He had not seen Courtney for two months; the threat that the girl had once presented was forgotten. So much had transpired in the meantime; so many new threats and demands had been fled from, that he no longer felt the need to ignore Courtney. He disliked litigation, and he disliked hurting people. Courtney's absence had mitigated the threat of possession and a real relationship, and he was pleased that he could relax.

"Well, tell me what you've been doing with yourself? How is Beverly Hills High?"

"Oh, it's ghastly, Barry." He had not asked her about her mother, and that was the natural question. He understood that if Sondra had disappeared from sight there was a reason for it, and the reason probably was that she was broke. So he did not embarrass the kid; these things were understood. Everyone knew that she did not get the part in Russell's picture, and everyone knew that the Garden had impounded their clothes. But then, the cellar of the Garden was full of impounded belongings.

"I didn't think you'd like it," he said. "You're so much older than kids your age, and the kids out here have lived a lot less than you have. That's not as true at boarding school."

"Yes, you're right, Barry. Christ, it's good to talk to somebody. I've missed being around here."

As she talked to him, she thought, I'm going to go on talking to him. I'm not going back to that room for a long time. I'm going to make him want to stay with me. And she remembered what she had heard an actress who had become a symbol through attractiveness to men say to her mother, "When I'm with a man, all I think is sex, sex, sex." She decided that she would try that.

"Tell me, Barry, what have you been doing with yourself? I read that you were on a couple of Kraft shows."

"Yes, I did two, and I'm doing another week after next. My work is really picking up, now, with television. I haven't much of a part, but it isn't really bad. It's the part of this taxicab driver. You see, when the thing opens, this girl is in the cab, and she says to the driver, 'Take me anywhere, just anywhere. Drive around the city.' And as he takes her through the city—it's about three in the morning—he starts to talk to her, to find out why . . ."

As he talked, Courtney watched his face, and she thought: I'd like you to kiss me, yes, I'd like that very much; your mouth is so full and petulant, and your body is very slim, your hands gentle and sensitive—and as she imagined, she ran through the daydreams she had about him, only now he was here, and she was looking at him, beside him, and the attraction that she first found with Al was there, the attraction that made her drop her fork that day.

" . . . but the girl is convinced that her brother really didn't murder this guy, so she has gone to the apartment . . ."

Jesus Christ, Barry thought as he talked, this girl is all woman. She's a real lovely young woman; this is no kid.

He felt the question, the searching, under the veil of conversation, and he found himself reciprocating.

Suddenly Courtney felt as though a wall had been removed. She was speaking wordlessly, and he heard her and was answering. She was no longer throwing her emotion against a block; he was reciprocating, and they were touching at a distance.

"But you're probably bored with this, anyway," he said. "Look, we've both finished our coffee, why don't you come up to my apartment for a drink?"

It had worked, by God; she knew it would. She didn't need the words of the actress to convince her that it would work; she sensed that she would win this man's interest, and that was all she wanted. She would never forget that first day, when she found that it worked.

"Barry, I would love a drink. You know, I've never seen your apartment?"

"No," he said. "I guess you haven't."

The apartment was well furnished, and somehow reminded her of Al Leone's apartment. Al wouldn't like her coming here. But the hell with Al.

"Is a martini all right?"

"I'd prefer Scotch—"

"You'll drink a martini, by God, because that's all I have."

"Okay," she grinned.

The apartment was not dim. Barry hated dimness. The door was open onto the balcony that ran on three sides around the pool, and the late afternoon sun was coming in. Her mother would think that she was staying late at school. She had done that sometimes, she had sat beside the big, ugly football field until it was dark, and her mother no longer worried, because she respected Courtney's moods. After all, she could not blame the girl for hating to come home to a place like theirs.

He handed her her drink and they toasted each other. She was conscious of his eyes upon her body. She looked boldly at him.

"When I had just met you," he said, "and I bought you a Coke at the Thespian, I asked you what color your eyes were. They looked almost gray then. Now they look very green, really green."

"They *are* green," she said. It was always a point of dispute.

"Let me see," he said, and he took her glass and set it down beside his own on the table beside the couch. He put his hand beneath her chin, so cleanly and strongly molded, and turned her face toward him.

"Yes," he said, "they are green." He put his arms around her and drew her toward him. She put her arms around his neck, as Janet had told her to. She was right; their bodies did fit together, and move together, and his hand ran down her back and pressed her close against him. The emotion was strong, overwhelmingly strong in the release from many months of solitude and want.

"Darling," he said. "Darling."

"Yes, Barry."

He was unbuttoning the pink Brooks shirt and it fell from her shoulders as he put his arms around her and unhooked her bra. She was aware, very aware, of what was happening to her, but she wanted it. She wanted it; she had planned it, planned it long before he had ever thought of it, and she had asked him silently before he asked her, because she wanted it so much.

He took her by the hand into the bedroom, and he did not pull down the shades to cut off the light. She took off the rest of her clothes and she waited, lying on the bed in the marvelous luxury of her own young body, she waited for him.

10

He was like a little boy as he slept in her arms. His face was young and relaxed. She didn't want to sleep. That terrible, dragging exhaustion was gone, and her body and her mind were clear and at peace, marvelously alive and relaxed. She ran her hand through the hair that was long on his neck. It was very soft, as she had imagined it to be, and he did not wake up. His body was pale and hard, a young man's body, sleeping with the peace of a boy. She was very happy. She was lost in her happiness. I have been loved, she thought. And this is my lover—she savored the word, formed it, lingered on it. An old and trite word, a word from historical novels, but the word was good to her.

She wished that he would wake up, so that he would love her again. Love. She had not known what it could be, and she would never live without it again. She had not known that she would know so much about love, the first time. The first time. She could never be as she had been before; she could never see life as she had seen it before, life with an entire sphere dimly seen.

He stirred, he was waking up as early evening came to the window. He kissed her shoulder; he was still half asleep, he probably didn't know who it was, but she didn't care. Then his eyes were open, and he looked at her for several minutes in the gentle silence.

He ran his hands along her body, along the ribs and the hips, pronounced but soft, and her body was relaxed. When he had first touched her body it had come alive where his hand had been.

"Court," he said, and his face was troubled. "Court, I honestly didn't know. If I had known—well, I've never done that. I'm not a very moral guy, but I've never done that."

"I wanted you to make love to me. I told you before, when you asked me, that I had never made love."

"I didn't believe you. You seemed to know so much, and in Schwab's—I've never known a girl like you," he said. "Honestly, this is no crap. You're so quiet, and warm, and—well, almost poetic. It's an odd word to use, but it suits you."

"Barry, do me a favor. Don't ever, ever say that you love me. Because that wouldn't be true, and I don't want you to feel you should say it."

"No," he smiled. "No, I won't ever say that. I don't love you, and you don't love me, and there won't be any pretending." He put his head against her in the growing dimness. "But I don't want you to go, darling. I don't want you to leave me."

"I won't go until I have to, Barry. Ill stay here with you."

She took him in her arms.

"You're like a much older woman," he said. "Not wanting to possess, not demanding anything from me. And yet you're young, your body is young, your skin is young and fresh, and you trust as a young girl trusts."

"Because no man has ever betrayed that trust." She saw the question in his face. "No, you never betrayed it, either. Of course I trust in you. I trust in you completely. I have to, anyway," she smiled. "Because I don't know anything. Because you're really the first, the first I've ever kissed, as well as the first I've ever made love with."

He smiled at her, "Yes," he said, "you kiss like a little girl kissing good night. I'll have to teach you to kiss." Suddenly he remembered. "Court, won't your mother be worried? Won't she wonder why you're not home?"

"Yes. Yes, I guess I'd better get back. It must be almost seven."

"I don't want you to go," he said again, and he meant it. "But I don't want you to get in trouble, either. You'll have dinner with me tomorrow?"

"Why, Barry, I thought you were famous for never buying anyone a meal."

"You're something else again. May I take you home?"

"No," she said hurriedly. She didn't want him to see where she lived. "No, I'd rather you didn't."

"Then I'll pick you up tomorrow."

"No—"

He understood. "Ill pick you up at school, and we'll swim, and then we'll have dinner. I don't want you to wander down here by yourself, like—well, I just don't want that for you. I'll pick you up, and I'll take you to dinner."

"Yes," she said. "I'd like that."

She got up and started to pick up her clothes. He got up, too, and he took her clothes from her. It had never occurred to him to do this before, but this was the first time, and he did not want her to do anything for herself. There would be many times, many years, of doing everything for herself in the love affairs that she would have. He did not want her to know the self-sufficiency now. He did not want there to be any mark of the tired and familiar love affair in the memory of this, her first. He wanted to treat her as something very special, which she was.

When she had left, the apartment was very still and empty. He poured out the now-warm martinis. Beneath the couch he saw a paperback Western novel. He picked it up in disgust and threw it in the garbage can. George. Ugly mementos of the thing in his life that made him hate himself, that made him feel he was not even the least that he could be, a man. He was an actor, an actor of talent, he knew that. But his talent did not make up for the fact that he was not a man. His talent could not justify his existence. He made himself a fresh martini and sat in the living room. He turned on a light because the room was now dim.

He had been a man with Courtney, by God. Her first. She chose him, this lovely and talented young woman. He was not a man with the others, he was a gigolo. A gigolo. But today, this afternoon, he had been a man. He wondered if she knew. She must know, she knew so much. He wondered how he had been able to rise above himself this afternoon. He wondered where he had gotten the courage to make love to her, to take the chance of failure. She knew so little. He wondered if he had been good. He could teach her, though, he could teach her a great deal, because she knew nothing. And she had chosen him. Why did he make this drink. This drink, this liquor, this Western pocket book. This lovely young girl.

"You're home late this afternoon, Courtney," her mother said to her as she came in.

"Yes," she said.

"What did you do, take a walk?"

"Yes," she said. "I took a walk."

"I worry about you when you're not home by dark."

"It's just barely dark," she said. "It got dark a little while ago, just a little while ago."

"It's a lovely evening. I don't blame you for taking a walk."

"It is a lovely evening," she said.

"Are you hungry after your walk?"

"No," she said.

"I think you ought to eat some dinner."

"I'm kind of tired," she said. "My walk relaxed me, and made me sleepy."

"I suppose so. Well, I certainly can't force you to eat dinner. Your walk seems to have done you good. You should do that more often. You don't look as drawn and strained as you usually do after school."

"Yes," she said, "I think I will do it more often. Is it all right, Mummy, if I have dinner at a drugstore somewhere tomorrow night, for a change?"

"I don't see why you want to eat at a drugstore."

"Well," she said, "it was so nice, just walking by myself. The streets are lovely in the evening. I thought I might go to a movie tomorrow night, after dinner—if it's all right with you."

"I don't like you spending so much time by yourself. It's not good for you."

"Well, as a matter of fact, Mummy, one of the boys in my Latin class asked me if I wanted to have dinner with him and go to a movie."

"Why didn't you tell me? I think that's wonderful. I'm so glad to see you starting to have dates."

"Well, I don't know, I—"

"Silly child, did you think I would feel you should stay here with me?"

"I guess so," she floundered.

"No, I'm glad to see you having some sort of social life. I'll be fine here. You know," she smiled, "I spent many years by myself before you were ever born."

"Thank you, Mummy."

"Just be home by midnight, because you have school the next day."

As Courtney took off her clothes and got into the bed beside hers, Sondra smiled to herself. What a thoughtful child. She put the world on her shoulders. She was afraid to tell me she had a date because she thought she should keep me company. What a wonderful daughter.

11

She went to Barry's apartment the next day, and they swam in his pool, and they lay in the sun, and she looked over at him many times, pleased and warmed by the thought that she knew the body within that bathing suit so well. They went to dinner at a steak house in downtown Los Angeles, a wonderful place. They did not eat in Hollywood because they did not want anyone who knew them to see them together. Then they went back to the apartment and had a drink, and they made love in the soft evening and it rained quietly and steadily outside the room.

The early winter passed in the newness of their love. Courtney developed a friend at school with whom she often stayed overnight, and her mother understood the fact that she never brought her friend home because she was embarrassed by her surroundings.

Courtney wondered what she would do when Christmas vacation came, how she would explain being out of the house all the days that she wanted to spend with Barry. Somehow, a week after vacation began and Courtney had spent many days sitting in the room reading, her mother's efforts paid off and she got a small part on a soap opera as a temporary replacement for an actress who was taking a two-week vacation. It was a sharp come-down for her, and a severe blow to her already weakened pride, but it enabled her to pay back a little money to Al. More important for Courtney, it kept her out of the house during the day so that she could see Barry.

Sondra wondered what was happening to Courtney. The girl was so distant, with a new sort of distance. The world that she kept within herself seemed to have grown completely out of proportion. It was difficult to talk to her, even simple conversation. For the first time she seemed to have little interest in her mother's fortunes, and she accepted her new job with little comment and no celebration. She took Courtney's distance as an indication that the emotional problems which had begun to show themselves at Scaisbrooke had become aggravated by their relative poverty, so unfamiliar to Courtney. She was worried by it. Although Courtney seemed happy these days, it was a happiness which grew from her inner world, and it did not reassure her mother.

Courtney had learned from Barry. He was a good and gentle teacher. Everything she knew, even the simple act of putting her arms around him, she had learned from him, and she no longer kissed him as a small child kisses goodnight. She had been taught by an older man, an actor, as she told Janet she would be. "I want to be charming," she had said in that room at prep school. "I want to be charming, to give in a charming way and to love in a lovely way."

Now that she was on vacation, he could not pick her up at school, so she had gotten into the habit of taking the bus down to his apartment. His apartment was as familiar to her as her own, and she often helped him clean it and cooked dinner for him. She liked that; it seemed to make her role as a woman a fuller one. He was pleased; he was always pleased when a woman took care of him.

She usually came down around noon, and Barry rushed as he walked down Havenhurst, because it was a quarter to twelve: He put the collar of his corduroy jacket high around his neck. There was a crispness in the air. It was the fourth of January. How quickly these two months had gone. He kicked the dead leaves on the sidewalk into the gutter. How different his life had been these last two months. Strange, the way he had come to accept Courtney's presence in his apartment, in his life. Of course they weren't in love with each other, but there was a fondness and an ease which was impossible to maintain whenever love played a part in a relationship. Only companionship, and making love. And Christ, she was good, for a kid who didn't know anything. It was a lovely life.

There were dead leaves in the swimming pool. He climbed the stairs to his apartment, and unlocked the door. The living room was dim; evening came early these days.

"Hiya, Barry."

"George! My God, what are you doing here?"

He came out of the bedroom, wearing his Levi's low on his hips, the Levi's that left no part of his body to the imagination, and a tee shirt. His leather jacket was on the couch, beside a can of beer.

"I couldn't find that Western I left by the couch," he said, settling himself with the can of beer. "Apartment looks very clean," he continued. "She's been cleaning it, I suppose."

"Now, look, George—"

'You've been eating in," he went on. "Not eating at Schwab's any more. She a good cook, this broad?"

"For Chrissake."

"You haven't called," he said, finally angry. "You haven't called in almost three months. I've checked my answering service every day to make sure. No call from Mr. Cabot. No call, because Mr. Cabot has been making it with a little girl. A snotty kid. He's ashamed of me, Mr. Cabot is. He's trying to forget he knows me, or that he ever knew me so well."

"I've been working," Barry floundered. "I've been busy as hell."

"Busy making love, you little sonavabitch. No time for me any more. The hell with all those months when you were broke and I supported you. And the time you went on that binge and I found you in a bar downtown with a fever of a hundred and three, and brought you home and took care of you, got a doctor and brought you your meals. You've forgotten all that, and you've forgotten the nights when you could sleep and you weren't afraid, because I was here. I don't mean anything to you any more."

"George, you're wrong. She doesn't mean anything to me. She's just—a convenience." Christ, where had it gone, his courage, his manliness, his loyalty?

"Then why haven't you called me? I sit home alone, and there isn't any call, there isn't anything. And I'm broke, I live on spaghetti for Chrissake, and there isn't even any call from you."

"George." And his face was solemn and tender. "George, look. I didn't mean to hurt you, God damned if I did."

"You know that when you don't call, and everybody knows you've got this little broad and I'm a laughing-stock—"

"Everybody knows!"

"Well, all right, they don't, but they know you've got somebody, because you just aren't around any more."

"George. Look, George, listen." My God, she was going to be here any minute, she would walk in, and what a helluva thing for her to go through, finding George here, this lovely young girl, and he had wanted to keep this ugliness from her.

"George, I'll call you tonight, and you come over for a drink, and everything will be all right again. I've been a son of a bitch, okay, but I'll explain it to you and I honestly—believe me, I didn't mean to hurt you."

"You trying to get rid of me."

"No, it isn't that, it isn't—for Christ's sake, I'll call you, but I can't talk to you now!"

"She's coming. She's coming here and you're ashamed of me. You're always ashamed of me."

"Get the hell out of here." He spoke quietly, the quiet voice in anger that he was famous for, the controlled and dangerous voice. "I said, get out of this apartment. I don't care if you have a key, this is my apartment, and get out of it."

George stood up in a fury, his husky body tensed. Barry was afraid.

"George, I didn't mean that. I didn't mean it, George." Maybe he could call her—but no, she was on her way. Maybe he could stop her before she came in, tell George he was going for a walk. No, that was crazy. There wasn't a thing he could do.

George smiled at the fear in the other man's face.

"I'll go, Barry."

Thank God, Barry thought.

"I'll go," George went on, "and I won't call you or come here again. I won't embarrass you in front of her, she's so Goddam special to you. But you'll wish to Christ you hadn't done this. You'll wish to Christ."

Courtney passed him on the street as she came to Barry's

apartment. He was wearing his leather jacket, and he was sweating. He pretended not to see her. When she passed him, she ran, past the swimming pool with the dead leaves and up the pastel stairs, to Barry's apartment.

He was sitting with a water glass full of gin, drinking it very quickly.

"Barry. Darling."

She had never called him "darling" before, a simple term; she had never used words of endearment. It slipped out. She went to him and put her hand on the glass to take it from his so that she could hold him in her arms.

"Let me alone. Let me alone, for God's sake."

He took her wrist with a grip so hard it hurt her, and he threw her hand down.

"Barry, don't drink like that. You're on the verge of another binge, a real bender. I thought you'd stopped that. Don't drink like that, I'll have a drink with you, and we'll make love—"

"I said let me alone."

She got up and went to the kitchen. She took the gin and started to pour it out.

He came in and took the bottle from her and he slapped her, three times, in his fury and confusion. At that moment he would have fought her for it.

She ran into the bedroom and shut the door, and she lay on the bed and cried uncontrollably. In a while she had quieted herself. She would leave when she had stopped crying completely, she would run through the living room where he was sitting so that he wouldn't talk to her, and she would leave him alone because there was no place for her here. If only she could stop crying. The room was so dark, the room was so ugly. She buried her head in his pillow. In his pillow. In the room, on the bed, where they had made love, and the room was so ugly, and she wanted to leave. If only she could stop crying.

A hand was on her shoulder, a strong and gentle hand.

"Court."

"I don't want you, Barry."

He turned her on her back, almost angrily, with his hands on her shoulders.

"It's all so ugly, Barry."

He took his hands away and sat on the edge of the bed.

"I didn't want you to see this," he said softly.

"It isn't just him, Barry. I knew about that even before I met you. It's me, too. It's getting on the bus and looking around when I get off and coming here and making up stories to tell Mummy."

"Everything would have been all right if George hadn't come here. But I sent him away. And now it can be just the way it was before."

She sat up and took a cigarette from his shirt pocket and lit it. She had stopped crying now.

"It's gray. It's gray and dim. Do you know what I mean? It's dead leaves in the swimming pool and smoke in the bedroom. But I guess that doesn't make any sense to you."

"Yes, darling, it makes sense to me. But life just isn't clear-cut and bright colors. There's the ugliness everywhere, and we just pretend not to see it."

"It doesn't have to be like that. I won't settle for its being like that. I won't live in the ugliness and subterfuge and making love just because we like it, and being so careful so that I won't get pregnant, and perverting everything."

"We're not perverting anything. It isn't like that with us."

"Oh, Barry, just stop talking."

"What do you want, darling? Do you want to stop?"

"No. No, I don't. But I don't want to live this way. Yes, I do want to stop, because it isn't young any more. It's middle-aged and gray and confused. But I don't want to stop coming here. Maybe I could just come and we could talk and—"

She looked at him, sitting on the edge of the bed, and she knew that it could never be like that. He wasn't looking at her, he was staring out the window at the naked branches of the winter trees and the room was dark and still.

"I need you," he said. "Help me."

"Help you. Help you to stop loving young men. Give myself for that. I'm worth more than that."

She didn't know why she spoke to him so angrily, why she wanted to hurt him. He sat in silence and then he turned to her, and his face was as it had been when he slapped her. He leaned across her body and held her wrists so tightly that it hurt her.

"You bitch," he said. "You whore."

12

It was a very cold day, and Courtney was wearing her Scaisbrooke polo coat. She was glad that school was out for the day; perhaps when she got outside and left the stuffy classrooms she wouldn't feel so sleepy. It had gotten worse again, the sleepiness that frightened her. She would walk to the bus stop, and go down to Barry's apartment. Not because she wanted to. It was a habit now, a hollow habit. They had never regained what they had had in the beginning, the discovery. It was no good any more; not the love, the love was always good. But she would go down there and they would pretend to talk to each other. It was as she walked down the steps with these thoughts, apart from her schoolmates, that she saw Al.

He was standing beside his car at the front of the steps. He had been waiting for her because, when she came down, he opened the car door.

"Al! How great to see you!"

"Get in."

"Well—"

He shut the door and got in the other side and started the car; he didn't turn toward Sunset but headed straight downtown.

"I'm taking you to dinner. I imagine you haven't had a good dinner in quite a while."

"Well, that's very nice of you, Al, but I'm afraid I have another date."

"Not tonight you don't."

"What's this bit?"

"I have a great deal to talk to you about."

"To me? What's wrong?"

"Look, we'll talk after we've both had a drink and we're sitting down. Not now."

Well, what the hell, thought Courtney. Maybe it would be good for Barry to sit and wait for her and not have her arrive, for a change. Al certainly had something on his mind. He was right, too, that she hadn't had a good dinner in weeks.

The restaurant was large and massive, with a lot of heavy wood, and they brought the cuts of roast beef around for their approval before cooking them. This wasn't so bad, after all. She was sure that she was going to get a lecture of some sort, but at least she would get a good dinner.

"All right, Al. We're both fortified with our drinks. What's the lecture?"

"It's not a lecture. I just want to get some things straightened out, and maybe get you straightened out."

"What about? I may not be doing much work at school, but I have a B average. I haven't had any fights with Mummy, I've been living within my allowance—"

"It's about Barry Cabot."

"What about Barry Cabot." She took another sip of her dry martini.

114

"You know George what's-his-name, the guy Cabot had this thing with."

"I met him once, why?"

"I was having dinner at Googie's last night, and he sat next to me. Now, this is a guy I never talk to, because he's just the sort of guy I never have dealings with if I can avoid it, and I usually can."

"Mmm." She sounded bored because she was worried.

"So he started to talk to me, and I didn't object because I have learned that it does not pay to be rude to anybody in this town. You never know when someone comes in handy."

"Yes, well get to the point."

"So he started to talk about your mother, and how he never saw her around any more, and he guessed she was broke. I thought, knowing I am her business manager, that he was trying to find some gossip, so I just said, 'Yes, she has left the Garden; she's living in Beverly Hills because her kid goes to school there.' I was not going to give him any satisfaction because I do not like the guy."

"So?"

"So he started to say what a great person she is, and right away I knew something was funny, because he doesn't know her particularly and I always thought he didn't like her. He doesn't like any woman Cabot likes. But I said, 'Yes, she is a great person,' to see what he was leading up to."

"You're taking an awfully long time on this story."

"So then he said, 'It's a shame her kid turned out the way she did.' Well then I had an idea of what he was going to say, because he knows I know your mother very well and take a kind of personal interest in you two. So I asked him what he meant. So, he said in a real offhand way, 'I mean the way the kid has been living with some actor.' Right away I shut him up. I said, 'I'm sure that's some lousy rumor,' and he had finished his coffee and saw I was not a good target for his gossip, so he kind of shrugged and pretty soon he left."

"Well, Al, you know what these fags are like. He doesn't like Mummy, and he has never liked me, ever since he saw me that night when I had a drink with Cabot at the Thespian, last summer. They're real bitchy, these fags."

"Look, kid. I'm no fool. I'm not Sondra Farrell. I know this actor he was talking about was Cabot, only he was too jealous to admit you were having an affair with him. Remember, I predicted this several months ago. George expected me to run to your mother and tell her, but I'm not that kind of a guy. Now, I want you to give it to me straight."

Courtney finished her drink.

"I'd like another, Al."

"You drink too much, for a kid. One is enough."

"Are you trying to legislate my drinking?"

"Somebody's got to legislate something."

"I said I wanted another drink."

"All right," he sighed. He signaled to the waiter.

"Another round."

"Yes, sir."

There was a silence. Al looked at Courtney. Five years he had known her, almost six. There was no question any more about her being a woman. She looked like a woman, even though she was sixteen. The waiter never questioned her being twenty-one. Well, she had the body, and she had that look, the absence of the hardness and unsureness of a kid.

"Yes, Al. You're right I have been having an affair with Barry Cabot. But I haven't been living with him," she added hastily. "I've just been having an affair with him."

116

"Sweetie, I thought I told you not to pin your need on a guy like Cabot. I thought I told you that."

"Yes, you did, Al. That day when we were moving out of the Garden. But you were wrong. I did pin my need on him, and he filled it."

"That bastard. A kid like you."

"No, Al. That's what I thought you would say. People always think a girl's first lover takes advantage of her. But I wanted it, nobody took advantage of me. You could almost say I instigated it. I don't know what this myth is about men seducing innocent young girls. It isn't that way at all."

"Look, doll. I can see this a little more clearly than you can. I saw the same thing, I saw the same young woman. But when I kissed you, I knew you were a kid, a moral, innocent kid, a little wooden doll. And I cared too much about you as a person to change that. This guy saw the same thing; don't kid yourself that you looked like a *femme fatale*. You looked like a helluva sexy kid. So he made love to you, this faggot, because if he was lousy, you wouldn't know the difference."

"Al, don't talk like that. He isn't that way at all. You're a man, and men hate him because he's a fag, but he isn't really—I used to think I knew what a fag was, but now I don't know at all. I don't know how I would have—I mean, I needed him. Not just anybody, I needed him. And he's a man, you know, my lover. He's a fag but I found that doesn't mean anything, it just means he's more sensitive, and he—well, he needs me. That's what's important to me. He needs me."

The waiter brought their drinks.

"Look, what you say about the guy's virtues doesn't interest me. You're obviously in love with him, for some reason. If you know what it's all about."

"I'm not a kid any more, Al."

"Yes, you are. Even though you've made love, you're still a kid. That doesn't mean anything, you know. Well, yes it does, but it isn't any indication of maturity, even sophistication. Other girls your age make out with boys, you just happened to go to bed with a guy."

"It makes a great deal of difference. Mostly with Mummy. I'm so conscious of being not her daughter but another woman."

"No. No, it won't make any difference in you yet. But it will if you go on with this. You know, it isn't any good for you, this bit. You aren't the kind of kid who can get away with it. You're too much of an idealist to do something shoddy."

"It isn't shoddy, Al."

He looked at the girl, his Manhattan part way to his lips.

"Well, all right. It is. You know me too well. But I tried to stop, Al, honestly I did."

He took a sip of his drink.

"I don't like it. It only increases the loneliness that made me start the whole thing. And worrying about getting pregnant, and watching the date, and all that grubby bit, that shabby, lonely bit. I don't tell Barry about that, I don't feel I can. I feel the worry and the guilt are my problem, and I have no right to inflict it on him."

"You have a lot of guts, Court, you always have had. Why don't you just pull yourself together?"

"Pull myself together! Pull myself together. That's a lousy line, it doesn't mean anything."

"I mean, stop hurting yourself. Because you are, you know. People are going to find out, and even if they don't, you'll know you have something you have to hide from people, a part of yourself that you can't let the world know about. It's easier to conform."

The waiter brought their dinner and Courtney ate as though it were her first meal in days.

Al smiled. "Hungry, kid? . . . Yeah, I guess you are. You aren't very used to being broke." Courtney continued eating. "You know, there isn't anything for your mother out here. When someone has hit the skids in this town, the only thing to do is to leave it, to re-establish yourself someplace else and then have them call for you. Here it is March, and your mother has had one lousy job. She ought to go back to New York, try some TV there. People know her there, and they aren't afraid of her the way they are here, they're so wary about people on the downgrade. This is no town for a comeback, people are too unsure of themselves."

Courtney was glad that the subject had shifted from herself.

"Well, it's a funny thing about Hollywood," Courtney said. "Once you've been out here awhile, it's hard to go someplace else, and it gets harder the longer you stay here. Takes some real propulsion to make you leave."

"It's always hard to change your way of life, but sometimes it's got to be done—like with you."

"Al, will you please stop lecturing me? I've had enough for one evening. I'm sick of your moralizing, as though I were a fallen woman or something."

"Court, stop feeling sorry for yourself."

Courtney didn't answer.

"Show some guts. Pull out of this."

She was very angry with herself then, because she started to cry. Not really, just silently, inside herself.

"I'm sorry, kid. Your mother's always telling me I have no sensitivity. I guess she's right. But I just don't like to see you waste yourself. I'm real fond of you, Court, and I hate to see you make yourself unhappy and guilty. There isn't any need for that. If you were middle-aged or something, it would be different, but everything's ahead of you, so don't screw your life up now."

"Al, please stop talking, just stop. Leave this up to me, will you? It's my problem. I know it isn't any good, it hasn't been for a couple of months now. But I just can't face being alone again."

"But isn't it better to like yourself? Isn't that more important than some guy's companionship just because he sleeps with you?"

She finished her dinner very quickly, because, after all, the food wasn't worth it. She hated to lose Al's respect. She hated to have him criticize her, to have him feel he had to help her. She wanted to go, though she didn't know where. She didn't want to go to Barry's apartment, not tonight. Maybe home would be the best place to go.

When she got home, her mother was asleep. She went to the bathroom and splashed cold water on her face because she had been crying in the car; leaning against Al she had cried. Al and Barry were the only men she had ever cried in front of.

It was after she dried her face and started to put the towel back that she saw the package of razor blades. She felt as she had at Scaisbrooke when she stood at the window of her room and looked at the ground. She was afraid. She could not trust her mind, she could never trust her mind. She looked back at the door. It was shut, and her mother never woke up when she came in. She held her hands in front of her under the light. She rested her left hand on the sink.

She took one of the razor blades from the package and held it above her hand. She was afraid, and, oddly enough, she was embarrassed. She felt foolish. She was too intelligent to hurt herself. But no, she would allow herself the luxury of self-punishment. She would give in.

She took the razor blade and she slashed one of her fingers at the first joint. Whenever she used it it would hurt, and it would remind her of her guilt, of her sensuality and her sin. It hurt, it was very sensitive, her finger, so she cut at the other fingers of her left hand very quickly so the pain would be over soon. It bled profusely, and she was pleased at the blood in the sink. What a beautiful symbol that Christ should have bled to expiate the sins of men, men of little courage. It took so much courage to be good, but it took even more courage to sin. She had neither. Al was right, she couldn't take sin. Living with her sin, living with herself in a state of sin, it was too much for her, and she had to punish herself. She hadn't even enough courage to destroy herself.

She took some toilet paper and wrapped it around her hand to stem the bleeding. What an awful lot of blood in her fingers. She folded her hand tightly, making a fist to stop the bleeding. Jesus that hurt. She wanted to show somebody what she had done to herself; she had a crazy desire to wake her mother up and show her. But that was one thing she would not give in to. She would maintain at least that much dignity. She got in bed very quietly so her mother wouldn't wake up. She had cleaned up the sink, and no one would ever know.

In the morning she woke up late, and the first thing she thought of was her hand. She looked at it. The bleeding had stopped in the night. That was good, she felt embarrassed at her weakness and childishness. Her mother had gone out for lunch. She got up and took off the toilet paper and with an edge of Kleenex she gingerly cleaned her fingers. The cuts were clean and, being in the joints, they didn't show. They would heal soon. Until then they would hurt, to remind her.

13

There was spring in the early California evening, and as Courtney left the sanitarium with her father she was glad to be among people again; she was glad that the psychiatrist had said she could leave. Two months ago there had been nothing that she had wanted more than to leave life, to be taken care of and not asked to decide anything. But now she was anxious to be a person again, and only a little afraid. She looked at her father, sitting beside her in the cab. She was glad that he had come to California for her release. She liked the way her parents seemed so anxious to be with her, and to do things for her, since she had gone to the sanitarium.

Robbie took her to a restaurant in downtown Los Angeles, a very good restaurant that he always went to when he came here on business. Courtney had never been there, because it was not a place frequented by Hollywood people. It was very New York, which she liked. Her father must know that she wanted to be far away from Hollywood and its associations. But, of course,

Courtney thought as she looked out the cab window, he couldn't really know that much about her. Probably he was just ill at ease in her mother's Hollywood world.

"I hope you like this place," he said as they got out of the cab. "This is your evening," he smiled.

They had talked little in the taxi, and they were uneasily silent as they sat down at the table. The things uppermost in their minds had been left at the gate to the sanitarium, and were forbidden subjects. Whatever had driven her to seek brief asylum was known only to Courtney, and though Robbie wished he could talk to her about it, perhaps help her, he knew that he must not invade her privacy. Perhaps it was just as well that he did not know it. They had shared so little— occasional afternoons and evenings over a span of so many years—that Robbie found himself searching his mind to make conversation with his daughter.

"What would you like to begin with?" he asked.

"I'd like a drink, please."

Yes, she drank now. He should have remembered that.

"A martini," she said. "Very dry, with no lemon peel or anything."

He ordered two martinis. He wondered where she had learned to drink martinis. With her mother, of course.

"It's good to be with you, Courtney," he said. "It's been a long time since we had dinner together."

"Yes," she said. "I guess it was when you saw me off to California. It's been about a year, I guess."

"You've grown up a lot in a year."

"Yes," she said. "I have."

The waiter brought the martinis.

"When I take you out to dinner now," Robbie said, "people

must wonder what I've got to be going out with such a lovely young girl."

"I don't know. You're very attractive."

"Thank you," he said. "How is your martini? Dry enough for you?"

"Yes, thank you. You know," she said, fingering the glass, "it's funny how a drink seems reassuring. Because of its associations, I guess. It's always been a permanent fixture of home."

"Well, I don't know about that. It's always been a permanent fixture with your mother, but you're a little young to find a drink reassuring."

"Daddy, really. Let's not have the New England morality routine."

"No, Courtney. You are too young to drink."

"I know," she grinned. "Have you ever thought that by the time I'm old enough to drink, I'll have been drinking for seven years illegally?"

"I'd rather not," he said drily.

Courtney sipped her drink defiantly.

"You're certainly your mother's daughter."

"Yes," she said leaning forward. "I'm Mummy's daughter, and I'm decadent, alcoholic at sixteen, blasé . . .

"Now, Courtney."

"Anything else you'd like to add?"

"Courtney, I didn't mean . . ."

Courtney leaned back. She took out a cigarette and he lit it for her.

"Why are you so worried about me? I remember when I was little, and insisted that you take me someplace nice like Twenty One or the Plaza when you took me to dinner, you always said ominously that I had my mother's extravagance. That's not such a bad thing, you know. To insist on good things, to be able to drink well. You know you wouldn't like to have a daughter who thought Longchamps was the height of elegance, and a furtive sip of ale or a cigarette in the john a great adventure."

"Let's not pursue the subject further."

"That's all right with me. You brought it up."

They were silent. Robbie sipped his drink and studied his daughter. He resented her sophistication. He resented her not being a little girl any longer. She argued with him just the way her mother always had. They even used the same phrases, the same images, as though the only alternative to their ways was a boorish conventionalism. Her mother always used the picture of the gray-headed mother, with knitting on her plump lap. It made him angry that Courtney should have become like Sondra, and that it should have happened so quickly. He resented having been cheated of the years that other fathers took for granted, dancing with their daughters at country-club tea dances, and surveying their dates with a protective and slightly jealous eye.

"You know," Courtney said looking around her, "I feel a little the way I used to when I came to New York from boarding school. I remember how I used to be surprised by all the colors on the street, and all the people. But most of all, it was the fact that the people weren't wearing Scaisbrooke blue that amazed me—like a man getting out of the army or something."

"Remember how you used to astound the waitresses at Schrafft's by ordering two desserts?"

"Yes," she said. But she was not interested in remembering.

She used to be so delighted at leaving school, Robbie thought. She didn't take things for granted then. He would take her to a play. Once he took her to "Pal Joey," and was disturbed because she enjoyed it. But what she liked most was the year the D'Oyly Carte Troupe was in town, before she went to boarding school, when he took her to a matinee every Saturday. They must have seen all the Gilbert and Sullivan in the repertoire, Robbie thought wearily. It was always an occasion for Courtney to see her father. That was too bad, in a way.

"Daddy," Courtney said suddenly, "what did Dr. Wright say to you? What did he tell you?"

"Very little," Robbie said. "That you were tired, that too much responsibility had been thrust upon you. I know your mother is a problem to you," he said.

"No. No, not at all. Only when I was very little, and she would go into tirades that I didn't understand, and get angry with me."

"I know," Robbie said. "It was always hard for you to understand that her tempers had nothing to do with you. I still remember the day you went into her room one morning to ask her if you could go into New York with a friend of yours to see the rodeo, and she got furious with you and wouldn't let you go, because you woke her up. She was in a play then."

"Yes," Courtney said. "I remember that very well. I remember I called you, to ask you if you would go with us so that it would be all right with Mummy, and you said no."

"I couldn't interfere with your mother's discipline, even if she was wrong."

"I was as angry with you as I was with her. I always thought you were the sane one, who would mediate."

"I couldn't take responsibility for your disobeying your mother."

"Of course you could. But that was years ago, let's not argue about it now." Courtney sipped her martini. Why did they always have to argue? Her father was always defending himself.

"You're still doing the same thing," Robbie said. "You're still playing one of us against the other."

"I play one of you against the other! You've got it backwards. You're always putting me in the middle, like a pawn. When I do something that displeases you, or when I need something that's a bore—like having to go to the dentist—you disown me, I suddenly become a child of parthenogenesis."

"What would you like for dinner?"

"I don't know," Courtney said petulantly. "I want another martini."

"One is enough."

"What are you trying to do? Suddenly legislate for me? You gave up that right a long time ago, you know. Maybe when you wouldn't take me to the rodeo."

"All right. Have another martini. Get loaded, I don't care. It's not my responsibility, since you refuse to do anything I say."

"I've never gotten bombed. Never in my life."

"What a remarkable record to hold at sixteen. How could you go all those years with an unblemished record? To say nothing of the pre-natal cocktail parties."

"You mean when Mummy was walking around pregnant and loaded, like *Tobacco Road*? You know she had never gotten tight, either. It just makes you mad that we can drink and spend money and never pay some black Protestant fee for it."

"Stop talking like your Irish mother."

"Look, why are you always maligning Mummy? You know I never believe what you say, anyway."

"I know. But your mother's word is gospel. It means nothing that I'm paying for your sanitarium, and the psychiatrist. I don't suppose your mother mentioned that."

"So what? Why do you always talk about money, as though money means something?"

"Because it does, to you. You're just like your mother. All you care about is what you can get out of me."

"You want another drink, Daddy? Do you feel a crying jag coming on? Nobody loves me, they just want to bleed me white, and leave me battered by the roadside?"

"Don't be disrespectful, young lady."

Courtney grinned. "You could at least have a sense of humor."

"I don't see anything amusing."

"You wouldn't."

"Now, look here—"

"All right. Let's drop it. I'd like another drink, please."

Robbie sighed. He had so looked forward to this evening with her. He had not seen her in so long, and he had hoped that now, since her mother's world had gone to pieces, she would want to trust in him a little. But he had had another daughter in mind, a prototype daughter who needed people, who depended on her parents and looked to them for help. Courtney was like her mother. If she were drowning, she would wave off the rescuers, in a last gesture of defiance, because they were fishermen in a rowboat and she wanted to be saved by a yacht. He ordered two more martinis.

"Daddy," Courtney said, serious again, "was that really all Dr. Wright said to you?"

"Yes," Robbie answered. "Whatever you told him was in trust. Whatever it is that you are so afraid of our knowing, you can be sure he didn't tell us."

He lit a cigarette. What could it be that it should weigh on her mind so? She was so young, despite all her sophistication. What could worry her so, at sixteen? It must be that she had told the psychiatrist things about her parents, feelings that she didn't want them to know. God knows, there was enough that she might have said. Something had gone wrong somewhere to make her so unlike other daughters. But then, how could she be like other young girls? There weren't many mothers like Sondra, fortunately for the future of the race.

"Your mother and I were talking about your future, Courtney," he said as their drinks were brought. "We decided that we should leave it up to you; you know better than we do what you want. There is one thing that we have decided, though. As you know, your mother isn't finding much work here in Hollywood, so she has decided to come to New York—TV is opening up a lot of work."

He took a sip of his martini.

"Now don't get defensive when I say this, but your mother's future will be very uncertain for awhile. We don't want you to have any more insecurity than you have already. In the fall you can go back to Scaisbrooke if you like—"

"I don't want to go back to boarding school."

"We thought you might feel that way. There are a lot of schools in New York just as good as Scaisbrooke, so that presents no problem. The question is—and I want you to think about this a little—we both know your mother's instability, and when she isn't working her moods are worse. Your mother realizes this, and our concern now is your welfare. We both think it might be a good idea if you stayed with me. Temporarily, until Sondra gets some good parts, if that's the way you want it."

Courtney ran her fingers along the stem of her glass. Robbie knew what her answer would be. Why was he put in this position, of begging for his daughter's favor? Why did he have to put his petition in her mother's mouth? He would never understand her devotion to her mother. Sondra had done so much to hurt Courtney, yet as he watched his daughter he knew her mind was made up and that she was only going through the pretense of making a decision because he had asked her to.

"Well," Courtney said, "I'd want to live with Mummy." She looked at her father and tried to think of a kinder way to put it. "You know, Mummy depends on me. And—well, even if she is unstable and moody and all, I'm used to her, and that really doesn't make any difference to me. It's all a part of the way I've grown up. This is the kind of life I'm used to. You know," she said hopelessly.

Yes, he did know. How could he expect her to stay with him, even temporarily? She had never known him very well. She had been brought up as her mother's daughter; he had let that happen from the first, when he had given Sondra custody of Courtney, and it was too late now to reverse his position. It was probably just as well. He wouldn't really know what to do with a daughter.

Robbie wondered when it was; he wondered if there was an exact date, when he had lost his daughter. Perhaps at some point he could have done something. Perhaps in all the confusion before Sondra married Nick, when she had been torn between Nick and Courtney's welfare. He had taken Courtney aside then, and tried to explain to her that when her mother got very angry with her it was not because she didn't love her daughter but because she was very unhappy. Perhaps then he could have done something, taken Courtney away to live with him instead of trying to explain her mother to her. But then he would have had to change his life for Courtney. He probably would have had to marry again, and moved to Westchester, to make a home for Courtney. He had never wanted to marry again, he had never fallen out of love with Sondra. This was his life sentence. He had never gotten angry or fed up enough with Sondra to want to take Courtney away from her. So now he had lost Courtney, too. Now Courtney would feel about him as Sondra did, that Robbie was always there if you wanted something from him.

"Well," he said, "what would you like for dinner?" He mustn't let Courtney know that she had hurt him; it wasn't the child's fault that she had stopped loving him.

"Roast beef, very rare. And a Caesar salad to begin with, please."

"Hollywood habits," he smiled. "We'll have to make a New Yorker out of you again."

"It's going to be good to be back in New York," she said. "I'll see Janet again, for one thing."

"Is she still at Scaisbrooke?"

"No," Courtney said. "She got kicked out last spring. She went to school in New York this year."

"She seems to have a habit of getting kicked out."

"Yes," Courtney said. "She's gotten the axe from every school she's gone to—except one, back in elementary school."

"Do you think it's such a good idea for you to start seeing her again? I remember your housemother used to say she was a bad influence on you."

"You worry so, Daddy. No, Fo-bitch never liked Janet, that's all. Janet's all right. She just has a grudge against institutions. I wonder what it will be like, being back in New York? For one thing, it will be nice to have a change of seasons. Perpetual blue skies drive me mad." She grinned. "I used to wake up in the morning and pray for rain, for wretched drizzle to break the monotony. Even the rainy season is monotonous."

"It will be good for you to get back to sanity, too," Robbie said. "Hollywood is the sort of town where you wake up in the morning and look out to see if it's still there. I expect the whole movie colony to pick up its tents one night and go back to whatever fairyland they came from."

"That's Mummy's line."

"I know. I have nothing to call my own."

When Robbie thought about the dinner afterwards, reproaching himself for not having said the things he had meant to say, he found it difficult to remember what they had talked about, although the dinner seemed very long. Yet there was really nothing he could have said. It was too late to undo what had been done, or to do what had not been done, and he could not ask his daughter to give him what he had denied her.

Robbie went back to New York that evening, and found a summer sub-lease in Murray Hill at a reasonable rent. He was so in debt now that he was at least determined that Courtney should have a nice home to come to.

Sondra and Courtney Farrell followed, a few weeks before Courtney's seventeenth birthday, laden with new clothes in new white luggage, all on charge accounts. They were very gay fugitives, heading for a life they could not know. As the lights of Hollywood fell behind the black California hills, Sondra opened the bottle of Piper Heidseck and they toasted each other and New York in paper cups.

"To a lovely life," Sondra said, and looked at her daughter a moment. "Darling—you do love me, don't you?"

"Yes, Mummy," Courtney smiled, and sipped her champagne.

14

The sublet apartment was not furnished in the wall-to-wall carpeting, solid-color taste of her mother, but it was pleasant and contained many antiques. There was a solid and secure feeling to it, and the building was only a few doors from Park Avenue. Courtney was pleased that they would live here, and she wondered, as they entered with their white luggage, what associations the apartment would come to hold for her.

That night, feeling adrift and isolated, Courtney called the only person whom she had cared to salvage from the many years at boarding school, Janet Parker. Janet was surprised and delighted to hear from Courtney, and being somehow without a date for the evening, she asked Courtney to come up to her apartment.

As Courtney took the taxi up Park Avenue, she felt a sense of peace at the reassuringly businesslike, gray buildings of New York. Hollywood, with its pastel buildings and lotus-shaped swimming pools, was behind her now, and except for the new consciousness which she carried within her, might never have existed.

The maid answered the door, pale and starched in her uniform, and looking somehow harassed. Courtney had just started to ask for Janet when she came out of the bedroom in her bathrobe. She was slightly tanned from spring house parties, but her tan was augmented by make-up too dark for her years. She rushed past the maid as though she were not there and flung her arms around Courtney.

"Court! Darling! How absolutely great to see you!"

The maid muttered something about taking Courtney's coat which passed unheard, and shuffled ineffectually into the kitchen.

"Come on into my room," Janet said. She lowered her voice. "The room is in an awful mess and the stupid maid refuses to clean it, but I hate to sit in the living room. Daddy is slightly bombed in there and he's angry with me about something—I'm not sure what—but if you really feel you ought to, you can come in and see him. Yes, I guess you should; you're about the only one of my friends he likes, but really, he's bombed out of his head."

"That's all right," Courtney grinned. "I'll go through the motions anyway. Jesus, it's great to see you, sweetie! You really look just the same."

"I'll bet you have an awful lot to tell me," Janet continued as she led Courtney into the living room. When she came into the room she stopped. There was only one light on, and Mr. Parker sat by the window with a glass of bourbon, staring out at Park Avenue eleven stories below. He was a heavy-set, gray-haired man with the weak eyes of the alcoholic. His face was square and determined, belying the ineffectual eyes. There was something alien about him as he sat beside the window with his drink. He was a man apart, one sensed a dangerous man, a man who no longer cared for the niceties of companionship or ice with his bourbon. He did not turn around when they came in or acknowledge their presence by any change in expression.

"Daddy, Courtney is here. She just got back from California."

He turned reluctantly.

"Hello, Courtney. I'm glad you're back. Maybe you can make some sense out of Janet. Are you here for the summer?" His voice was harsh and strong, as though he were giving instructions to a subordinate.

"Hello, Mr. Parker, it's good to see you again. No," she answered his question, "I've moved back to New York."

He nodded briefly and retreated to the world beyond the window.

"Come on, Court," Janet said. "Do you want a drink? Oh, I guess you still don't drink."

"No, I'd love a drink, Jan. Scotch."

"Sweetie, you're becoming domesticated."

She went into the pantry and fixed the drinks. The harassed maid was doing the dinner dishes and humming abstractedly to herself. Then Janet took Courtney to her bedroom.

Janet's bedroom, like the rest of the apartment, had a slightly brocaded look to it which Mrs. Parker mistook for elegance. The walls were light blue and the furniture was upholstered in pink with overtones of gold. There was a large mirror above her dressing table which reflected the bed, unmade and covered with records and clothing, and a lighter space on the door leading to the bathroom which indicated that a full-length mirror had been there. The room was more than disarrayed; it was chaos. Crinolines, dresses, a bedspread, letters, and photographs littered the floor. On the bureau was a silver shoe, standing in solitary splendor among the perfume bottles and photographs, undoubtedly placed there while Janet was trying to locate something on the floor.

"Are you hungry, sweetie? The maid could bring us something, along with a lecture on my room—whenever she comes in here she lectures me. Mother should have fired her, but she's a little afraid of maids, and Daddy doesn't care."

"No, Jan, that's all right. Well tell me, what have you been doing with yourself in the past year?"

Janet was sitting at the dressing table taking off her make-up with cold cream. She looked at Courtney in the mirror, pausing dramatically.

"Court, you're going to flip. Or maybe you won't. It finally happened."

"Did it *really*?" With Janet, Courtney was beginning to resume the staccato prep-school speech which she had fallen away from.

"Yes, it was when I was in Bermuda. I got bombed one night and the son of a bitch did it. I really didn't know what was happening until afterwards, and I was mad as hell, but it had happened. Then I met this guy—this drummer from Harvard—and I figured what the hell, and we made it. Then it was different and it really had happened. I had an affair with him for months—two—he has this beautiful body, his neck sort of *blends* into his shoulders—really beautiful."

It never occurred to Courtney to ask Janet if she was in love.

"Is it still going on? I mean, this drummer?"

"No, after he went back to Harvard I didn't see him. I went up there once and looked him up, but he had a date for the weekend. He simply *ignored* me. Bastard."

Courtney leaned back against Janet's pillow. Now was the time for a roommate's confidences, now that she knew Janet would understand.

"Well, you know that actor I wrote you about?"

Janet nodded in the mirror.

"Well, I—we—I had an affair with him."

Janet got up and sat on the bed.

"Oh, sweetie, how great! Well, so you're not a kid any more."

Courtney shook her head.

"But isn't he the one you said was a fairy?"

"Yes . . ."

"Well, doesn't that—I mean—"

"No, it doesn't make any difference." Courtney was feeling very much like a woman of the world.

Janet grinned and shook her head.

"Well, I never would have thought it of you. I mean, that both of us—well, it's really funny, the way you were so naïve in school, and now we've both made it. Funny, the way things work out."

"But it's only one with me." Somehow Courtney felt a need to re-establish her moral superiority.

"Yes, I've had two." A note of pride came into Janet's voice.

This wasn't at all what Courtney meant. Somehow, too, she felt that telling Janet cheapened what she and Barry had had. But she was glad that she had told her, so that she wasn't alone with it any more. Each of the girls felt a justification in the other's complicity. As Janet talked, Courtney felt somehow that Janet had missed something, and she was glad that with her it had been Barry, and not some tight college boy. Then suddenly she didn't want to talk about it any more.

"Hey, Jan, what about putting on a record or something?"

Janet looked around the bed until she found the record she wanted. She grinned as Kenton's "Abstraction" filled the room with the familiar sounds.

"Court," she said, "want a banana?" And suddenly, it was as though they were back at boarding school, before they had known all this.

"Janet, sweetie, you're an idiot."

They both laughed. Janet handed Courtney a cigarette and lit one herself. She nodded approvingly as Courtney smoked hers. They lay on the bed in familiar silence. It was good to be with Janet who knew her so well, and with whom she did not need to explain herself. They formed a happy world when they were together, a world without censure or criticism. It was good that in their separation their lives had followed similar patterns, so that they could be with each other with no strain or lack of under-standing. They resumed where they had left off, their friendship strengthened by the new knowledge that they held in common. They both had been alone for a year, and it was good not to be alone any longer.

It was Courtney who broke the silence.

"Where is your mother?"

"Oh, didn't I tell you? No, that's right—that last letter I wrote you was returned." Janet did not ask why her letter was returned, why Courtney had left Beverly Hills without a forwarding ad-dress. If Courtney wanted to tell her, she would.

"Mother is in the sanitarium again," Janet continued. "You know, she just can't take Daddy's drinking, and I guess my stay-ing out on two-day parties and all doesn't help. She's been there for six months now. She just cried all the time, and had all these obscure ailments."

"Do you know when she's getting out?"

"It's kind of indefinite. She may be back in July. You know, every once in a while she just has to leave."

"Yes, I remember at Scaisbrooke when she left for a few months."

"Well, nobody can take Daddy without some relief. Of course, I'm home as little as possible. You see that door, the one that leads into the bathroom between my bedroom and the parents?"

Courtney nodded.

"There used to be a full-length mirror there, when they first moved in. This room was the nursery, and my crib and all was here. Mother used to run in here at night sometimes when Daddy was really drunk and lock that door. She always was kind of afraid of him, even then," she mused. "And he used to try to break that door down, and he knocked off the mirror and cracked it so often that finally Mother decided there wasn't any use in getting it fixed any more."

"Kind of violent of him."

"Well, Daddy and I have an understanding. I'm not afraid of him the way Mother is. He knows if he ever tried to hurt me, I'd kill him. We respect each other, in an odd way. We're kind of alike. Once he slapped me and I threw my shoe at him and called him a son of a bitch, and I came in here and locked the door and wouldn't let him in. He was mad because I had stayed out two nights on a party—you know, we all fell asleep on the floor and then woke up and resumed the party; one of those—and he was sure I had slept with somebody. I hadn't," she added.

This was the ugliness in Janet's life, a life of wealth and endless dates, of subdeb and then deb parties, of superficial glamour and gaiety. Courtney knew of the ugliness at Scaisbrooke, and when Janet mentioned it now, she reacted as she had with the ugliness in Barry's life. She did not want to know about it, to talk about it, as though by ignoring it, it would disappear. The dead leaves were in this swimming pool as well, but perhaps by walking by very quickly she would not see them.

"You know," Courtney said, "I really love being in New York, but the trouble is I don't know any men here."

"Well, sweetie, I can take care of that. Look, give me your phone number—no, better yet, stay overnight here—and I'm going to a cocktail party tomorrow night, and I'll get you a date."

"Oh, Jan, that would be marvelous. I adore cocktail parties."

"Now that you drink, you know, I can dig up lots of parties. I couldn't before, because you were sort of out of it. I think you'll like this party, it's going to be a real blast, and the whole crew will be there. You'll probably get some dates out of it, and once the crew gets to know you, you'll be all set."

And so, almost by inadvertence, Courtney began to adopt Janet's life. She called her mother and told her that she was staying overnight with Janet, and her mother was pleased that Courtney would not be alone. Courtney was happy that she would be going to a cocktail party the following night, she was happy that she had such a good friend in Janet. The days of spending her life with adults were over; she was about to discover a group of young people who, like Janet, had led lives similar to her own, and the guilt and solitude that she had known with Barry Cabot were far behind her now. She was sure of these things as she lay in bed beside Janet, who was already asleep. She was sure that with Janet, and with Janet's friends, she would find herself.

Mr. Parker awoke before them and had escaped to his Wall Street office by the time they got up for breakfast. It was almost noon, and the maid muttered to herself that Miss Janet always wanted breakfast when she was in the middle of cleaning the house, and she never could have breakfast when Mr. Parker did, to make things simpler for her.

"If you don't like my hours, Peggy, you can always quit," Janet said curtly. The maid didn't answer but went into the kitchen to fix their breakfast.

"Mother is always talking to Peggy about my getting up late, so she feels she has some right to criticize me. Mother always spoils the maids, but when we get new ones, they usually quit because of Daddy's tempers or my room or something, so we have to put with second-rate maids," she explained.

Janet was able to get Courtney a date with a Yale junior, George Keyes. She assured her that George was very attractive and a great drinker—never got bombed. In short the ideal date for a cocktail party.

Courtney went home to change and Janet went with her. Mrs. Farrell was pleased to see Janet. Despite Scaisbrooke's insistence that Janet was a bad influence on Courtney, Sondra had always liked Janet. She admired the courage, however misdirected, that caused her to rebel against the school's students and faculty, and she felt that Janet's determined gaiety was good for Courtney, who tended to get so moody.

After they changed they went back to Janet's apartment and their dates picked them up. George was attractive, as Janet had promised. He was a sailing enthusiast, and was tanned from weekends spent in the Island on his boat. Courtney warmed to the evening. They had two drinks at the apartment—Courtney wanted Scotch, because she always felt that she could drink Scotch better than gin, but George said, "Really, *Courtney*—Scotch in the summertime? Like a weenie!"

Courtney winced. She knew that "weenie" was Yale's term of derision—applied to those who do not behave like Yalies—and this was enough for her. She followed George's lead, and had a gin and tonic against her better judgment.

The cocktail party was being held at the apartment of one

of Janet's friends, which the parents had vacated for the occasion. When they got there it was four o'clock, and the room was already almost full. Courtney was enchanted. All the boys were from Harvard, UVA or Yale, and somehow they all looked attractive and self-assured in their gray flannels and cord jackets. The girls, too, seemed to be in uniform. It was not that they wore the same clothes, but they wore the same expressions, and talked in the same staccato rhythm which Nick Russell once described as the "boarding-school speech impediment."

Courtney, being an attractive girl and a novelty, with her dark glasses and her air of Hollywood, was soon surrounded by the uniformed young men. She had a few more drinks, the room filled with people and cigarette smoke, and she began to talk more freely as the windows darkened and the lights were put on. Someone began to play the piano and a few couples danced absently. Some of the extra men gathered around the piano and sang. The party got gayer; girls were sitting on the gray flannel laps of their dates and other girl's dates. When Courtney went to the bathroom she saw two boys passed out on a bed among the coats and jackets.

When she returned, she was handed another drink and she began to hold court.

"Of course," she was saying, "Hollywood can become an awful drag after a while. You know, you get tired of the movie stars who can't talk about anything but their last picture . . ." She felt a little odd. No, she wasn't going to be ill, she simply couldn't do that. She dismissed the sensation.

George took his arm from her waist and called to one of the boys who was sitting by the window, engrossed in intense conversation with a girl who had lank blonde hair and was wearing a red dress and getting slightly tight.

"Hey, Pete, it's getting hot as hell in here, open that window."
Pete obliged and someone came around with more drinks.

". . . and you just get starved for some good conversation, and some intelligent people, and there's nothing to do but come back to New York," Courtney continued.

George was looking at her steadily. His eyes moved down her body. She knew the black cocktail dress she was wearing was well cut and fitted her very closely.

"Well, you know," another boy was saying, "sometimes I get the same feeling when I'm away from New York. I've never been in Hollywood, but even when I was in Europe last summer . . ."

"You're a very attractive girl," George said softly as he put his arm around her. Courtney concentrated on what the other boy was saying, ignoring George as he kissed her forehead and then her neck.

"You never realize how much you miss New York," Courtney said to the boy, "until . . ." But some girl was talking to him now and he was listening to her, and it was somehow rather confusing the way there was nobody but George there. The other boys were still in their vicinity, but they were split into different groups. She concentrated on George, because she had that odd sensation as though she were falling asleep again. Through determination she was now facing him and his arm was no longer around her, but he was talking—something about his fraternity parties at Yale.

"You would really enjoy them," he was saying. "I'd love to have you come up there some time . . ."

Courtney was concentrating very hard on what he was saying now, because she had waves of not feeling very well. It was awfully hot.

"You know, I'm glad Janet found you for me, you're really a

game girl," he was saying, and then he looked very surprised because as she stood there listening to him she was suddenly sick.

"I'm terribly sorry," she said, hardly able to believe that she had actually been sick. "Awfully sorry, really—"

And he was rushing her into the bathroom, past the bedroom in which a girl had been added to the two boys passed out on the bed. There was somebody in the bathroom, a boy standing outside said.

"This girl's sick," said George.

"It's really never happened to me before," Courtney said dazedly. "Really, never in my life—"

The girl had come out of the bathroom and Courtney was pushed in. She was abruptly ill again and then she felt all right. She splashed her face with cold water. Her black cocktail dress— oh, how ghastly.

When she emerged George was standing outside and the girl who gave the party was there.

"Are you all right?" the girl said.

"Yes, I'm fine. I'm terribly sorry—only my dress—"

"I'll lend you one of mine," she said, and Courtney was back in the bathroom changing her dress. It was a very pretty dress, and it fit her. At least there was that much luck.

"That dress looks great on you, sweetie," said George gallantly when she came out. "You should always wear a low-cut dress."

"I'm horribly embarrassed," Courtney said. "Did anyone see me?"

"No, they're all too bombed to notice."

"It never happened before," she said wonderingly.

"Well, it's hot out, and the room is kind of stuffy. It happens to everyone." He grinned. "I'll never forget the time when I was just out of Andover, and I was on a beach down in Florida. I was eighteen, and feeling terribly sophisticated, and I was talking to Mrs. Astor. She was a friend of Mother's and I was trying to be awfully charming. It was awfully hot and I was drinking gin, and I knew I was going to be sick, so I simply said to Mrs. Astor, 'Excuse me,' and I turned around and barfed, and then went on talking. She pretended she never noticed, but I was mortified."

Courtney laughed. She felt all right now.

"You have a glass of ice water, and then you can have another drink," George said.

Courtney felt like a fool, and she was sure that George would ignore her now because she had obviously acted like a kid. Instead he said, "You know, you're real game. I think the party's moving on to somebody's apartment with a swimming pool. Would you be my date?"

"I'd love to, George." Courtney grinned. She was going to like Janet's crew.

15

The cocktail party broke up at four in the morning, so Courtney stayed overnight again with Janet. They woke up in the early afternoon and the maid protestingly gave them breakfast. Then they retired to Janet's room. Courtney lay on the bed and looked through some of Janet's photographs from Bermuda, and Janet sat at the dressing table and polished her nails.

"Did you have fun at the party?" Janet said.

"Yes, except for barfing. That was awfully embarrassing."

"Nobody noticed."

"I liked George. He was awfully nice about the whole thing."

"Yes, you seemed to get along."

"Mmm-hmm."

Janet got up and gingerly opened the closet door, careful not to smear her nails.

"I thought so," she grinned. "Last night I carefully hung my dress up, feeling very proud that I was sober enough not to leave it on the floor. Only," she added, "I hung it up inside out."

Courtney moved to the foot of the bed to observe this. She looked up at the top of the closet.

"What a lot of purses you have," she commented.

"Yes," Janet said. She looked at Courtney. "I—acquired them."

"What do you mean?"

Janet sat at the dressing table and looked at herself in the mirror. She wiped a smudge of mascara from beneath her eye.

"Well, you might say I stole them; I say I acquired them."

"*Stole* them?"

"Mmm-hmm," Janet said nonchalantly. "It was really awfully easy. Like the dress I wore last night. I acquired that from a store. Just wore it out."

"Aren't you afraid of getting caught?"

"Oh, I did once, by one store. A detective came up and took me by the arm, and led me into some manager's office. He said since I was so young, he didn't want to press charges. It was funny, I felt like a J.D. or something. I carried it off well, though. I told him I was under a psychiatrist's care and had him call my psycho. Then they let me go after I gave back the dress. They never even contacted Daddy."

"You were lucky," Courtney commented.

Janet looked at the silver perfume bottles in front of her and the pair of long white gloves that she had left on the dressing table.

"I guess so," she said.

"You get an allowance of over two hundred dollars a month. You could buy the clothes."

"I figure the stores have more money than I do," said Janet.

She pushed the bottles of perfume around, rearranging them like chessmen. Courtney lit a cigarette, and stared up at the ceiling. Janet picked up a small bottle of Sortilège, one of the token bottles that Billingsley sent over whenever she went into the Stork. She set it down again and took a silver flask. She shook it. It was almost empty. She picked up a bottle of obscure and expensive French perfume and the Sortilège, and poured them both into the silver flask.

"What did you do that for?" said Courtney, who had been watching the operation with detached interest.

"I get tired of the same perfumes." She got up and handed the flask to Courtney.

"Like it?" she asked.

"Smells ghastly," Courtney answered.

Janet put the flask in the center of the table. Then she shoved it almost angrily behind the mirrored Kleenex container.

"Oh, screw them all," said Janet.

"Who?" said Courtney.

"I don't know." She turned to Courtney. "I'm bored," she announced.

"What are you going to do about it?"

"I don't know." She thought a moment. "Have a drink, I guess. Want one?"

"I suppose so."

They roused themselves and went into the kitchen.

"Maid's out," Janet observed. "She's always going out on obscure errands. I think she has a lover."

"The elevator man?" Courtney inquired.

"Probably someone's butler. That sounds logical. A somewhat indigent butler, who works for an alcoholic couple. The son is dying of leukemia, and the parents are always in the bedroom, bombed. And the butler slips out, abandoning the dying son, to make mad love with Peggy under the El."

"Under the El." Courtney thought a moment. "The rhythm of the trains makes them mad, like Spanish fly or something. And it's all like a Bellows painting."

"Who?"

"Bellows."

"Oh. And then the son dies," Janet continued, "but nobody knows it for weeks because the parents are out of their head and the butler has taken Peggy to Coney Island in the heat of passion."

"Finally a window washer sees the body and it's all in the *Daily News*," said Courtney.

"You want ice, don't you?" asked Janet.

"Mmm-hmm. I'll get the Scotch." She opened the cabinet. "Nothing but Scotch and gin in here," she observed. "Where does your father keep his cache of bourbon?"

"Locked up in his bedroom closet," Janet said. She looked through the icebox. "Six full trays of ice," she said. "Some roast beef from last night. Some impotent cucumbers. Cocktail onions. A dead salad. Hard-boiled eggs," she said with pleasure. She took one from the bowl and peeled it. "Want one?"

"No, thanks."

"Here's the ice," Janet said with her mouth full. Courtney made the drinks and handed Janet one. The phone rang and Janet went in to answer it. Courtney followed her.

"Oh, sweetie!" Janet exclaimed. "Pete, it's great to hear from you." She listened a moment. "Yes, I'd adore to," she said. "I've got a friend with me from California, she's staying with me. A really neat girl. Do you think you could get her a date?"

Janet nodded to Courtney.

"Oh, in about an hour. Thanks, sweetie, I really appreciate your getting the date. Bye-bye."

"Remember Pete? He was at the party last night. They're all sitting around drinking beer at his apartment and they want us to come over."

"I'll have to go home and change—"

"Oh, that's a drag. Wear a dress of mine."

"I'll call Mummy."

"You're always calling your mother."

"Well, she worries when I'm not home and she doesn't hear from me."

"Thank God my parents don't," Janet said. "There are some advantages to having an alcoholic father and a psycho mother."

Courtney was provided with many dates by Janet, and stayed overnight with her often because her mother would not have tolerated the lateness of the hours she kept. Coming into the summer there were many cocktail parties. Those of the "crew" who stayed in New York to work during the heat met regularly in the evenings to commiserate with one another about the humidity and the injustice of having been kicked out of college and into the working world ahead of their time. Courtney learned that almost none of the boys in the group had been able to finish college, or, that if they were still in college, were on probation—usually for drinking. She enjoyed the closeness of the group, who seemed banded together in their rebellion against something—she could not yet ascertain what—and she enjoyed the quantity of liquor and the relaxed air of the impromptu parties. With them, she found a warmth that bordered on acceptance. The casual affection, the frequent passes, the drinking companionship—these things, for the time being, filled her need, and eased the solitude that had driven her to seek oblivion. Sometimes, when she lay in bed at night, she missed the love she had known with Barry. She had been so important to him. But she had many dates now, and she was seldom alone. That was better, much better, she reminded herself. She didn't want another love affair, she didn't want to hurt herself again. This life was good, this life would keep her from continuing in the self-destruction and escape. She was happier with herself this way. June passed quickly, in a haze of gin and grapefruit juice, and Janet gave Courtney a party on her seventeenth birthday.

The party was large and loud—word had gotten around New York that Janet was giving a "Bad Actors' Ball," and all the "bad actors" in town showed up, anxious to defend their reputations for excessive drinking and rather easy morality. Somehow Janet and Courtney found themselves early the next morning in the apartment of two of the noblest drinkers. The two boys sat bravely with them until it became apparent both that the girls would not go to bed with them and had out-drunk them. They retired to the bedroom, promising Janet and Courtney that they would return in an hour and match them for drinks after they had had a nap.

The girls sat in the living room and smoked cigarettes until they had used up all that they could find. At this moment of crisis, Courtney looked at her watch.

"Seven fifteen," she announced.

"No more cigarettes," Janet observed glumly.

"No." Courtney shook her head. "No more cigarettes."

"Boys still asleep," said Janet.

"Yes," said Courtney. "Still asleep. Asleep for over an hour."

"Won't wake up for ages."

"No. Passed out."

"Passed out," Janet agreed.

"More liquor still," Courtney suggested.

"No," said Janet. "Shouldn't have any more. Don't want to get bombed."

"No," said Courtney solemnly. "Don't want to get bombed."

"Drank them under the table," Janet said proudly.

"Under the bed. Maybe on the bed." She was puzzled.

"Anyway, they're passed out and we're still sober."

"Sober as judges." Courtney thought a moment. "Why are judges always sober, church mice always poor, and lords always drunk?"

"I'm hungry."

"And horses always hungry."

"Let's eat," Janet said.

"It's Sunday," Courtney said.

"I'm still hungry. What does Sunday have to do with it?"

"Church day," Courtney said solemnly. "Nurses and maids and things getting up now and going to early Mass. Good drinking day, Sunday."

"Good day to make love."

"Why?"

"I don't know," said Janet. "Everything is so sober on Sunday. People going to church. Eating big dinners in the Bronx."

"I see what you mean," Courtney said thoughtfully. "That reminds me," she said suddenly. "I'm hungry. Haven't eaten since breakfast yesterday, at two. Mmm, I'm awfully hungry."

"Gotta eat," said Janet. With that they both rose and went out the door.

They wait to a drugstore which seemed to be populated with Irish policemen. They bought some cigarettes.

"Cigarette tastes good," said Courtney.

"An *enormous* orange juice," said Janet to the man behind the counter. "And a glass of milk. And black coffee now. And eggs. And toast, and bacon, I suppose. And a glass of water."

"I'll have the same thing," said Courtney.

One of the policemen said something to the policeman next to him. They both looked at Courtney and Janet and chuckled. The man smiled when he brought the juice and coffee.

"Do you suppose," Courtney whispered conspiratorially to Janet, "that they know we've been on a party all night?"

"No," said Janet. "We're too sober. I wish they did," she said wistfully. "I like to shock people."

"So do I," said Courtney.

When they left the drugstore their spirits were considerably higher. It was a lovely morning late in June, and a church across the street was ringing its solemn chimes.

"What shall we do?" said Courtney.

"Can't go home now. Only quarter to eight, and the elevator man will know we've been out all night and Daddy will raise hell. Cut my allowance or something. It's much better if we come in around nine thirty and say we stayed overnight with some girl."

"Where shall we kill the time?"

"Let's go to the park," said Janet. "There's a nice lake near here where my governess always used to take me on Sundays. Let's sit there."

"Okay," said Courtney. She nudged Janet. "Look at this woman in front of us, in the little white hat. I bet she's going to church."

"Let's shock her," Janet said.

Courtney grinned.

"I always think," Janet said in a loud voice, "that there's nothing wrong in going to bed with boys."

"No," said Courtney. "And they take you to dinner, and buy you things."

"Yes, and you don't really pay any price for it, it's so enjoyable."

"You don't have to look at them, really, so it doesn't make any difference what they—"

The woman turned quickly and gave them a fleeting glance, and continued walking with a purposeful step. Courtney and Janet grinned at each other. This was great sport for a Sunday morning.

156

"—look like," Courtney finished.

"No, it's really a great life," said Janet.

The woman turned very obviously and cut diagonally across the street toward the church. Courtney and Janet laughed triumphantly until they came to the entrance to the park.

It was a lovely lake, very quiet and empty on the Sunday morning. A man was walking his dog and whistling. Courtney picked a furry bud and rubbed it against her cheek.

"Reminds me of a pussy willow," she mused. "I always loved pussy willows, when I was a little girl."

It was funny that she should think of it now, that she could remember the morning as though it were this morning, and she was once again the little girl of ten in her first year at boarding school, about to go to the plane that would take her to California to meet the stranger who was her new father. She had known so much since then; she had known a lover, she had known fear and the desire to escape. And yet this early morning in Central Park could almost be that morning, seven years ago.

She was frightened that morning. She wondered what he would be like, and whether she would like him. She wondered whether he and her mother loved each other, and if they did, she wondered what it would be like to share her mother's love with this stranger. Before she left for the airport she had gone for a long walk around the school grounds, because she was frightened and she felt very alone. It was very early in the morning, and the mist hung heavy on the stubble of winter grass. She even walked off bounds that morning, because she figured that no one would be up that early to report her. She walked across the street and down the hill to the rusty field, and then she saw the pussy willows. She had always loved pussy willows. She picked one and rubbed it against her cheek because it was very soft. Then as the thin winter sun began to displace the mist she walked back to school to get her bags ready for the taxi.

When she got off the plane in Hollywood it was warm, and the palm trees and the bright, blue sky made the airport look unreal to her, so soon after she had left the rusty field and the thin winter sun. As she walked across the airfield she still held the pussy willow in her hand, vestige of a world that was real. Even when they got into the car she did not let go of it. Finally, on the long drive from the airport to Hollywood, she fell asleep on her mother's shoulder and the pussy willow dropped to the floor.

She was silent and thoughtful in the soft morning sunlight, fingering the bud and remembering. It was Janet who finally broke the stillness.

"You know," she said, "it's funny, the different times I've come here, to this lake." She had been remembering, too. "When I was little my governess used to take me here to play with the other little children. And when I was in elementary school we used to be taken on walks past the obelisk and the teacher would tell us how it was brought from Egypt. And last year a friend of mine and I used to come here from school on our lunch hour with a bottle of Scotch, and go back to history class slightly bombed, because it was such a bore." She threw a stick into the water and watched it float away. "I wonder what the lake thinks of me, watching me grow up. I wonder what it would say to me this morning if it could talk."

"It must be nice," Courtney mused, "to spend most of your life in the same place, and have associations with physical things like lakes and buildings. And go out with boys you've grown up with, that you used to play with in Central Park."

"Yes," Janet said, "it is nice. That's how I know most of the boys I go out with. It's too bad you didn't grow up in New York, so you could have a group like that."

"I really appreciate the way you've introduced me to so many boys," Courtney said. "I'd have gone out of my head this summer if it hadn't been for you."

"Well, sweetie," said Janet, "you're about my only good friend, and I couldn't just sit around and let you be lonely. I always said, even in Scaisbrooke, that what you needed was to go out more." She picked a thistle from her cocktail dress. "You know," she went on, "that reminds me. There's this boy I know—he's not one of the crew, he's a very unusual person. Awfully charming, and very intelligent—rich, too; he doesn't even bother to work—and I was telling him about you. He keeps saying he wants to meet you."

"Is that the boy you told me about, the one who owns that island off Florida and the villa on the Riviera?"

"Yes, that's the one. Well, I was thinking, those boys won't wake up until just about the time they pick us up for the deb party tonight, which will be around ten. So what about going by the Pierre, where he stays, and meeting him? We could have a drink with him and our dates could meet us downstairs at the bar."

"Well, that sounds great, sweetie."

"I really think you two will get along—I'm afraid. But he insists on meeting you"—she grinned—"so I really have no way of keeping him to myself. But prepare yourself," she added. She threw a pebble into the lake and watched the circles grow. "He's really a madman, so be prepared for anything." She smiled to herself. "I really couldn't describe him to you."

16

Mr. Anthony Neville was fortunately to be found at home that evening, at his suite in the Pierre. When he opened the door, Courtney understood immediately why Janet had said with a smile, "I really couldn't describe him to you." He stood at the door, a pale young man in his early twenties, with delicate features, an abundance of black hair, and challenging, brooding dark eyes. He was wearing a white terry-cloth robe, and in his left hand he held absently a single long-stemmed rose. He bowed deeply and theatrically to the two girls.

"Anthony darling," Janet said. "Isn't this a new pose?" She smiled. "And didn't Oscar Wilde use a sunflower?"

Anthony ignored her, his expression unchanged.

"This, of course, is Courtney. How marvelous of Janet to bring you to me. Courtney's enchanting," he said to Janet, who had walked past him and was taking off her coat.

Courtney, who was accustomed to the staccato Ivy League speech of Janet's friends, was surprised by the quiet languor of the young man's voice. His speech seemed, like the red rose, cultivated to defy categorization. He took her coat.

"Anthony," Janet said abruptly, "we can't stay long. Our dates are meeting us downstairs to take us on to a deb party."

Janet's matter-of-fact voice temporarily dispelled the aura of eccentricity which the young man had cast upon the room.

"Here," he said, walking to the oversized bed, "lie down."

He cleared a silver tray with two wine glasses from the bed and sat on the window sill.

"Wretched heat," he commented, opening the window. "I've been lying here pretending I was on the Island, and feeling terribly Byronesque." He set the rose upon the tray. He didn't bother to explain the second wine glass. "Do you know," he said suddenly, "Byron watched from a carriage while they burned Shelley on the Beach at Via Reggio. Royal Road. I like that. And watching from a carriage until stench and grief overwhelmed him, and he left. That appeals to me. Such a death makes burials seem terribly prosaic."

"Anthony," said Janet, "my tongue is hanging out for a drink." She straightened her evening dress beneath her on the bed. "I'm hung over as hell."

Anthony sighed and walked over to the telephone.

"Two Chivas Regals on the rocks," he ordered. He looked over at Courtney. "Scotch?" he asked. She nodded. "Make that four. And a half bottle of Pommard. André knows what I want. Mr. Neville." He hung up and sat on the bed beside Janet.

"Jan," he said, "you're heaven. We really should see each other more often. Why do you insist upon going to that deadly deb party?"

He rested his hand on Janet's hip. Courtney looked uncomfortably at a print on the opposite wall.

"I asked you to a party last week," he continued, "but you never showed up." He stared nostalgically at the tray of wine glasses. "It was a marvelous party," he said wistfully. "Hordes of girls naked above the waist, and mass fornication."

Courtney looked sharply at him. He pretended not to notice.

"You really should come to one of my parties," he said with a slight smile which was his only recognition of Courtney's stare. "Courtney should come, too." He looked over at her. "Irish girls have such lovely skin," he said. "You look so terribly Irish," he said to her. "Those enchanting green eyes." He turned to Janet. "You're marvelous to bring Courtney. I'm sure we shall get on famously. She sits there so silently." He leaned toward Janet with a conspiratorial air. "Do you suppose," he said to Janet, "that your friend is shocked by me?"

Courtney smiled uneasily.

"No, not at all. No," she said.

Anthony sighed. "What a pity. I do so love to shock people."

He rose and sat again on the window sill, leaning moodily against a corner of the window.

"I've been writing a story," he announced. "It's about two lesbians who are married by a homosexual priest—" He paused and looked at Courtney. "You're Catholic, of course." She nodded. "—by a homosexual priest in a terribly floral ceremony in Switzerland. Up to this point they have been living quite happily in sin, but now their idyll has been destroyed. One of the lesbians develops a pathological jealousy of the priest . . ."

What am I doing here, Courtney thought, listening to him. Why does he assume he can say these things to me. But I mustn't seem to be shocked. It would seem so childish to be shocked, and I mustn't let him realize that I am that young, that I know so little.

"Of course," he was saying, "the priest is defrocked, and is wretched because—"

Courtney studied him, leaning languorously against the window in a careful pose. He had an arresting face. He might have been an actor. He might have been a great many things. She wondered what he was. Janet had talked about him while they were on their way to his hotel. He was legendary among her friends. They played at dissipation, theirs was a child's game. His was not. Courtney glanced quickly at Janet, who was enjoying his story. He had been her lover, this extraordinary young man who was a symbol of decadence even to Janet's friends, a young man whom every one knew of and no one knew. And yet he had asked to meet *her*, he had asked Janet to bring her to him.

"And the lesbians go to live"—he smiled reflectively—"in Denmark." He broke his pose and stood before them, pleased with himself. He looked triumphantly at Courtney. "Did you like it?"

"It's ridiculous," she said defiantly. "Wallowing in childish perversion."

"Oh," he said, offended. "You feel perversion is childish."

"No," Courtney said with a studied nonchalance. "But your idea of it is."

"My dear girl," he said patiently, "I have been accused for years of being homosexual. Actually," he said, rearranging a fold of his robe, "homosexuality bored me. But I am by no means a child when it comes to perversion."

Courtney was spared further comment by a knock at the door. He answered it and took the tray from the boy. Courtney watched him. They were playing a game now, a game of sophistication, and she must hold her own. She was a little frightened, but she could not let anyone know that. She could have backed out by letting him know that she felt like a child beside him. The stakes were high, she sensed that without knowing why. She knew so little, and this decadent world of his was a dangerous one. Yet somehow it was a point of honor not to withdraw. She scorned herself for feeling afraid. So she couldn't handle this after all, she was still a child. No. No, she couldn't admit that. This was her world, a world she wanted without knowing why. Janet excused herself as he set down the tray, and as the bathroom door closed Courtney remembered what Janet had said to her as they got out of the elevator. "Don't be surprised by anything he says or does," she had said. She must remember that. He looked at the closed door and then at Courtney, and lay beside her on the bed.

"I like you," he said quietly. "You're rather of a challenge, lying there so silent and so voluptuous."

He rested his hand easily on her breast, and his breath was warm against her ear. My God, she thought, and she was frightened as the emotion she could not control built up inside her, as she felt his challenge and answered it without being able to do anything about it. She felt so helpless, at the mercy of his sophistication and her own body.

"Why do you insist" he murmured, "on going to the foolish deb party? Stay here and go to bed with me instead. I know you want to, darling. As much as I want it."

Desperately, she tried to rise out of herself. Why isn't there a little door, she thought, that closes on our emotions when we can't close them off ourselves, a little door of morality? Suddenly she thought of Janet who would come out in a moment. Thank God, she thought, and in remembering Janet she was able to rise out of herself.

"No," she said. "Our dates are meeting us."

He was annoyed. "Why didn't you come earlier?"

"We were out all night last night," she explained. He was look-ing very steadily at her. "My birthday," she added.

"How old are you?"

"Seventeen."

"Seventeen. My God."

"And we fell asleep around ten this morning," Courtney con-tinued. "The maid didn't wake us until seven, and we had to eat. We were hung, you see. That's why we had to eat, to feel better."

"When are your dates meeting you?" he said. She could feel that he had withdrawn from her. It was not so tense now, and she was glad.

"In about fifteen minutes. At nine thirty."

"They're"—he spat out the word—"*Yalies,* I assume. Most of Janet's friend are."

"Yes," she said. "Ex-Yalies."

"Very well, then." He rose, petulant. "Go on, then. Leave me here to seek lesser forms of amusement. I hope I have gotten you"—he paused and looked at her—"so that you will lay your little Yalie in the woods somewhere."

So I have won this round, Courtney thought. I refused him and he is not used to being refused. She was pleased with herself. She had met the challenge and won; she did not need to be afraid of him now. Janet came out and quickly surveyed the situation. Courtney was lying on the bed, the white skirts of her evening dress spread out around her. Anthony was pouring himself an-other glass of wine. Janet was pleased. She went over to him.

"Anthony, darling," she said with an air of triumphant posses-sion, "I'm awfully sorry that we have to go so soon."

"So am I," he said wryly. He put his arms around her and kissed her on the neck. Courtney got up and put on her long white gloves. He walked over to her, and held out his arms.

"Good night, angel."

He kissed her lightly and softly on the mouth.

"Toy kiss," he murmured, looking steadily and appraisingly at her. "Before you go," he continued, "I want your address. It has been many years since I asked for a girl's address and phone number," he informed her. He looked at Janet for corroboration. She watched them silently. Courtney took a piece of paper from her evening bag and wrote her phone number for him. He wrote her name above it. He looked at her suddenly.

"Where did an Irish girl get a name like Courtney?"

"My parents read it in a magazine serial," Courtney said drily.

"Yes, I do like you," he said, putting the paper into the pocket of his white robe.

"Now, sweetie," Janet said with a smile, "don't fall in love with Courtney."

"Jan," he said softly. He walked over to her and put his hand on her shoulder. "Promise me one thing—that you will never, never get jealous. Because if you do, it will be all over between us." He turned to Courtney. "Janet is the most marvelous girl," he said. "Never jealous or possessive. That's why I love her."

Their dates had been waiting only a short time in the bar, but long enough for them to have a drink to ease their hangovers. They were in high spirits as they drove out to Long Island. Courtney was in the back seat and her date, Eric, put his arm around her.

"Did you have a good time last night?" he asked.

"Mmm-hmm."

"Sorry we faked out," he said. "You drank us under the table."

"Yes, we certainly did," Courtney smiled.

"That won't happen tonight," he assured her. "We'll match you for drinks, since they're free."

"Hey, Eric," said Janet's date, "do you think we'll be able to get in?"

"Sure," Eric assured him. "This will be a real blast, Pete. They'll never be able to check at the door. I could name you ten other people who are going to crash this party, and I know there are a lot more."

"I met the girl who's giving it," Janet said. "There are two of them, and I met one of them a couple of weeks ago at one of those teas."

"Hell," said Eric, "the girls who are giving this won't know half of their guests anyway. It's one of those pre-Tuxedo Park things where they just ran down a list of approved guests, chosen because they could drink well and their fathers were giving them big parties during the Christmas season."

"It's all such a farce," Pete said in a bored tone. "Coming out. A real farce. What the hell do girls come out to nowadays that they haven't known since they were fourteen?"

"Well, it's free liquor," said Janet. "And the more people you can invite, the more parties they have to invite you to later on."

Courtney wasn't listening as the white-jacketed Yalies talked in bored, staccato voices. Everything that they were saying she had heard before. Debutante parties were a farce. Drinking was the finest of all institutions, second, of course, to that other. Any man worth his liquor was kicked out of Yale within two years, otherwise he was sure to graduate to a very mediocre career on the stock exchange. These were the axioms which provided conversation as they drove through Long Island to crash a major debutante party of the summer season. Courtney knew the dialogue by heart. She had learned the language in boarding school, and she had needed only a few weeks to learn the idioms. She now spoke the dialect like a native, and was therefore freed from listening to it. She thought instead of the extraordinary young man she had just met.

Anthony Neville had succeeded in being the first man who had ever overwhelmed her. She couldn't even know if she liked him, but she was fascinated by him. Beside him they all looked like dilettantes at this game of love-making and dissipation, at this game they all must somehow play. She was a little afraid of him, afraid that he might draw her into his world, whatever that world might be. She somehow didn't trust herself with him. Courtney was glad that she was not alone tonight. This, at least, was a world she knew and which she could handle. How sane and reassuringly conventional the country club looked as they drove up to it. She would forget Anthony for the evening. He probably would never call her anyway. He knew how young she was.

They were able to crash the party successfully, as Eric had promised. They avoided the front door, where a man with a list of guests was standing guard and checking invitations. Pete surveyed the setup of the country club while they stood by the car. He came back triumphantly from his reconnaissance and announced that he had found a side entrance. They opened the door, Pete in the lead, Janet and Eric following, and Courtney standing uneasily behind. Pete pushed aside a preoccupied waiter and they found themselves behind the bar.

"Pardon me," Pete said to the astonished bartender.

"Feeling a little sick," Eric explained to the man, who stared after them, absently rubbing an empty glass. Someone called for another drink, and he dismissed the incident as he answered the order. "Young people these days," he muttered wonderingly to one of the waiters. "We used to get such a different group at coming-out parties."

They danced and they drank until dawn came to Long Island and the band, exhausted, retired from the floor. Reluctantly the last remaining guests left and stumbled into their cars. On the way back to New York, Courtney was vaguely concious that Pete was driving on memory and luck, and she distinctly felt that, once they got to the city, they traveled many blocks going the wrong way on a one-way street. A policeman stopped them, but decided not to hold them when Eric rose with great dignity from the back seat and announced that he would drive the rest of the way. The policeman was soon to be relieved and had no desire to be detained, so he left them with a warning. Somehow they got back to their homes, and Courtney was left off at her house. Her mother had been informed that she was going to a deb party and would be home late, and was asleep when Courtney made her way to bed as New York rose to another working day.

Courtney was awakened late in the afternoon by her mother.

"Courtney, someone on the phone for you. Some young man—he had his secretary make the call." This had impressed her mother.

"Who is it?" she said sleepily. "Tell him I'll call him back."

"Mr. Neville, I think she said."

"Anthony!" Courtney reached for her bathrobe, tying it as she went to the phone.

17

Anthony took her to dinner at Chambord. She was pleased at being with him; she liked the obsequious attention of the waiters and the glances of women at other tables. He was wearing a powder-blue tie with a white dinner jacket and dark trousers which fit tightly at the legs, although Edwardian trousers had not yet come into fashion. He was a striking young man, with his challenging face and his slim, athletic body. She felt more at ease with him now, after what she had decided about him last night. He didn't seem so extraordinary, in the conventional and familiar setting of the restaurant.

"I know almost nothing about you," Courtney was saying. "You don't seem to have any relation to any group or any background. It's almost as though when the lights came on full I found you on stage, in a careful pose, without any explanation of why you were there."

He smiled. "What is this passion for categorization?"

"I'm curious, that's all."

"Very well," he said. "I shall tell you about myself. My father's family is from Boston, although he dislikes the fact as much as I. He is an architect, and when he finished college he went to study in Rome. My mother is from a vaguely aristocratic Italian family. After they were married they went to Florence, where I was born. I was sent to school in France as soon as possible, since my only talent as a child was disrupting my parent's lives, and I suppose I was rather a bore. I ran away from school at seventeen and became a steeplechase jockey. I've always liked to risk my life," he added. "I really don't know why. Boredom, perhaps. In a few months I was broke, and I didn't like that, so I was reconciled with my family. I lived with them for a while in Florence, and when I was eighteen I came into my own money and fled to New York."

"I'm not sure that I believe you," said Courtney.

"That's your privilege. What I say is in substance true." He shrugged. "I don't know why I feel prompted to tell you this much, but somehow I like to talk to you. You actually seem interested in me," he said reflectively. "Perhaps that's why."

"What are your parents like?"

"What is this, a cross-examination? Really, my dear, you must be careful or you will be a great *bore*. My parents are wealthy, of course. More of the money comes from their families than my father's work. Some land in Italy, and a great many excellent investments. That's what I live on. The parents are charming, well-educated people, and," he added, "terribly busy. I was always sort of a nuisance to them, so I left as soon as possible. And that, Courtney, is as much as I care to tell you."

Courtney studied him in silence. She had felt an ease and companionship in the easy morality which seemed to pervade Janet's group. With Anthony she sensed an amorality, a greater freedom from the criticism of society and the Catholicism which she had been born to and had betrayed. She envied him his ease, his ability to function, as she saw it, apart from society in his own foreign world, safe from the rejection which she had found whenever she tried to join society. She liked being with him; she was only a little ill at ease now.

"What thoughts could be so solemn?" Anthony asked with a smile.

"I was thinking about you," she said.

"A very excellent occupation," he said, "but it's not advisable to take me too seriously. I might have a corruptive effect on the mind of an innocent young girl like you."

"Not so innocent," Courtney smiled.

"No?" He appraised her leisurely and boldly. "How is your dinner?" he said abruptly.

"Oh, excellent," she said. "And I like the wine."

"Not so harsh as Scotch," he smiled. "Not as coarse and abrupt. I do like subtlety," he said looking at her steadily. "Americans tend to overlook the value of subtlety." He was silent, and he did not take his eyes from hers.

"What would you like to do after dinner?" he said softly. "We will do anything you like."

"Oh, I don't know. You make a suggestion."

"We could go somewhere amusing for a drink," he said. "I know some iniquitous little caves in the village. Or, if that doesn't appeal to you, one of those brightly lit, communal places where mirrors and heavy wood pass for elegance. Or, we could go back to the Pierre and have some wine brought to the room. Whatever you choose."

She didn't really think before she answered him, it was almost as though the decision had been made when she didn't realize it, some time ago, in timelessness. In the back of her mind she thought, I don't need to be afraid. I refused him before, and he is not the sort to press the matter—there are too many women for him. I can handle him, and I would like to talk to him, and find out more about him. At the same time she was not really convinced of this, but somehow it didn't matter. There were no crises, no decisions, with Anthony. Everything just happened.

The question was raised so simply, as the cab took them to the Pierre. They were silent as they were driven along Park Avenue. Courtney was looking out the cab window, and thinking of that first day when she had looked out the cab at New York, so strange and unknown to her, and had wondered what the city would hold for her. She could never have imagined that it would hold Anthony, that she would be driving this same route with him. He was studying her in silence. He put his hand on her thigh. She didn't object to the gesture, it was only casual, not compromising.

"When did it happen?" he said softly.

"When I was sixteen," she answered. Why did she tell him so easily, without hesitation?

"Sixteen," he repeated. "How marvelous. Like the Greeks."

Not so marvelous, she thought wryly. Not so romantic as all that. A little desperate, perhaps.

"How many?" he went on.

She was embarrassed. She didn't want to tell him that it was only one, that she was that young.

"That many?" He smiled.

"Oh, no," she said hastily. "It isn't that, it isn't that I can't count them, or something." Now she had blundered, but she didn't go on. She was so damned young.

He smiled, but he said nothing else. Nothing else needed to be said. It was decided so simply; there was no crisis.

It happened so simply; it happened so easily in the natural course of the evening. She still did not know how it happened, and she did not bother herself with the question of why it had happened, as she ran her hand languorously along her arm. She was conscious of his eyes upon her, watching her silently as he lay beside her. She looked around the bedroom of his suite, furnished in conventional hotel elegance. His white robe was tossed carelessly, like discarded virginity on the floor beside the bed. She lay back against the pillow. He got up and turned on the victrola. He put on a record of Bach, listened to it for a moment, then took off the record.

"No," he said to himself. "Not Bach. My God, not Bach."

He put on a record of Gregorian chants sung by Benedictine monks. He listened a moment and smiled.

"Yes," he said. "That pleases me." He turned to her. "If you will excuse me, darling, I shall take a cold shower."

He returned, rubbing a towel across his shoulders.

"What a beautiful body," she said.

"Of course," he said. "It is immoral not to be beautiful."

"Immoral?"

"Yes," he smiled. "The morality of the body."

"Pagan," she said.

"Not necessarily." He stood before the mirror, running a comb through his abundant black hair. "It is embodied in your Catholicism. You know," he added, "I was born Catholic. Of course," he went on, "the morality of the body was overshadowed by the monastic denial of the body—flagellation and abuse of it. But the theme still exists in Catholicism. Even in the fact that suicide is a mortal sin. Abuse of the body is discouraged. You see," he said, "I have simply cut the head off religion. I cannot divorce myself from all of its teachings. I have simply rearranged those which I have salvaged. The morality of the body," he repeated.

"In rearranging them, you have necessarily perverted them."

"What is your preoccupation with perversion? Why do you insist that I am perverted in my view of life?"

"You are," she said, suddenly angry. "You make love to yourself."

"To myself?"

"Yes. You're not able to make love to another human being."

He sat down beside her on the bed, his body young and graceful.

"Of course," he said. "I can't love. You're very right."

"I don't ask for love," she said angrily. "I'm not talking about love. I'm talking about making love."

"Then I don't know what you mean, angel."

She ran her tongue along her lower lip. "I mean you're crippled. I mean you loathe yourself, and that makes everything backwards."

"Oh, dear," he said. "This isn't the way it should be at all. You should be lying back in marvelous ease, and all that. You certainly shouldn't be angry with me. No, this just isn't right."

"You fancy yourself a lover," she said.

He looked steadily at her, her body pale and lovely against the pillows.

"My dear Courtney, have you ever been beaten?"

"It's all a great farce, you know," she continued. "A pose. You're incapable of living up to it. I imagine, invariably, you fail."

The mask of composure left his face. He looked as though he had been struck.

"Why are you trying to hurt me?" he asked softly.

"Because there's the ugliness," she said hopelessly, turning her face into the pillow. "The ugliness, the dead leaves, they've followed me. Because I can't escape them."

His face was hurt and boyish as he looked at the girl. He put his hand on her softly molded shoulder. The body was so very young, and she was so very lost.

"It's not ugly," he said quietly. "There's nothing ugly in it. Believe me. There's only beauty in making love. It may be the only beauty, and it may be of brief duration. But there is no ugliness."

He took her hands in his.

"Get up a moment, Courtney. I want to show you something."

She looked at him. His face was solemn and tender, and for the first time she trusted him. She got up and followed him to the side of the room. He took off his robe and let it drop on the floor.

"Look," he said. "Look into the mirror."

"No." She buried her head in his shoulder. "No, I don't want to. Don't make me look."

He put his hand on her back and ran his fingers along her neck.

"I said, look." His voice was stern.

She turned obediently and looked into the mirror.

"What do you see?" he asked.

"I see myself. And I don't like what I see."

"That's not what I see," he said. "I see two beautiful young bodies. I see no ugliness in the mirror. It's a simple reflection, you know, and there is no ugliness in the reflection."

He put his arm around her and led her hack to the bed. She put her head against his chest and he held her to him.

"Poor darling," he said. "Poor, moral child."

She smiled to herself.

"You know, I didn't undertand you when I met you. Now I understand a little. You dislike yourself so."

"I do dislike myself," he said. "And you were right when you accused me of being crippled. It is impossible for me to love, because I don't love myself. You know," he said thoughtfully, "I can ride a horse at top sped over a dangerous course, and not be afraid. But being alone at night, and in the dark, terrifies me."

"I have to go soon," she said. "And I'll be frightened when I go, because I betrayed myself again, and I know I can't trust myself. For a little while, I thought I could. Then I met you, and I wanted you, because I thought you had a secret world, a world without ugliness, that you could take me into. But you don't, and I was wrong."

"We'll have some wine," he said. "And promise me you'll forget the ugliness for a little while. You know, as long as you remember the ugliness, you might as well live in oblivion, because there's nothing for you in life. The ugliness is everywhere, and you just have to overlook it."

"Someone else said that to me once," she said.

"It's quite right," he said. "And you have to face that truth before you can live with yourself even for a short time. Otherwise you will be in constant search of escape."

"I know," she said quietly.

He got up and poured the wine. He handed her a glass.

"That's what I love about Janet," he went on. "She has no compunction. She is totally unable to love," he added. "You, even though you are her closest friend, couldn't know that. I am in a position to realize it. Nonetheless, even if she is conscious of ugliness, even if she dislikes herself, she never lets any one know it. She is perpetually gay, she visits her unhappiness or dissatisfaction upon no one. That wretched home she has. The group of boys she goes out with, who laugh behind her back at what an easy lay she is, while she thinks she has found in them a respite from a loveless home."

"I probably shouldn't have said all this to you," Courtney said soberly. "I suppose I had no right to let you know, and to hurt you because I was unhappy with myself."

"No, darling, that isn't what I meant. You and I talk to each other, even a little. She talks to no one. I don't even think she talks to you."

Courtney shook her head.

"And she certainly doesn't talk to her lovers. I would make a prediction, with absolute certainty, that within a year she will have a serious nervous breakdown."

"Janet?" Courtney smiled. "No, not Janet. She's so terribly gay and courageous. She has life a little under control."

"Well, that is only my unprofessional prediction. Nonetheless, we were talking about you. I want to see you tomorrow. If I could help it, I wouldn't let you go now. I may not have much to give you, but I don't want you to be alone when you're feeling like this. I feel vaguely responsible."

Courtney smiled at him. "You're not so wicked, are you? Not so different."

"Angel," he smiled. He put his arms around her and ran his hand through her hair. "When will I see you?"

"I'll call you when I wake up."

"Promise me," he said. "As soon as you wake up." He sighed. "I can see now that my social life will be shot. Becoming the lover of a moral child. I never envisioned such a fate. I should have known better than to get involved with an Irish girl. They're all so moody and passionate, and so terribly conscience-stricken about the whole thing. You know," he said, "I can't go on seeing you constantly. Only for a while, then my polygamous self will be reasserted."

"You think so," she smiled. "We'll see. You haven't made such an auspicious beginning, you know. Dropping your pose. You've made yourself vulnerable."

"Courtney," he said, "have you ever been beaten?"

They laughed and it wasn't ugly any more.

18

When she went home that night Courtney was not afraid, and her first thought on waking was: I have been loved. She was surprised and pleased that she felt neither the burden of loneliness nor the consciousness of sin. Because there had been no love, because, actually, there had been not even desire, there was no guilt. It had simply happened. She looked forward to seeing Anthony, and she thought again: Perhaps this is what I have been looking for. Perhaps this is love without evil, without the ugliness.

She cleaned her room, a thing which she had not done in days, and then she called Anthony. Her mother was not in; she had gotten a featured role on a TV dramatic show, and was at rehearsal. Courtney was reassured by her absence. It was good to have her mother working again, it was, as Sondra said, "Like the old days." It was different now, though. Courtney no longer felt dependent on her mother's success, and her ability to pay bills and take her to dinner. While Courtney made breakfast for herself, as she had so often when her mother was working in Hollywood, she realized how, first with Barry, then with Janet's friends, and now with Anthony, her life had become separate from her mother's. The feeling of independence reassured her. Centering her life around men rather than around her mother was more secure: men were at least replaceable if they failed.

Although Anthony offered to pick her up, Courtney chose to go to the Pierre by herself. Even though her mother was not home, the doorman might mention to her mother that she had left with a young man, and Courtney did not want her mother to know how much time she spent with Anthony. She left a note that she and Janet were going to the movies and would probably go on to dinner and then to a cocktail party. She was careful to account for the whole day in her note to her mother. How we deceive our parents, she thought as she propped the note beside the telephone. But it's kinder this way; it would hurt them to know us better. She took the subway, because the contrast between the subway and Anthony's suite amused her. As she walked into the Pierre, she thought to herself with pleasure, "I always live in glamour." But then she cut herself short because she was beginning to sound like her mother. She knocked on the door.

"Hello, darling." He greeted her casually and without presumed familiarity. "Come into the living room, the bedroom depresses me in the morning. Beds in the morning," he said as they walked into the other room, "are merely something to be gotten out of." He looked at her. "I've been thinking of you all morning, angel. Oh, have you had breakfast?"

"Yes, before I came."

"Well, then, have some coffee with me."

"Anthony, did I wake you up or something? You haven't shaved."

"No." He smiled. "I've decided to grow a beard. I had a three-day growth a couple of weeks ago, and it had a marvelous effect on the elevator men. I really couldn't find suitably iniquitous occupation, though, so I shaved it off."

"Well, I think you should shave it off again. It looks foolish."

"Oh, dear, you're always deflating me. Do you drink your coffee black?"

She nodded.

"I'm terribly bored this morning, angel. But I can't think of any hope for it as I consider making love in the morning a barbaric practice."

Courtney suddenly wondered what she was doing here, but the sensation passed quickly. She sipped her coffee.

"Are you depressed this morning, Courtney?"

"No, I don't think so."

"Come sit by me," he said as he put down his coffee. She sat beside him and he put his arm around her. She leaned against him and felt at peace again. "Tony will tell you a story," he said.

"Oh, no," said Courtney. "Not another tale of deviation."

"No," he said. "This is the story of a child."

She settled comfortably in his arms.

"This is the story," he said in his low, gentle voice, "of a little boy who lost his childhood. The boy was bred to wealth and boredom and his nursery was a little pocket of a private beach on the prewar Riviera. It was a lovely beach, with fine white sand and quiet waters, and there was always sun on the beach. There were some caves in a cliff at the end of the beach, very mysterious. It was really an ideal nursery. He and his childhood used to play with each other there, swimming and building intricate castles, and his parents were content to let him play without his governess because he had his childhood to keep him company.

They got along so awfully well. So his parents had lavish lunches for charming people, and never needed to worry about their little boy."

"Wasn't there ever anyone else on the beach?" asked Courtney. "You mean, he just played by himself all day long?"

"I told you," said Anthony patiently, "it was a private beach. Besides, he had his childhood to play with him. Now, don't interrupt me with these academic enquiries."

Courtney nodded, chastised. He brushed her hair gently from her forehead as he resumed his story.

"He was ecstatically happy, this little boy. He was terribly fond of his childhood, and didn't go anywhere without it. One day, he was exploring the caves in the cliff. Now, he had never been off the private beach, so exploring was very exciting to him. It was dark in the cave, and darkness was something he wasn't used to. You see, it was always sunny on his beach. When he went into the cave he was a little frightened, but he soon got over that in his excitement. He even forgot to pay attention to his childhood as he wandered through the tunnel. Well, he found to his delight that the tunnel went all the way through the cliff, and he saw sunlight ahead of him. He came out at the other end and found himself on one of those ghastly public beaches, with men rubbing sun-tan oil on women's backs and lying with the *Times* over their heads. It was a shocking sight, so he hurried back into the cave. When he came out on his own beach, he looked behind him, and suddenly realized that he had lost his childhood somewhere between the two beaches."

"Didn't he go back to look for it?"

"No, of course not," Anthony said crossly. "If you must know, he called into the cave, but there wasn't any answer, so he simply walked wretchedly back to his villa and had a Brandy Alexander."

"He never found it again," Courtney said despondently.

"No," said Anthony gravely. "It was lost for good."

"What a sad story. What's the moral?"

"Now, the moral is obvious, angel, and if you're so thick you can't see it, I refuse to explain it to you. Did you like the story?"

"Yes," she said. "I like it very much."

"Do you feel better now?"

"Yes," she smiled.

"I thought you would," he said. He ran his fingers along her mouth, tracing its curves. "Perhaps it's not so barbaric to make love in the morning," he said thoughtfully.

"Perhaps not."

The sun was soft, spilling through the partly closed Venetian blinds. It was very still, with no indication that life existed beyond the room.

"I want to lie here for years," he said. "Just like this. Making love and then lying here like this."

"And people will walk to work in the morning," said Courtney, "and come home to nag their wives and pay their bills, and everyone will grow old outside our room. And we'll just lie here like children in a secret place."

"Building sand castles." He smiled. "Did it ever occur to you that we might sound a little foolish?"

"No, not really," said Courtney thoughtfully. "The people who sit and pay their bills are the ones that sound foolish to me."

"Think of it," he said. "Never living to excess, never taking a chance, never touching the heights."

"I don't know that we would touch any heights, either," said Courtney, thoughtfully. "Maybe we would go as far as scaling the walls of our secret garden, but that would be all."

"And drop back in horror at the sight of the outside world?"

He put his head against her breasts like a child and ran his thumb absently along her arm. "Possibly you're right. I've done my damndest to find the heights. Making love, risking my life, occasionally—in my wayward youth," he smiled "—getting involved in slightly illegal dealings. None of it really worked, though. Something was still missing."

"I don't know, really. Sometimes I think it's necessary to be a child to find the heights—you know, illusion is necessary. Then sometimes I think the harsh light of adult reality is what's needed, and that children only climb sand hills."

"We haven't any choice in the matter," he said. "If it takes an adult to know the joys of excess, I haven't any hope. So I like to think that only a child can come upon euthanasia, that isolation at the height of ecstasy. But the question is academic," he said crossly, "and it depresses me."

"We need some wine," she said, "and some lunch, to descend from fantasy for a moment."

"Yes," he said sadly, "I suppose we do."

"Where will we go? Some place special, heavy and dark, where we'll drink marvelous white wine and have things flambeau."

"I know a place," he said. "You have expensive tastes, my dear."

"Not always," she said. "But I have always eaten either very expensive food or terribly cheap food. I refuse the in-between. Both poverty and wealth are excellent things, because they are extremes, but the middle ground is damaging to the soul."

"Schrafft's," he said. "Good, wholesome food at a moderate price."

"And three women haggling over the check."

"I agree with you," he said. "Far better a fifty-cent meal served by fugitives from an early Bogart picture, in filthy aprons."

"You know," she said, "we're going to have a delightful life."

The restaurant was exactly what Courtney wanted. They walked down stone steps to enter it, and when they sat down they lost all awareness of the fact that it was daytime.

They were the only young people in the dimly lit room, which was half filled with leisurely diners. Courtney had not known that such places existed in New York, and she was enchanted. She did not have to think of the cost of the meal, because she knew that, somehow, the world gave Anthony his living without his having to work for it.

Courtney sat with studied nonchalance while the waiter set her roast duck afire in solemn ceremony. When he had left she sipped her wine, and then looked over at Anthony. Her face was relaxed and very young, and her eyes were green indeed in the dimness.

"I'm marvelously happy," she said.

He watched her silently for a few minutes.

"You know," Anthony smiled, "if I'm not awfully careful I shall fall in love with you."

"Oh, no," she said solemnly, "you mustn't do that."

"You object?"

"You must promise me never to fall in love with me."

"What an odd child," he said. "I'll promise, if you wish."

"And you must keep your promise, like a monastic vow."

"I'll do my best, angel. Because you're quite right; if we ever fell in love we should fail miserably in our quest. Great phantoms of doubt and jealousy would slip into our room. We must hold to our vow, and keep ourselves pure."

"This is a marvelous wine," she said suddenly, "and an enchanting place. I like it here." She looked at him thoughtfully. "No, I mustn't say that. I mustn't say that wherever I am with you seems enchanting."

"No, you mustn't say that."

"We're idiots, do you know that?"

"The thought had occurred to me once or twice today," he said. "Now eat the dinner that you were so anxious to get."

"And then what will we do?"

"I don't know. Does it really matter?"

"No," she said thoughtfully.

19

Time passed in timelessness, and the city settled down under the oppressive heat of July. In almost a month not a day had passed when Courtney had not seen Anthony, and as she lay on her bed with her clothes off in a vain attempt to keep cool she felt strange at being alone. Anthony had called her when she woke up late in the morning, and had told her that he would have to have dinner with his lawyers that evening. They were conferring about his estate, and he would be with them for several hours after dinner as well. Courtney was faced with the prospect of having dinner with her mother, or alone. Neither appealed to her, so she decided to call Janet. Janet was delighted to hear from her.

"Courtney, sweetie, what has happened to you? I called a few times, but you were always out. Have you been having a mad affair with someone?"

"I've been awfully busy," Courtney answered. She did not want to tell Janet about Anthony, because she felt a little disloyal, knowing about Janet and Anthony when Janet had visited his island last winter. "I really meant to call you," she went on. "Look, I wondered if you were tied up this evening?"

"I'm not doing anything for dinner, except the family, but after dinner I'm going to Pete Murray's cocktail party. You remember Pete?"

"Vaguely. Well, what about my seeing you for dinner, then?"

"Sweetie, that would be great. Then maybe you could come to the party. I know Pete wouldn't mind."

"I don't have a date—"

"That doesn't make any difference. You'll know the whole crowd. It's going to be a real blast—the whole of Pete's house is turned over to us. His family is away for the weekend, and every bad actor in town will be there."

At its wildest, Courtney knew that at least the party would be better than sitting at home. Courtney felt more and more ill at ease with her parents these days, conscious that somehow she was betraying them, and painfully aware of how careful she must be to keep them, for their own sakes, from knowing of her life with Anthony. It was a difficult duality that she must maintain at home, and she avoided contact with her parents as much as possible.

"Jan, I really would love to go to the party," Courtney said finally. "Are you sure your parents won't mind my coming up for dinner?"

"Well, *I* would be delighted to have you, sweetie, and it's as much my home as theirs. I'm afraid dinner will be a real drag, though. Mother is back, and Daddy will be there, too."

"That's all right, Jan. It will be great to see you, and I'm really sorry I haven't called before."

"Don't worry about it, Court. You can come right on up—it's about five thirty, isn't it?"

"Yes. I'll be there about six. So long, sweetie."

The familiarity of Janet's apartment was reassuring to Courtney; it was reassuring to be reminded that she had a group to return to if somehow her world with Anthony should dissolve. Although she could see no reason why her garden should wither, the caution that she had learned at such great cost remained with her.

Courtney had not seen Mrs. Parker in almost three years, but Janet's mother was just as Courtney had remembered her. She was a slight woman, with the small, regular features and the almost formless face of the women whose pictures can be found every day on the social page of *The New York Times* with the caption: Benefit Aides. She was wearing a nondescript black suit and clutching a glass of sherry as though it were a period prop which she had just been handed and was not yet accustomed to. When Courtney came in she rose with great agitation to greet her, as though she was anxious to take Courtney's attention from Mr. Parker, who was sitting beside the window with his usual glass of bourbon.

"Courtney dear, I'm so glad to see you, it has been such a long time. Thanksgiving vacation a long time ago, when you and Janet were in Scaisbrooke, I think it was, you *have* changed, you look so much *older*, but then I suppose you are"—this with a little laugh—"I was so glad when Janet told me you were coming to dinner with us, I've been looking forward to seeing you so much," and by this time her speech had carried her across the room and she kissed Courtney on the cheek, a gesture which Courtney had objected to since she was a little girl.

"It's good to see you again, Mrs. Parker. You're looking very well," Courtney managed to say.

"David," Mrs. Parker addressed her husband, "*isn't* it nice to have Courtney with us."

"Mmm-hmm," he said, not moving from his chair. "How have you been, Courtney? Janet tells us that you're going to a tutor in the fall."

"Yes," Courtney answered, "Mummy thought it would be good for me to have intensive schoolwork without all the rules I had at Scaisbrooke."

"You know," said Mrs. Parker with her head to one side, "I was saying to my husband that it might be a good idea for Janet to go to a tutor, rather than going back to that school she went to last year, because she didn't seem to be very happy there."

Janet laughed. "They just sent Daddy a letter saying that I might be happier somewhere else, and indicating that they might be happier, too. The polite axe."

"It might be a very good idea," said Courtney.

"We'll have to look into that, won't we, David?" Receiving no response, she continued, "What is the name of your tutor, dear?"

"Mr. Bigelow," Courtney answered. "I'll write it down for you."

As she wrote the name and address of her tutoring school, Courtney looked over at Mr. Parker. What a strange, angry man, she thought. He looked very sorry for himself, sitting with his glass of bourbon. She remembered that Janet said he was worse when Mrs. Parker was home, that the rest of the time they had a sort of understanding, but when the third person entered the house his rages and his crying jags were more frequent. "I hear him getting up at five in the morning," Janet had said, "and when I go into the kitchen in the morning there is almost always an empty fifth of bourbon on the counter."

The maid came out of the kitchen.

"Dinner is served, Mrs. Parker," she said as though unfamiliar with the phrase and her new mistress.

"Thank you, Ann," said Mrs. Parker. "I do hope there is enough, Courtney. Janet told us at the last minute that you were coming and I did wish she had given us a little more warning, but she is so vague about these things, springing guests and parties on us without *any* warning. I do wish she would be more considerate of Mr. Parker and myself," she said to Courtney in a confidential tone.

"Court, do you want to wash up or anything—in other words, go to the john?" asked Janet.

Courtney was enough at home in the Parker household so that she would have excused herself had she cared to, and she sensed in Janet's unnecessary remark that Janet had something she wanted to tell her.

"Yes, I think I will," said Courtney. "Please excuse us."

When she entered Janet's room, Janet closed the door and took a letter from the jumble of clothes in her top drawer.

"It's been so long that I haven't had a chance to tell you anything," Janet said. "I've been having a *thing* with this really great guy, Marshall Richards, for weeks now," she explained. "We're madly in love, and he wants to marry me and all, and Daddy can't stand him—he's a really bad actor—bad news all the way—and he wrote me this letter from Newport last week." She opened the letter. "This is the part you've really got to hear. 'I hope that your father, that Babbittesque caricature of Samuel P. Insull, is sufficiently steeped in drink so that the next time I see you we won't have another scene like the last.'"

"Very amusing," Courtney said, "but what is the point of all this?"

"Well, I've suspected for a long time now that Daddy has been reading my mail, so I stopped leaving letters around the house. Last night though, when I looked in my drawer for this letter to get Marshall's address, it wasn't there, and this morning it had somehow returned. There's a whole lot more in the letter, too, about my body, and how much he loves me, and all that."

"This is all your father needs," said Courtney.

"Well, he knows about me already, because once when we were having an argument I threw it up at him because I knew it would make him mad. But the thing I'm glad about is that I caught him in the act this time. So at dinner I want to let him know that I know he's read the letter. That's why I wanted to tell you before dinner," Janet said. "Now we'd better go out so we don't hold up dinner. Daddy is drunk as a lord," she added as they went out the door.

Courtney and Janet took their appointed places at the dinner table, beside each other. The maid brought the first course, and they ate in strained silence. Mr. Parker was contemplating the centerpiece with a fixed and moody gaze, and Mrs. Parker was nervously alternating her food with sips of water, because she drank only one glass of sherry, never more or less, a day. Mr. Parker's fresh glass of bourbon was beside him.

"How are your parents, Courtney?" asked Mrs. Parker in an attempt at conversation.

"They're fine, thank you."

"I would like to meet them some time. They must be very talented people."

There was another agonizing silence as the first course was cleared and the soup brought.

"Daddy," Janet said suddenly, "who was Samuel P. Insull?"

Mr. Parker fixed his gaze upon his daughter.

"Why do you want to know?"

"I ran across his name in a book," Courtney said hastily, "and I asked Janet who he was. She thought you might know."

"He was a very great man," Mr. Parker answered gravely.

"But what did he do?" asked Janet.

"He controlled utilities in Chicago."

"What was he like?" asked Courtney.

"A great public benefactor," Mr. Parker said solemnly. "He gave his fortune to the Chicago Opera. A very generous and great man. A man who should be the model and inspiration for any businessman," he continued.

Courtney was delighted. Knowing the game they were playing, Mr. Parker was extolling the virtues of the Chicago tycoon. He was really getting quite worked up, she thought as she listened to him, quite personally involved, as though he were defending himself against his daughter's thrust.

"Yes, a very great man," Mr. Parker repeated, taking another sip of his drink. "He had very little education, Samuel P. Insull, but he never forgot where he came from, and how he got to where he was. That's a thing a great many people overlook," he went on. "Janet with her debutante parties and her friends and her snobbery, she's forgotten the value of hard work. Hard work, and humility. That's why she can have all these things, because I worked so hard. Started as a messenger in the firm I work with, just a clerk when her mother and I were married, worked my way up. My own hard work, humility, and God's help."

Courtney was beginning to get a little embarrassed by the man's alcoholic intensity. Their game was getting out of hand.

"God's help," he repeated. "Young people these days forget to thank God. To thank God for what He has given them, to respect their parents and fulfill their obligations. Ungrateful, the whole generation. Worthless." He started to weep quietly as he talked.

Courtney said nothing.

Now, David," said his wife in agitation, "don't upset yourself."

He turned to her angrily. "Shut up."

There was a silence broken only by Mr. Parker's heavy breathing. He blew his nose loudly. Courtney looked at her dinner with fleeting distaste.

"You read that letter." Janet broke the silence. "You went into my drawer and you took out a letter written to me, and you read it."

He didn't answer.

"You know you had no right to do that," she said triumphantly. "And it was because you read that letter, because of what it said about me and the boy who wrote it, that you cut a hundred dollars of my allowance this morning. You weren't fining me for coming in late last night. You were taking almost half of my allowance, because that was the only way you knew of hurting me, because you knew I didn't care what you said or thought of me any more. The only hold you have over me is money, and you know it. You know that's the only reason I stay in this house, because the food and the bed are free!"

He looked up in fury, struck in his most vulnerable point.

"Yes, I read that letter," he said. "I have a right to know what you're doing, as long as I pay the bills. I have a right to know what everybody else in New York seems to know, that my daughter is nothing but a whore!"

They knew how to hurt each other, these two.

"Sure I sleep with boys!" Janet was almost shouting. "What do you expect me to do? At least they care what happens to me, at least I know I'm wanted. Do you expect me to stay in this house at night, when all I get is abuse from a drunken father? Do you think I feel this is a home?"

The maid came and cleared the dishes, bringing the main course unnoticed. Mrs. Parker had started to cry, and got up hastily, running into the bedroom. Courtney was very hungry, and tackled her dinner with relish.

"You can leave," Mr. Parker was saying. "You can leave whenever you feel like it; you're eighteen. I'll be glad to see you go. How do you think I feel when I sit here alone at night and I know you're off sleeping with some drunken college boy?"

"Just the way I hope you feel. Just the way I want you to feel."

The lamb chops were a little too well done, Courtney noticed.

"All I worked for all my life," he shouted. "I wasn't working for myself, I was working for you, and your mother—"

"Crap," said Janet calmly.

"—you and your mother, and you drive her into a sanitarium with your promiscuous life. To see you a laughing-stock, someone mothers and teachers point to—was that what I worked my fingers to the bone for? Was that what I spent my life for, to give you enough money to sleep with college boys instead of poorer juvenile delinquents?"

"Who are you to criticize me, you, an alcoholic, a person I am embarrassed to have my friends meet. What kind of a father do you think you are? What do you think you have ever given me? Money. Hell, I can make money, I can marry money, I can get money in a thousand ways; it doesn't mean anything, if I live in a place I can't bring my friends to. I might just as well live in a tenement as Park Avenue."

With dogged determination, Courtney finished her dinner. She wanted desperately to leave, to flee this scene as Mrs. Parker had, but her loyalty to Janet made her stay.

"Then get out. Then leave, if I embarrass you so!"

Janet looked at him, suddenly silent and thoughtful. Courtney wondered what she was going to say.

"No," Janet said quietly. "No, I'm not going to leave. You owe me something as your daughter. You haven't given me anything but a family I'm ashamed of and a house I hate. I'm going to make you give me something. I'm not going to leave. That would be the easy way out for both of us. I'm going to stay, and you're going to support me until I'm through high school. I'm not going to let you off that easily."

Mr. Parker lurched from his chair in fury. He gripped the glass in his hand and threw it at the girl. In his anger it missed her and hit above her head on the wall, shattering and spilling its contents on the thick carpet. He was defeated, out-bluffed, and he knew it. He knew that his impotent devotion to his daughter, so like him in her combativeness, unafraid of him or anyone else, and his own terrible loneliness would not permit him to drive her from his life. She had beaten him. He left, defeated, as she sat in triumphant silence watching him. He took the bottle of bourbon with him and a new glass, and walked out to the living room.

His wife was in the bedroom, undoubtedly in hysterics at this evidence of the dissolution of her family, and the fury of her husband and the daughter who was so like him. It was the fury and self-destruction in each of them that she could never understand, and it frightened her. She had locked the door to her bedroom, locked herself in as she had for so many years.

There was a silence over the whole apartment. The maid stood in a corner of the kitchen, and as she realized that the terrible fury had once more abated, she started to wash the dishes, humming tunelessly to herself because the sound reassured her.

It was Janet who spoke first.

"My dinner isn't cold, thank God."

When they had finished dinner, Janet went into her room and put on her make-up while Courtney put on some lipstick. Janet put on some Kenton records and turned up the volume loud to fill the silence of the apartment. Then they left, carefully avoiding the living room. As they went out Janet tried her key in the front door.

"That's good," she said. "He hasn't changed the lock again. Whenever Daddy is mad at me," she explained, "he changes the lock so I will have to ring the bell to get in, and he can know what time I come home. Then I have to get a new one made. The locksmith around the corner and I are great buddies by now," she grinned. "But I guess Daddy won't get a chance to change the lock until tomorrow."

And they got in a cab and headed down Park Avenue to their cocktail party.

They were greeted at the door by a young man in Bermuda shorts and matching gray flannel jacket, and they walked into an enormous living room filled with young people. Drinks were thrust into their hands and, armed, they advanced into the center of the horde.

"Dapho," shouted Janet as she rushed over to a young girl in black, "how great to see you. Did you and Al ever get back from that party on the Island last week? Someone said he found Al marooned in Oyster Bay—"

"Yes," someone was saying at Courtney's elbow, "the Count lost his job on the Street; they got tired of his being either bombed or hung over—"

"He got out of the army because of cirrhosis of the liver," a young man was saying. "The doctor really flipped, at the age of twenty."

"And, my God, did they make out, right in the living room, which was all right except that the girl who used to be mad for him was right there, and here this was practically a *seduction*, she was really throwing the make on him—"

"She wouldn't let you go out for a week? Oh, is your mother a bitch, too?"

"Oh, my date passed out, as usual, so they won't let him in any more—you know, some gun-happy cop pulled a gun on him once when he tried to slug the cop, that sobered up Davidow, thank God, so—"

Through the milling conversations Courtney, seeing that Janet was occupied, made her way to the kitchen to put a little water in her Scotch. After all, this was going to he a long party.

The only other person in the kitchen was a tall young man in gray flannels, wearing a somewhat detached air, who was fixing himself a martini.

"Hello," he said, "we haven't met, but as you're the only other sober person I've seen, I think we should make each other's acquaintance. I'm Charles. Cunningham."

"Courtney Farrell," she said. "Everyone else seems to have arrived before us and gotten an edge."

"Us?" he said, gently stirring the martini. "Did your date get lost in the throng?"

"No," she reassured him. "I came with Janet Parker."

"Oh. Yes, Janet."

"You know her?"

"Who doesn't?" he said with a quick smile. "I see you have some of that abominable Scotch they are serving. Some remote brand that they forced on me when I came in. I couldn't stomach it, so I'm making a martini. If you'd prefer one, there are about four in this shaker."

"Yes," she said, "perhaps I shall. I usually drink Scotch out of habit. A martini would be nice for a change."

"Just leave your drink on the counter," he said. "Someone will take it."

Courtney made the quick appraisal of the young man that she always made of cocktail party acquaintances. He was tall and self-assured, and seemed somehow older than the others at the party. His hair was brown, lightened by the sun, his skin was tan, making his quick, easy smile more noticeable by contrast. His eyes were blue and direct, with the disconcerting quality of never leaving his companion's face. He had a slightly critical and self-contained air, the air of the observer. She decided that he was worth staying with, and accepted the martini that he handed her.

"You in school?" he said.

"Yes. And you? Yale, I suppose. Most of the people here are."

"I went to Yale," he said. "That's where I met our host. I'm just finished with Harvard Law."

"Oh," she said. He was older, then. Probably about twenty-five. She liked that. "You're not a member of the Crew, I see."

"No," he said with the smile which relieved the direct intensity of his expression. "No," he repeated. "I like to drink, but I find no charm in passing out and getting sick all over my dates. The routine doesn't appeal to me. I'm afraid I find being sober a little more enjoyable. I may be lost, but I refuse to be so blatantly lost."

Supercilious, she thought. Although she agreed with what he was saying, she felt in his words a criticism of herself for being with these people. She didn't say anything.

"Is Janet a good friend of yours?" he asked.

"Yes," Courtney answered. "Since we were in Scaisbrooke together." She was aware that whenever she said she was a good friend of Janet's there was always a slight reaction, a sidelong glance, but she refused to deny Janet because of her notoriety.

"She's a very game girl," he said. "But game girls become tiresome. There are so many of them."

"Say, you're awfully critical, aren't you?" said Courtney finally.

"I might make a similar remark about youthful cynics."

"All right," he smiled. "Touché. How is the martini?"

"Excellent. And I am a harsh judge."

"So am I. Of martinis and people."

"I gathered that."

"Well, it's not that I'm cynical," he said. "I am probably too much of a perfectionist. I set high standards, for myself, and the people around me. It doesn't endear me to people," he smiled. "But there's really nothing I can do about it. Say, what about going into another room? It's awfully hot in here."

"It's hotter in the living room," Courtney said.

"I know. Let's go into the library. It's quiet there, and we can talk."

Although it was against all her principles of coktail party behavior to confine herself to one person, Courtney agreed. The young man, for all his critical airs, interested her. The defense of cynicism was one she often applied when she felt ill at ease, or when she was meeting someone. She ignored it and sensed that, at least, Charles was more intelligent than most of the boys at the party.

There were two other couples in the library, and the quiet conversation was a relief from the noise and congestion of the living room. Charles brought the shaker of martinis with him.

"You know," he said as they sat down, "there's something about this crowd that always puts me in a sort of cynical mood. I knew Peter would be upset if I didn't accept his invitation, though."

"You probably feel a little ill at ease with them," Courtney commented.

"No," he said thoughtfully, "I really don't think that's it. For my first two years at Yale I was very much a part of the Crew, as you put it. Then I looked at my marks, and I looked at my friends, and I suddenly asked myself, why this self-destruction? Why this drinking to get drunk? We're not middle-aged and beaten; there really isn't any reason for it. So I stopped seeing them and set myself to the task of becoming a lawyer. There's something about the conviction that they're lost, and the self-pity, that makes me angry whenever I'm with these people. It's not that I don't like them. If I disliked them, I wouldn't be here. But they're wasting so much by being angry with the world. That's what makes me mad."

"Yes," Courtney said. "You have a point. I've felt a little the same way myself."

"I hope you don't think I'm being supercilious when I say all this," he said with a smile.

"Only a little," she said.

"Well, it's just such a damned waste. There isn't any reason for it; they just lack courage. They criticize their parents, and blame them for their own drinking and sleeping around, and still they allow themselves to be supported by the parents they despise."

Courtney thought of Janet. "Well, there might be a little more to it than that."

"Not if they have any real self-respect," he said. "After I got in trouble with the deans at Yale, when I got in with this crowd, the parents sent me a long letter telling me that as long as they were paying the bills I was there for an education, and I'd better mend my ways or they'd withdraw their support. My father is a very conservative Boston lawyer," he added, "with all sorts of ideas on the importance of education and the fact that education has to be earned, and he wasn't going to put up for a moment with high bar bills and low marks. So I told him to go to hell," he smiled, "and continued my pattern of life, putting myself through by writing papers and tutoring other students."

Courtney looked at Charles with a new interest. He was not as she had first thought a "straight arrow," a supercilious prig. He had simply refused to compromise. Courage was something she had always admired, and she liked his reaction to the situation which all Janet's friends had met and had answered simply by getting themselves kicked out of college.

"You know," she said, "it's a funny thing, but the fact that you continued living it up makes me respect you more than if you had gone straight-arrow."

He studied her for a moment. "Yes, I suppose that is what would appeal to you. Not that I earned my own way, but that I continued to be an alkie. I suppose you measure a man by his fondness for alcohol."

"No," she said hastily. That wasn't the impression she had meant to give at all. Now he was classifying her as one of the Crew he despised. "That isn't what I meant."

"Well, I had thought somehow that you weren't one of the group. I suppose I was wrong. That's the trouble with young girls, they think the measure of a man is the measure of alcohol in his blood."

Courtney stood up, angry.

"The martini was delightful," she said, "but the criticism I can do without."

"And now you're going to leave," he said. "I didn't mean that as a criticism, really. I'm always putting my foot in my mouth."

"Yes, I'm going to leave."

"Well, there's nothing I can do about it," he sighed. "Women always take things personally. But I do wish you wouldn't go."

Courtney shrugged and went with her martini into the living room. She had enjoyed talking to Charles, his sanity and his ability to hold an intelligent conversation were refreshing to her. She felt that she would have liked to get to know him better. He was very attractive, too. But she didn't need criticism from anyone; there was no necessity to take that, and certainly not at a cocktail party. For the first time since she had walked into the kitchen, she missed Anthony. She wished he were here. There was no criticism from Anthony.

"Yes, Cynthia is coming out at the Cotillion. Well, face it, all it takes to come out at the Cotillion is money, and that's about all she has—"

"Look, darling, I promise I won't pass out on you, really. We'll just go up to the apartment and have a couple of drinks—"

"The Stork. Oh, God, no, I'm getting so sick of the Bird; it's just filled with a lot of prep-school kids these days. What about going to P. J. Clarke's?"

"Yes, sweetie, you really have lost weight, you look marvelous in that dress. I've been on a diet, but unless I go on the wagon, I don't suppose I'll ever lose weight, and I simply can't be on the wagon in the summer, the heat is too ghastly, and in the fall there are so many parties, right into the Christmas season—it's really a drag—"

Again Courtney retreated into the kitchen. She hadn't really wanted a martini after all. She poured the dregs of her drink down the drain and fixed herself a Scotch.

"My God, Court, was that a martini you threw out?"

"Oh, hi, George, I didn't see you," she said.

"Perfectly sinful, to waste a good drink. Say, we haven't seen you in a month. Where have you been keeping yourself?"

"Oh, I'm being kept by a mad Italian nobleman," Courtney laughed.

"Really? Congratulations, darling, but you should try the French." He grinned. "Seriously, we have missed you. Say, how long have you been here?"

"Oh, about half an hour."

"Well, why haven't I seen you? Who took you away to make mad love upstairs?"

"I was talking with Charles Cunningham, in the library."

"Oh, Charlie. He's a great guy, brilliant lawyer. He's turned kind of straight-arrow lately. Used to be a real alkie, but he shaped up."

"Yes, he is kind of straight-arrow," Courtney agreed. This was more like it.

"Hey, sweetie, don't *nurse* that drink!"

"The last time I saw you, as I remember, I drank you under the table."

"Well, try again. I'll match you. But nursing drinks is not allowed."

"All right; I'm game."

"Come on out into the living room, and I'll watch you get bombed."

"No, I'll always outdrink you, sweetie."

Courtney and George proceeded to match each other for drinks in quick succession, and Courtney found that very soon the conversations did not seem quite as trivial, and she no longer missed Anthony. In fact, she found that she was enjoying herself. Several hours later, she again found herself in the kitchen, taking George's brief absence as a chance to drink some ice water.

"Courtney, sweetie"—the Count wandered in unsteadily and kissed her passionately—"I love you."

She disengaged herself from his embrace.

"I love you too, sweetie, but don't be so vema—*vehement* in your demonstration."

"Oh, God, those syllables are too much for me," the Count responded. "I'll go make love to Janet."

"Mmm-hello, darling," Peter put his arms around her and kissed her, taking his cue from the Count. "Why haven't we ever had an affair?"

"You're never sober enough," Courtney laughed.

"Everyone seems to be kissing Courtney," said a quiet, familiar voice. Charles held his martini to one side and kissed her on the forehead. "I've been looking all over for you. I see you've been catching up with the rest of the party," he observed.

"Oh, the straight-arrow again," said Courtney. "I'm just about to leave."

"Marvelous. Then I'll take you home. I've canvassed the group and found no one quite so intelligent or attractive, so I've been in search of you."

"George is taking me home," Courtney said coolly.

Charles smiled. "I just passed George on his way to the men's room, and he seemed a little bombed. I think I'd better take you home."

"I appreciate your solicitude," said Courtney, "but George is taking me home."

Charles shrugged. "The offer is still open, if you change your mind."

George appeared in the doorway, and leaned his arm against it, taking the opportunity to kiss the forehead of a girl who ducked under it as she made her way back to the living room.

"Ready to go, George?" Courtney asked him.

"Go? Hell, there's still some liquor."

"Well, I'm ready to go, sweetie," she said.

"Then go. I'm going to drink," George said without concern.

"Offer's still open," said Charles.

"All right," she sighed.

When they got into the cab, Charles looked at his watch.

"Twelve thirty," he remarked. "Twenty One," he said to the driver.

"That's not my address," said Courtney.

"No," said Charles, "but that's where we're going. I'm hungry as hell, and I think you could use some food."

"I'm not bombed," Courtney said distinctly. "And I was under the impression that you were taking me home."

"I know you were," he smiled. "Marvelous late supper at Twenty One."

They were seated in the bar, at one of the small tables with red-checked tablecloths. The last time Courtney had been to Twenty One was with her father. She and Anthony went to the more obscure restaurants, but Twenty One had always been one of Courtney's favorites. Somehow it was a place that none of the young men she knew took her to; it was somehow too established and conservative, and she felt hesitant at suggesting it. There was something straight-arrow about Twenty One. She was glad they had come.

"You know," she said, "despite my objections, I'm glad we came here. This is a marvelous place, and I never come here as often as I'd like to."

"It doesn't appeal to your Crew," Charles said. "You can neither get loudly drunk or make out here."

"I do wish you'd stop referring to them as my Crew," Courtney said wearily. "As a matter of fact, tonight was the first time in a month that I saw them."

"Well, congratulations," he said. "Seriously, it's not a good group for a young girl. No matter how well she behaves, if she goes around with them she is suspect. And I can sense that you're not a Janet Parker."

"Janet's a marvelous girl," Courtney said. "I told you she was a good friend of mine."

"Oh, stop defending her," he said with annoyance. "I think she's a great girl, too, but you know perfectly well what I'm talking about."

"Yes, as a matter of fact I do," Courtney said soberly. "It's really too bad that she's so confused, and that she's gotten herself the reputation she has."

"You know," Charles said, "a girl could live as Janet lives—and more so, because you have to discount eighty per cent of the stories about her, and nobody would have to know about it. I really think that she wants people to know."

"That's one of the first intelligent things I've heard anyone say about Janet," said Courtney. "She does want people to know. Most of all, she wants her parents to know, to hurt them."

"Damned shame. With the family she has, though, it's not awfully hard to understand. Not that I endorse her behavior," he said hastily, "but I can understand it."

The waiter came over to them.

"I think I'll have a chicken sandwich," said Courtney.

"Oh, darling, don't be so unimaginative. This is Saturday night and I have my check in my pocket. Let's have something gay like crepe suzettes."

"That's a marvelous idea," said Courtney.

"And if you're not averse to mixing the grape and the grain—"

"No."

"—two cognacs."

Courtney was delighted. Somehow the gesture reminded her of Anthony, but Charles had a reassuring air of solidity and command about him. She was not acquainted with men like Charles, not young men, anyway—he somehow reminded her of Al Leone—and she felt a little unsure of herself. The idiom of the cocktail party was out of place here.

"I'm sorry I annoyed you earlier this evening," he was saying. "I wanted to apologize. I really wasn't referring to you in particular. I was just in a lousy mood, probably because I felt sort of out of place."

This reassured her.

"Well, please don't let it bother you. I guess I am kind of young, as you said, reacting the way I did. But that isn't important. I care much more about the fact that I adore Twenty One and we're having crepe suzettes. That's delightful."

"Say, Courtney, you have marvelous eyes."

She sighed. "Yes, they're green. Green. It has been a point of contention all my life. They're green, they're unusually large, and I have never yet been out with a boy who didn't comment on them."

He laughed. "You're great, you really are. I am stopped cold. You know, you must get awfully bored with the boys who were at the party tonight. I can see you're not one for cocktail party conversation."

"As a matter of fact, I love cocktail parties. I never have to think. I never have to say anything I really mean, and I know that nothing I say can be held against me because nobody will remember it."

"You have a good point there. You know, I'd like to see more of you. Could you give me your phone number? I'd like to call you, and take you out for a real dinner. We could just sit and talk, and you wouldn't have to say anything you really mean if you didn't want to. I promise, despite my forbidding air, to be content with bubbles of conversation." He smiled.

20

I had a lovely time at the cocktail party," Courtney said, stretching her arms above her in smugness and then folding her hands behind her head. "And afterwards I went with that charming boy to Twenty One, and we had crepes suzettes and brandy."

"Philistines," Anthony snorted. "Philistines. I'm glad I got you back before they corrupted you."

He stood in front of the window a moment, holding aside the hotel drapes in an attempt to draw some relief from the oppressive midday heat. He turned to her, and she watched him from her front-row seat on the couch. He never turned just his head; his whole upper body turned when he shifted his attention, as though he were conscious of maintaining a sculptural balance of line.

"I've languished without you," he said sadly. "An evening of wretchedness, pretending to listen to those deadly lawyers. And all the while you were enjoying yourself thoroughly, no doubt being made love to or something."

"I like to watch you move," Courtney said without concern at his petulance. "Come over here and sit beside me."

He walked obediently to the couch. She ran her hand with proprietary ease along the narrow, sculptured line of his ribs and hips. He took her hand in his and studied her a moment.

"I come at your call, don't I?" he said. "I've really lost all my command. My art is being corrupted. I'm behaving like an *American* lover."

"You certainly are," Courtney smiled, "and I'm enjoying it thoroughly. You're getting jealous."

He rose with studied grace, and leaned on the mantel, watching himself and the girl through the mirror.

"Where shall we have lunch?" he said abruptly. "At the Plaza?"

"I suppose so," Courtney said without enthusiasm.

"Now look." He walked over to her and took her hands, pulling her up. He stood slightly apart from her and regarded her steadily.

"I don't like you this morning," he said levelly. "You don't amuse me. You're behaving very like a woman, which you haven't since that first evening. I'm afraid I am a little jealous, but that is no reason for you to hold my jealousy aloft like a laurel wreath, proclaiming your triumph. Shall I name you the single greatest error that women make in love affairs? After the first flush has faded from the lover's face, after they are no longer treated with the deference paid to the new conquest, they attempt to make him jealous, they play the coquette. Particularly American women, who can't bear the subordinate position they find themselves in."

He put his hands on her shoulders, resting his thumbs against the softly modeled collarbone.

"They end up by spoiling everything," he said softly. "They

make a game of love, they corrupt it, and from that point on everything disintegrates."

She watched him solemnly. He dropped his hands and turned away from her, as though it were easier to speak when he was not looking at her.

"Whenever I have found that happening to me, I have simply ended the affair. Right there. I refused to let it end in ugliness, on the decline, so to speak." He turned slightly toward her. "So, my dear, you must be very careful. You must guard against your latent feminine wiles. That would be a costly indulgence."

Courtney regarded him steadily, running her tongue between her lips for a moment.

"Do you think that you have so much control over me, that you are so desperately important to me? Do you think that I am so unsure of you? Just because you are my lover, you think you have the right to tell me what to do when no other human being can? You had better watch your step as well. You can't afford to lose me," she said defiantly. "After knowing me you'd find yourself quite adrift, my darling Anthony, for all your masculine arrogance."

He stood silent, in anger and surprise, and Courtney wondered idly if he were going to hit her. Suddenly he laughed, sincerely laughed, with no malice in the laughter.

"What's so amusing?" Courtney said levelly.

"Angel, you look so terribly Irish, a little Irish banty cock, ready to fight anyone." Still smiling, he put his arms around her. She didn't move.

"Now, darling," he said in that soft, low voice, "don't be angry with Tony."

His face was solemn now, like a child who has suddenly realized that his teasing has made his mother angry, and is anxious to atone for it. He gently kissed her chin, still thrust out in defiance. She looked at his face, boyishly solemn. As suddenly as she had gotten angry, she smiled, and slowly put her arms around him. He picked her up easily, and looked down at the girl, resting in his arms. He kissed her cheek as he would a child's.

Suddenly the phone rang, insistingly, demandingly, in the adjoining bedroom.

"We won't answer it," he said in a conspiratorial tone. She shook her head and smiled.

The phone still rang, harshly, jarring their mood and shattering it, dropping its crystal fragments to the floor in disarray.

"Damn," Anthony said softly. He set her on her feet and she followed him into the bedroom.

"Janet, darling," Anthony said. "How marvelous to hear from you." Courtney looked at him sharply. "I know, I've been out of town for a couple of weeks, Jan. Courtney? Yes, she is here, as a matter of fact." He handed Courtney the phone.

"Hi, Court," Janet said, "your maid gave me this number. I'm awfully sorry to bother you, but something awful has happened. A real crisis."

Anthony lit a cigarette and handed it to Courtney. She nodded. He went into the bathroom and she heard the shower running. Courtney grinned.

" . . . so Pete and I didn't get out of the after-hours club until about six this morning," Janet was saying. "I was kind of bombed when I got home and so was Pete, and there was Daddy, waiting up for me with his bourbon. He practically drove Pete out of the house, I thought he was going to slug Pete or something. Daddy was really out of his head. Well, the point of the whole thing is, I was just bombed enough to pack my clothes and pull out. Daddy was even threatening to put me into the hatch, and he could put me in a sanitarium if he wanted to, you know, I'm not twenty-one yet. So I'm at Pete's now, but his family is back and is mad at him because the house is a shambles, so I'm hung, I can't stay here. I wondered if I could stay with you for a couple of days. I really can't go home this time."

Anthony was standing in the doorway of the bathroom, drying his body with a Turkish towel. Courtney watched him a moment. This would mean a curtailment of their seeing each other so constantly, because Courtney was determined not to hurt Janet by letting her know.

"Sure, Jan," Courtney said finally. "I'll tell the maid, and you can come over about five. Mummy won't be through rehearsal until six, but I'll be home."

Anthony looked at her sharply. She shrugged. "Thanks, sweetie," Janet said. "I knew I could count on you. Give Anthony my love."

Courtney hung up and turned hopelessly to Anthony. He sat down beside her on the bed and kissed her softly on the shoulder. She was hardly conscious of him. She reached across him and flicked the ash of her cigarette in the ash tray beside the bed. He sat up and sighed.

"Damn," he repeated.

He handed her the ash tray.

"So Janet is moving in on you," he said finally. "That will complicate things."

"I know," Courtney answered, grinding out the cigarette.

"Did that alcoholic father of hers finally throw her out?"

"I gathered it was a sort of mutual agreement," Courtney said. "She says she's only coming for a couple of days, but I know Janet. Much as I love her, she plays the Man Who Came to Dinner whenever she stays with anyone. She has no consciousness of imposing on anyone, of overstaying her welcome. It's all a part of this conviction that the world owes her everything."

"Courtney, I know how fond you are of Janet, and I know this ridiculous obsession you have about not letting her know we're having an affair. I know you feel you betrayed her somehow because our on-and-off affair ended the night she introduced you to me. I trust you realize it will be awfully hard to keep this from her when she is staying with you and realizes how much we see each other."

"Well," said Courtney, "I'll just have to do what I do with Mummy, and let her think I see you only every couple of weeks, and have fictitious beaux."

"No, angel," he said patiently. "Janet knows every one of the boys you tell your mother you go out with, because she introduced you to all of them. That won't work. You'll just have to kick her out after a little while and dispatch her to some other friend, or your kind deception will fail."

"No," said Courtney thoughtfully, "I can't do that. Jan has done too much for me, I just can't kick her out when she needs me. Besides, I'm very fond of her, and when she's in trouble, I want to help her. There's only one solution," she said, turning to Anthony. "And that's to see less of you, darling, and maybe go to some of those cocktail parties with her, though I don't want to, to erase any suspicion."

"Now, Courtney," said Anthony, suddenly worried. "Don't be rash in your loyalty. I know you have a very great sense of responsibility, and I know how you hate to hurt anyone. Janet was half in love with me for a year or so, I know, but it was no grand passion. Neither of us bothered even to be faithful to the other."

Courtney looked over at Anthony. "She wanted to marry you, you know. She told me that about a week after I got back into town, and she would talk about it often."

"Oh, she didn't really," Anthony smiled. "We would talk of marriage, but that is just one of the conventions of the love affair. I used to say that in a couple of years we would get married, but in the most offhand way. You know, 'After you have your first husband and are broken in, we really must get married. We get along so well.' That sort of thing."

"Nonetheless, angel, you meant something to her. Don't you see, all of Janet's friends habitually betray her. Her lovers laugh at her to other boys, her friends use her to get introductions and dates and, after their purpose is accomplished, take over her beaux and drop her. I want her to think she has one friend who is loyal; I want her to believe that, whether it's true or not. She introduced us, and I proceeded to take you from her, after an affair that had lasted through a year. I know how it would hurt her to think I followed the pattern, too, and cared that little about her."

"A friend is that important to you," Anthony said.

"Yes. Janet is. Janet needs my friendship."

"You really think you want to see less of me," Anthony said quietly, "and you really think you will be able to go through with it?"

"Darling, for a purpose that I am convinced is right, I can go through with almost anything. I don't want to. You know that, you know that what we have, the world that we create when we're with each other—well, you know that I'm almost afraid of seeing less of you. But for Janet, I'll do it. Not in any great altruistic sense, but because I'm never happy with myself when I compromise on something I know is right." He studied her for a moment in silence.

"Angel." She smiled and took his hand. "Only for a couple of weeks. Until her father calms down; it never takes longer than that. Then, when I know she can go home, when I've fulfilled my obligation—we'll see each other constantly again, and we'll make up for all the days we've missed. All right?"

"All right," he smiled. "Let's get decent, darling, and get over to the Plaza."

Janet moved in at five as she had promised, with two suitcases and a colossal hang-over. She took over Courtney's room, establishing herself in the other bed and putting her numerous cocktail dresses and her three evening gowns into Courtney's closet. In the top of the closet went all her collection of "acquired" purses, and Courtney's notebooks and assorted letters were summarily dispatched from their shelf and put on the floor of the hall closet. Janet called her home and instructed the maid to transfer her phone calls to Courtney's number. Then she sat down in the living room and announced to Courtney, "My tongue is hanging out for a drink. Hair of the dog and all."

Consequently, Courtney fixed two Scotches on the rocks, although she had not the remotest desire for a drink. As she set the drink in front of Janet and sipped her own, Courtney resigned herself to the fact that, through her own decision, her life for the next two weeks would be tailored to Janet's.

"Daddy is getting really unbearable," Janet was saying. "I don't know what the hell I'm going to do. This drink tastes good, ecstasy. I called Marshall from Pete's house—you remember Marshall, the boy I have this thing with, who wrote the letter . . ."

Courtney nodded and lit a weary cigarette.

"Anyhow, I called Marsh out at Newport and he said he'd be back in town in a few weeks and said I could stay in his apartment—his roommate is spending the summer in Connecticut. So I guess that's what I'll do when I leave here."

Courtney looked up, startled. "Sweetie, don't do that, really—I'm no one to moralize, God knows," she said. "But you would be an idiot to live with this guy, openly. That's very different from an affair. That means committing yourself to the affair, resigning yourself to it—announcing to society that this is what you want?"

"What's the difference? You're drawing a thin line."

"Not thin at all, Jan. You know yourself. You know that once you start with something that hurts you, you go on with it, taking more and more important steps to hurt yourself. You sleep with a guy by inadvertence when you're bombed one night. Then you can't stop. Drinking the same way. You know what it's like. Once you live with this Marshall for a few weeks, that will be it. You'll leave him and go on to the next, anxious to show everybody your degeneration or something. You can't stop yourself once you take the next step, you know that."

Janet looked sharply at her.

"Look, Court, are you trying to give me a sermon or something?"

"No, Janet," Courtney said wearily. "Never in my life have I lectured you or moralized to you—or anybody, for that matter. I haven't any right to, and I haven't any desire to."

Courtney looked at Janet for a few minutes. How much older she looked than eighteen, how much more—well, tired she looked than she had any right to. Maybe it was just the hang-over.

"Jan," Courtney said quietly, "do you remember when we were at Scaisbrooke? Remember when you broke so many rules and were warned that you would be campused for the rest of the year, I didn't say not to break the rules. I broke them, too, as much as you did, but I had an A in conduct because I got staff permits from my friends on the staff for being on the grounds at sunset when I used to like to walk on the hockey fields. I had illegal food, and I read after lights, but I was careful about breaking the rules. I broke every rule that inconvenienced me, but I never got caught. And I used to try to tell you, not to obey the rules, but to break them carefully, and not get penalties. To watch out for yourself."

Janet nodded.

"You didn't pay much attention to me then," Courtney continued. "You got kicked out anyway, because you wanted to, I guess. You probably won't pay any attention to me now. I still break all the rules, sweetie, all the rules that you break. But I don't get caught. Nobody knows about it because I keep my life to myself, or else entrust it to people who won't betray me. I don't hurt myself in front of society."

"I don't give a good God damn about society," Janet said angrily.

"The hell you don't! Look, eventually you want to marry some Yalie and have kids and all that. You know you do. You don't want to be frequenting the same bars in ten years that you frequent now, you don't want to be walking into the Stork and Twenty One and the Plaza with an escort a little more aged and probably a little less desirable than those you have now, knowing that if you're not gay, you'll be alone. That's not the life you want and you know it."

Janet sat in silence, contemplating her drink.

"Look, Janet, don't go on destroying yourself. You're only eighteen. You still have grace, but there isn't much time of grace. There aren't many years which we are allowed to refer to as years of 'youthful indiscretion' or whatever. People are too harsh, too ready to condemn. Don't live with this guy. That will be the beginning, and you know it, and then—"

Courtney stopped herself because Janet was looking away from her, with an expression that to anyone else would have looked like anger, but Courtney knew it wasn't.

"Sweetie," Courtney said gently. "I'm only going out on a limb like this because you're really a good friend of mine, and I can't sit by and see you hurt yourself. I'm no one to talk in one sense; I'm no saint. But I think that gives me a reason to talk. You've got too much on the ball for this, you're too great a person."

Janet, embarrassed, took a sip of her Scotch and lit a cigarette.

"It will be amusing as hell," Janet said with a brittle brightness, "when I come out at Tuxedo this fall and I'm not living at home. You know, this is the thing Daddy has planned for since I was little, a kind of symbol that he gave me what he never had. It means so much to him, and I won't even be living at home when it finally happens. It's all paid for, too, and there isn't a thing he can do about it."

Courtney sighed and took Janet's glass, in which the ice had melted. She freshened Janet's drink and made herself another.

"I should have known better," Courtney said finally. "Somebody talked to me like that once, too—a guy out in California. It didn't do much good. I learned once that you can't stop a man from drinking. I guess it's the same way in this."

"Your mother should be in soon," Janet said.

"I guess so. It's close to six. She'll be home a little after."

"Does she know I'm here?" Janet asked.

"I called her at rehearsal. She was delighted."

"She really has been doing a lot on TV lately, hasn't she?"

"Yes," said Courtney. "She has this summer soap-opera thing, and then she has some appearances on shows and so on. Nothing very much, but enough to have the maid. That's a real psychological boost to her, to be making enough to have the maid. Of course, she wouldn't be able to do it without Daddy's help, but it still is important to her."

Courtney sat down and lit a cigarette.

"You know," she said with a slight smile, "I really love to see the difference in Mummy when she's working. It's a funny thing, and hard for most people to understand. The actress is the only part of herself that she loves, the only thing that holds the pieces of her life together. When she isn't working, she just isn't a person. She feels she hasn't any right to show herself to society, so she's a recluse, the way she was out in Beverly Hills. But now, even though this TV bit is a real comedown for her, she's almost the way she used to be. Funny the way it works. Symbols of her acting success, like the maid, Marie, and the clothes she buys, make her feel she's a success as a person, almost—the way a devoted husband would reassure another woman, or something."

"Marie is an awfully good maid," Janet said. "Well-trained."

"Mummy always spends a couple of days breaking in a new maid. The first thing she does is sit down and have the maid serve her, in mime, a full-course dinner. Then she sits the maid down and serves her. She's a real perfectionist about her maids." Courtney grinned. "We had this wonderful German maid once, Gretchen. Gretchen worked for us for three years. Poor Gretchen. One night Mummy had this big dinner party, when we were in Scarsdale, and I was a little girl, and the dessert was a chocolate soufflé. The soufflé fell and Gretchen was fired on the spot."

Janet laughed for the first time that evening.

"She fired the maid because the soufflé fell?"

"It was the *pièce de résistance*," Courtney explained. "The great gesture. You have to understand Mummy, really it's quite a logical reaction—not excessive at all."

A key turned in the lock and Courtney's mother swept into the room.

"We were just talking about you," Courtney said, but her mother did not hear her.

"Janet darling!" Sondra said, rushing over to her as though Janet were, at that moment, the only person in the room. "Courtney told me what happened," Sondra said in her low, dramatic voice, "and I was *so* glad that she asked you to stay with us."

"A Scotch, Mummy?" Courtney broke in.

"Martini, darling. No show tonight," she said, as though it were extraordinary that she should have an evening free. "Courtney, Marie knows that Janet is staying with us—"

"Yes, Mummy. Of course."

"Good. We're having roast beef tonight. You like roast beef," Sondra said to Janet. Janet nodded. "Courtney, darling," Sondra exclaimed, "don't drown it in vermouth, for God's sake!"

"No, Mummy," Courtney said patiently. "I make an excellent martini, you know."

"I thought you had a date this evening, Courtney," her mother said. "With that charming boy, the—"

"No," Courtney broke in hastily. "I saw him for lunch. I haven't any date tonight."

"Courtney has been having a mad social life," her mother said to Janet.

"Oh, really?" Janet said. "You must have found new bars, Court."

"Yes, I have," Courtney said. "I get tired of the same places."

Marie came in.

"Dinner is served, Mrs. Farrell."

"Marie, I shall want another cocktail. I will be in in about fifteen minutes."

Marie nodded. "Yes, Mrs. Farrell. I didn't mean to hurry you."

Fortunately, her mother was soon off on the subject of herself, and her television work. Courtney breathed easily. Life was going to be a little difficult for the next two weeks, that much was obvious.

The phone rang, and Courtney rushed to answer it, thinking it might be Anthony.

"I'm not in," her mother announced. "I refuse to be bothered with agents and business during the cocktail hour," she explained to Janet. Courtney smiled to herself as she picked up the phone.

"Is Courtney in?" said a deep, self-assured voice.

"This is she."

"Courtney, this is Charles Cunningham. I'm terribly sorry to call you at the last minute like this, but I called you from the office several times and you weren't in. I wondered if you were free this evening."

"Well, I had—" Courtney looked toward the living room, where her mother and Janet were sitting "—as a matter of fact I am free this evening."

"Wonderful! I was so afraid you wouldn't be. Could I pick you up around seven thirty then?"

"Yes, that would be fine. You have the address?"

"Of course I do! I'll look forward to seeing you, then."

"Thanks for calling, Charles."

Janet certainly was succeeding in screwing up her life, Courtney thought as she hung up. She had determined not to see Charles, but his coming in while Janet was there would be ideal. Janet seldom saw Charles, and this would be a convenient name to use when Courtney wanted to see Anthony. Well, his coming over this evening would be all that was needed—then maybe a couple of more times to reassure Janet, and the rest of the time she could see Anthony. Charles might turn out to be convenient.

"Jan, you did say you had a date tonight, didn't you?" Courtney said as she came out.

"Yes, with Pete. We're going to the Bird."

"That's what I thought. Good, I won't be walking out on you then."

"You have a date after all, darling?" her mother asked.

"Yes, Charles Cunningham. You remember him, don't you?"

"I'm afraid I don't," her mother answered.

"I guess you've never met him somehow," Courtney said. "That's odd."

"Have you been going out with Charlie?" Janet asked.

"Yes, for quite a while now," Courtney answered.

"We'd better go in to dinner," her mother announced. "You may take your drinks in with you, children."

Pete arrived first, and when Charles came, Janet suggested that they all go to the Stork. Courtney was delighted; she was determined that Charles should remain unimportant to her, and a double date made her feel less that she was betraying Anthony by seeing someone else and enjoying herself, as she knew she would.

"You know," Charles said to her as Janet and Pete left the table for the dance floor, "I really didn't want to come here. I can't stand the place."

"Why?" Courtney smiled. "Filled with children or something?"

"As a matter of fact, yes."

"This is a real obsession with you, isn't it?"

"No," Charles frowned. "I'm just more interested by people who are doing things, who are out working and living. I enjoyed prep-school kids when I was in Andover, and college kids when I was in Yale. One simply progresses, you know," he smiled.

"I adore the Bird," Courtney said haughtily.

"You know you don't," he grinned.

"Well, all right, I don't really, but your attitude annoys me.

Tell me, haven't you any weaknesses, are you totally self-sufficient and impregnable?"

"People often ask me that. Of course I do," he said, lighting a cigarette. "I just don't choose to display them, that's all."

Janet and Pete returned, interrupting them.

"God," Janet laughed, "that was a crazy number. Hey, what happened to my drink?"

"You finished it," Pete smiled. "Here, take mine while I get you another."

Charles looked up and studied Pete a moment.

"Double Scotch on the rocks," Pete said to the waiter, "and a Scotch and water for me."

With no change of expression, Charles lowered his eyes and flicked the ash off his cigarette. A noisy group of white-jacketed young men and their dates came in, and Janet looked up.

"Hey, Count," she called. "Come on over."

The Count looked up and headed to their table, detaching himself from the group.

"Hiya, sweetie," Count said as he unsteadily dropped his arm around Janet's shoulders. "We've been at Our Club, but Third Avenue didn't appreciate us, so we came over here. Slugged some guy," he explained, "and they threw us out. I was sitting over there getting horny, anyway." He leaned down over Janet. "Hey, sweetie," he grinned, "what about getting laid tonight?"

Janet laughed.

"Stop bird-dogging my date," Pete said.

"Oh," Count said, raising his eyebrows. "Possessive, aren't you?"

"Go to hell," Pete said.

"Say, Count," Charles said hastily, "what about a drink?"

"I'd love a drink," Count said.

"What about it, Court?" said Charles. "Shall I buy Marcel a drink?"

"Sure," Courtney said. "Buy the Count a drink. It can't make any difference."

"Y'know," the Count said proudly, "I was rejected by the army for cirrhosis? Funny as hell, the reaction that doctor had when I told him I was only twenty. Funny as hell."

Courtney looked up at the Count, and studied his aristocratic features, the hair brushed back from his face in a European manner, except for a loose strand that escaped and fell on his forehead. He looked even younger than twenty.

"Count," she said, "why do you drink so much, anyway?"

"Hell," he shrugged. "I don't know. It's a comfortable way of life." Then, as though suddenly becoming aware of the question, he turned angrily to Courtney. "What's the matter, you turning straight-arrow, too? You're with a goddamn moralist, you know. Cunningham. He's out of it. You're a pair."

Courtney didn't answer, not wanting to provoke him. Charles broke the silence as the waiter came over.

"Count, what can I buy you?" he asked quietly.

"Double gin on the rocks. I'll pay you back some day, C. Cunningham. You're a good man after all, God damn." Solemnly, Count shook Charles's hand. He took a chair from the other table and sat down next to Janet.

"Hey, Jan darling," he grinned. "Let's make it, hmm? Really, baby, I know you're great in the hay—"

Pete shoved out his chair and stood up.

"Count, for Chrissake, shut up. We've had about enough of you."

"What's the matter?" Count said, still grinning coolly. "You're getting real possessive. You're not the only guy who's slept with her."

As Pete lunged for the Count, who was still composed, waiting for Pete, expecting his anger and enjoying it, Charles got up and held Pete's arms to his sides. A headwaiter looked up, from across the room, watching them anxiously.

"For Chrissake, Charlie," Pete said, "will you let go of me? Let me shut this bastard up. Count, I'm not sleeping with her and you know it. You're just sore as hell because you're always so bombed you never make it, that's all. You sonuvabitch, Charles, let go of me."

Count's expression still had not changed. With his slim, graceful hand, still smiling, he slapped Pete twice.

"I don't take that crap from anybody," he smiled.

"Look, Count," Charles said, looking steadily at the headwaiter who was coming toward them, "will you get the hell out of here before they throw you out? You want to get thrown out of here, too, you want to get thrown out of every bar in town?"

"Yes," he said. "That's it, that's just it. I want to get thrown out of every bar in town, I want to get thrown out of every lousy corner of the goddam world. That's just what I want."

As he felt Pete's body relax, Charles let go of him. Janet stood up. The headwaiter, reassured, turned to a group that was coming in the door.

"How many abortions are you going to have," Count said to her, "before you finally get married, darling?"

Pete put his arm around Janet's shoulder.

"Good night, Charlie. Court," he said steadily.

Janet smiled at Courtney. "I'll be in later, sweetie. Just leave the door open."

"Thanks, Charlie," Pete added as they turned to leave.

Charles sat down. There was a silence. The waiter came over.

"Here's your drink, Count," Charles said. "Courtney?" He

held out her chair for her. Charles paid the check and they left the Count staring moodily at his double gin on the rocks.

"I wish we had gone out with Janet," Courtney said as they went out. "She was really upset; usually a drunken incident like that doesn't bother her."

Charles looked up the street into the night, and turned back to Courtney.

"Maybe you don't know her so well, sweetie," he said. "Where they're going, we would hardly be welcome."

Courtney looked sharply at him.

"We were at a party once," he said. "The second time I'd seen her. I don't know whose date she was," he said musingly, not looking at her, "but if she had a date he had either passed out or faked out. Somehow we were maneuvred into one of the bedrooms. She sat on the end of the bed and put her hand on the bed, and looked up at me."

"Don't say things like that, Charles," Courtney said angrily.

"It's very true, darling. I didn't, though," he continued. "I took here out of there, and took her to dinner. I talked to her for a long time, trying to shape her up, straighten her out." He looked at Courtney. "It didn't do any good, of course. I suppose you've tried." She nodded. "Ever since then she has disliked me," he said. "Straight-arrow." He smiled. "It's like the Count, who used to be a hell of a good guy. I've known him for many years. He started drinking at thirteen, just like Janet. The liquor was in the house, and like a kid wearing her mother's high heels, they emulated the parents. Count's father was a good man, though, a fine lawyer. Died when Count was ten, and Count was man of the house to his mother. I don't know how it begins."

He turned to her and smiled, folding her arm in his.

"But it's not up to us to solve the problems of the Lost Generation. We've lost so many of them," he smiled. "What's one more here and there. Let's go someplace decent and conservative for a drink. Like Twenty One. Speakeasy to the last generation, symbol of convention to us."

"You're getting awfully philosophical," Courtney smiled.

"I know. That's why it's time for a drink."

"No," said Courtney wearily, "I really don't want a drink. You know what I want? I want to go home. I know that's odd, and I know it's only ten o'clock. But all I want to do is go home, for some unfathomable reason."

"Not so unfathomable," he smiled. "All right, little girl, I'll take you home—on one condition."

"What's that—that I give you a drink at home?"

"No, I understand the way you feel—even if you don't. My condition is that you let me take you to dinner and the theatre tomorrow night."

"All right," Courtney said without enthusiasm.

"I think I *had* better get you home," Charles said, and hailed a taxi. "And tomorrow night I promise," he said as he opened the door for her, "we will steer clear of the Lost Generation."

21

The steady August rain was incessant and depressing, even though it brought relief from the heat. Courtney lay in bed, smoking a cigarette and looking around her at the disarray of her room. In the two weeks that Janet had been staying with her, Courtney's life, like her room, had been thrown into confusion. As she smoked the first cigarette of the day, the before-breakfast cigarette which always tasted awful and which, therefore, Courtney enjoyed more than any other, Courtney looked at the still-empty bed beside her and at the clothing and perfume bottles which littered her room, and wondered when she would be able to put her life back into the careful order which Janet had destroyed.

Janet had certainly raised hell with her love life. She had been seeing more of Charles than she had ever planned to. Janet knew that she saw Anthony occasionally, and almost deliberately, it seemed, she was always proposing that Courtney and Charles accompany her and whatever date she had. Courtney enjoyed being with Charles, but—she mused as the smoke of her cigarette rose to meet the gray, damp air of the morning—when she did allow herself to see Anthony, something seemed to be missing. It was as she had feared, the fragile structure which they had created could not be exposed to the threatening reality outside. Inadvertently, Courtney had allowed herself to venture a little into another life, and was startled to find that it was not as stark and terrifying as she had made herself believe. Despite herself, she enjoyed the calm, almost protective maturity of Charles, and when she did see Anthony she felt almost ashamed at having enjoyed herself away from him; she felt almost as though she were betraying Anthony. But that, she thought as she ground out her cigarette and lit another, would all be changed when Janet finally left, and she and Anthony could return to their secret garden.

There was a knock on the door.

"Come in," Courtney said listlessly. Perhaps it was Janet, finally getting back from that party. It was nine o'clock.

"Courtney, this *room*," her mother exclaimed as she opened the door.

"I know, Mummy, I'll clean it up after breakfast."

"You're always cleaning up after Janet," her mother said angrily. "She isn't in yet, is she?"

"No," Courtney said.

"Look, I just can't have that girl disrupting the household like this. She comes in at all hours of the morning and sleeps through most of the afternoon, so Marie can't clean the room. She leaves her clothes all over this room, it looks like a pig's pen."

"It's my room," Courtney said.

"Yes, but it's my house," her mother replied. "And I am sick of seeing it filthy all the time. It's all well and good for you to say it is your room that is filthy, and your life that is complicated, and that Janet is your guest. But as long as you're living under my roof I am going to have some say. I won't have you living like this."

"I said I'd clean the room after breakfast," Courtney said wearily.

"That's not your responsibility, Courtney. I refuse to have my daughter act as a personal maid to Janet Parker. Tell her to clean her own mess. Don't let her walk all over you."

"But, Mummy," Courtney said patiently, "I do tell Janet to clean it up. But you know how she is, she feels everything should be done for her. She can't help that, really—she doesn't mean to be a nuisance."

"I don't see how you can even find your own clothes in this mess," her mother continued. "Did you ever find those two bras and the slip you asked Marie about?"

"Yes," Courtney said. She didn't want to tell her mother that she had found them in Janet's open suitcase beside the dresser. The clothes weren't that important; Courtney didn't want Janet to know that she had discovered the theft. Courtney knew that Janet had a far larger clothes allowance than she, but Courtney had determined not to meddle and blunder in Janet's psychological problem. She let the clothes go.

"I still don't see how," her mother said wearily. "Look, Courtney, I really can't stand this any longer. I'm not a very easy person to live with—two husbands can attest to that—and I have hesitated to say anything about this because I am aware that I am too demanding. But I must draw the line; I refuse to live like this and I refuse to have it inflicted on you. Janet may do what she likes, but there is no necessity for you to live with her sleeping around and never getting in and making your room unfit for human habitation. Janet simply must leave."

"Oh, Mummy." Courtney sat up. "I can't—"

"I won't have any argument. This is not the way I want my daughter to live, and that's all there is to it. I'm fond of her, too, but I happen to care a little more about you. If Janet at least were appreciative, I might hesitate. But there is no reason to put up with this. And unless you ask her to leave, you know, she'll stay forever. I know I can't ask her to be considerate, because she isn't capable of it. There's no alternative. She can't conform to our way of living, and you must ask her to leave."

"But she can't go back to her father and all that—"

"You'll have to demand that she show a little courage, that's all. It's not up to you to assume the burden of her home life."

"All right," Courtney said finally. "When she comes in, I'll ask her to leave. But I hate to have her feel that I've let her down, too, the way everyone else does."

"Put the blame on me," her mother said. "Tell her that I am unbearably temperamental or whatever you want. As long as she goes."

With finality, Sondra turned and shut the door behind her, ending the discussion. Courtney felt almost relieved that the decision had been made for her. Now her life could be the way it was. The only reservation was Courtney's fear that Janet would go back to Marshall. She had spent the night there, Courtney knew. But perhaps the many discussions Courtney had had with her since that first evening would help. Courtney had to wait and see; the outcome depended on Janet. For once, there was nothing Courtney could do; for once, her mother had made the decision for her.

Janet was strangely depressed when she came in half an hour later. She took off her red cocktail dress and put on her bathrobe and sat on the unmade bed in silence. She lit a cigarette.

"Do you want some breakfast?" asked Courtney. "I've eaten, but I'll have some coffee with you."

"No," Janet said, staring out the window at the murky city. "I've had breakfast."

There was another silence.

"What's wrong, Jan? Didn't you enjoy seeing Marshall again, and the deb party and all?"

"The deb party was deadly," Janet said. "And Marsh was in a lousy mood. So we left early and went to his house."

"Did you stay there last night?"

"Yes," Janet said. She turned in confusion to Courtney. "He refused to make love with me," she blurted out. "It was awful. It was so late I didn't want to come back here and wake up your mother, and I kept thinking if I stayed he would shape up. Finally he told me about this girl in Newport that he's known for years, a real drip, who cooks him dinner and all that crap. He asked her to marry him, and they're going to announce their engagement next month. Next month." She smiled to herself. "Everything happens next month. Marshall gets engaged and I make my lousy debut. I don't know what the hell I'm coming out to. I don't even want the debut now."

Courtney was silent. She didn't want to tell Janet what her mother had said. What a lousy break this was.

"He slept on the couch," Janet said suddenly. "On the couch, for Chrissake!" She started to laugh, and laughed hysterically, burying her head in the pillow as the laughter gave way to tears. "Why is it always this way?" Her words were muffled and Courtney couldn't understand the rest of what she said. Nervously, Courtney lit a cigarette.

Finally, Janet sat up, a little composed. "Now what do I do," she said hopelessly.

"Do you want a drink?" Courtney suggested.

"Ten in the morning. What the hell."

Courtney brought Janet a glass of brandy and had a cup of coffee for herself.

"That's better," Janet said after a little while. "I guess I was an idiot to let this guy mean so much to me. What the hell, there are lots of other men. But now I'm hung; everything seems so confused. I can't stay here forever."

I might as well tell her now, Courtney thought.

"Mummy threw a fit this morning," Courtney said. "She's been in a lousy mood, and she just blew up. She said—"

"She wants me to leave?" Janet asked.

"Yes," Courtney said, relieved. She watched Janet's face closely, but could see no emotion.

"I wondered when she would," Janet said dully. "I never am very popular with parents. Not even my own," she smiled.

"I'm glad you aren't upset, sweetie," Courtney said. "You know I don't want you to go."

There still was no reaction on Janet's face.

"I really think your father will be all right," Courtney continued. "He should have shaped up by now."

"Is it all right if I stay here until tonight?" Janet said aggressively, as though waiting for rejection.

"Of course, Jan. I haven't any date tonight. You stay for dinner, and go home later. Maybe your father will be asleep, so it'll be easier."

"Maybe," Janet said.

Janet was strangely silent all that day, as she packed her clothes. Courtney noticed that she did not return the bras and the slip, but still said nothing. Janet had had enough for one day. Thank God, Courtney thought, Marshall had broken off with her. Now she didn't have that to worry about. Janet would go home, peace would be made—or at least armed truce—and Courtney's life could return to normal. It almost seemed that what her mother maintained, in her Irish philosophy, was right—all things *did* work out for the best. But wasn't that Voltaire? Anyway, it was all right, and Courtney breathed easily as the problem of Janet was taken off her hands.

She was bothered, though, by Janet's silence. Janet never gave in to depression, unlike Courtney in her Irish fluctuation of mood, yet this silence was very like depression. Depression, as Courtney knew it from her mother and herself, was violent and stormy, but Janet's listless, passive acceptance of the sudden reversal of her plans and the fact that she was again forced to return to her father was new to Courtney. This was the sullen acceptance of misfortune of a tired, middle-aged woman, a mood Courtney had never seen in Janet. Janet's resentment was harshly vociferous, screaming at her father, getting drunk. Her new silence perplexed and worried Courtney, presenting the only cloud in Courtney's bright, newly washed sky.

Janet carried her silence even to the dinner table, and her mother was as affected by it as Courtney was. Sondra felt that it was an expression of resentment toward her, because Courtney had put the responsibility for asking Janet to leave on her.

Sondra was greatly relieved when, late that evening, Courtney accompanied Janet downstairs and put her in the cab which would take her home.

"Well," Sondra said as Courtney came back, "thank God that's over with. Shall we have a drink and celebrate the liberation of our home?"

Courtney made the drinks and handed her mother her Scotch. She sat on the couch and lit a cigarette.

"Don't tell me you're angry with me, too," her mother said, "because I made you kick out Janet. I don't have to put up with your mood, too, do I?"

"No," Courtney smiled. "I'm actually just as glad Janet finally left. It will make my life a lot easier, too, and I never would have had the initiative to do it by myself. I'm worried about Janet, though. She was in such a strange mood, not angry, not really depressed. She just sort of accepted the whole thing as though she expected to be rejected by me, too."

"Darling," her mother said as she put her hand on the back of her daughter's neck, "Janet is not your problem. Neither is your father, neither am I. You're only seventeen and you have enough to worry about just thinking of yourself."

Courtney looked up, surprised.

"What prompted all this?" she smiled.

"I had dinner with your father last night," Sondra said, "and we had a long talk about you. Don't think that we aren't aware of what's happening to you." She sat down. "You have a lot in your own life to resolve, things that you can only resolve by yourself. We haven't said anything to you, because we have no right to interfere. That's the hell of being a parent," she mused. "Someday you'll find that out for yourself. You don't want to see your child hurt, you want to take the pain and make the decisions for them. But you can't do that. You have to let them work out in their own stumbling way what you learned a long time ago—what you could tell them in fifteen minutes but what takes years for them to find out for themselves."

Courtney studied her mother's face, the sleek hair, the skin that still looked young from careful care, the knowledgeable, self-assured expression that people who didn't know her called arrogance. How much she knew that Courtney took for granted, the years of living and fighting her own way in a harshly competitive world. Because Sondra had never made a success of her own personal life, Courtney assumed that she could do it so much better, and fought her own way through the tangled web she spun about herself. She had underestimated her mother; she had assumed that her parents were deceived by her careful explanations of her actions. So they knew, so they had known for a long time, but had never said anything because they, wiser than most parents, had known there was nothing they could have done. Courtney studied her mother's face with a new respect.

"Don't think your father and I haven't been aware of the wall you have put up around yourself. This estrangement, your fumbling attempts toward becoming an adult. Children are so foolish, insisting on doing all this themselves, refusing their parents' help."

"I have to do it myself," Courtney said finally. "You wouldn't want me to let you live my life for me. I'm sure you have more respect for me as a person because I make decisions by myself."

"I suppose so," her mother said. "But this discussion gets us nowhere; it's the eternal discussion between parents and children. There is one thing your father and I can do, though, and that's what we talked about last night. I haven't told you before, but there is a very good chance that I can get a part in a Broadway play this fall."

"Oh, Mummy, how marvelous!"

"This is no pipe dream, like the Nick thing. The producer and the director are both people I have worked with before, before I went to Hollywood. They know me very well, and they know my work. I think this is the break we've been waiting for. If I get this part," Sondra continued, "—it isn't a big part, but a decent featured role—your father has just gotten that raise, and I think when we have to move out of here in September we can move into a place on Fifth Avenue, with your father's help. I really owe you a lovely home again, and I think we'll be able to manage it."

"Everything happens in September," Courtney mused.

"What?" her mother asked.

"Nothing," Courtney said. "I was just thinking."

Everything happens in September, Courtney repeated to herself. Janet finally makes her debut, and she's living at home after all. And our life finally gets back to what it used to be. Funny how everything really does work out for the best.

And several blocks north of the apartment where Courtney and her mother sat talking, Janet Parker and her father were standing at opposite ends of the living room. Janet's suitcase, still unopened, sat in the hall with her raincoat thrown hastily across it.

"Yes," Janet was saying, "I did come back. But it wasn't because of you. I didn't want to come back any more than you wanted me back. But you might at least pretend that you're glad to see me."

Mr. Parker said nothing, but stared down at the drink in his hand.

"Your mother left," he said. "When you went to that girl's house, she was hysterical. I called her psychiatrist and he said it would be best to send her back to the sanitarium." He stared at the girl, dressed in the simple black dress which fitted close to her body, her mouth full and petulant, anger and contempt in her eyes. "How can I be glad to see you? You've destroyed your mother, you've destroyed me."

He set down his drink and walked across the living room to her. His eyes were cold and totally without emotion. For the first time in her life, Janet was afraid of her father. She held her ground, refusing to move as he came up to her. Coldly, with the full force of his body, he slapped her. She fell back a step and suddenly, she didn't know why or how, something deeper and more basic than emotion took command of her and she found her hands around his neck in anger, and she knew that she wanted to destroy him, this man whom she loved and so hated, her father. He fell upon her and forced her onto the couch and lay above her as a lover might, and she was terrified. This was too strange and too strong for her, her father lying on her body in control of her. Emotion left her in a sudden exhaustion and she turned her head away and wept. As her body went limp in his arms he rose and walked over to the window. Thank God, she thought. Thank God he got up. He leaned against the window sill in shame and hatred of himself and buried his face in his hands. The intermittent and lonely sounds of the taxi horns and a train leaving Grand Central deep beneath the street rose to the window from Park Avenue. Dazed, Janet got up and ran into her room, locking both doors. To fill the awful silence of the apartment she turned on her victrola to its full volume. The one record on the victrola, Stan Kenton's "Capitol Punishment," filled the room in unreal cacophany, as the girl lay on her bed, beyond tears, beyond emotion, in the starkness of what had happened.

The record played over and over and finally Janet rose and walked to the window. She looked down at Park Avenue in the early evening. She watched the cabs travel down Park, the cabs that had carried her to mid-town bars and restaurants, each a world in which she had found, for an evening, the illusion of companionship and warmth. This was the hour when the city stood up, brushed the soot from its shoulders and waited, tense and expectant, for the night. This was the loneliest hour in the day. She knelt on the window sill, beyond fear, beyond emotion. For a moment she hesitated, but there could be no hesitation, no emotion. With a single, simple thrust, she flung herself toward the street below.

22

The rain had stopped during the night, and as Courtney turned in bed and looked out her window at the fresh, clean-washed morning sky, and then at the empty bed beside her and the room in some semblance of order, she lay back on her pillow with a great feeling of relief. Janet had finally gone home, and Courtney could pick up her life where she had left it two weeks ago. She got up, eager to start the day, and put on her bathrobe. Before she went into the dining room, she stopped and picked up the *Times*. Her mother, sitting at the breakfast table in her white robe, looked up as she came in.

"Good morning, darling."

"Good morning, Mummy," Courtney said brightly.

"You're in a good mood this morning."

"I'm in a wonderful mood. Marie," she called into the kitchen, "could I have some scrambled eggs and toast and some orange juice? I picked up the *Times* from the door," she said to her mother.

"Isn't it wonderful," her mother said, sipping her second cup of coffee, "to have the house to ourselves and life back to normal? What does the world have to say for itself this morning?"

"'Fair and warm today,'" Courtney read. "Somebody attacked the administration—the Mau Mau are raising hell—some Park Avenue girl—"

Courtney stopped and read it again, a story in an obscure corner of the front page:

Janet Parker, Park Avenue socialite, jumped or fell to her death last night . . . her parents could not be reached for comment . . . to make her debut in a month . . .

"What is it, Courtney? What's wrong?"

Courtney put down the paper and stared, shocked and bewildered, at the window across from her. Suddenly she got up and ran into her room, slamming the door behind her, as her mother picked up the paper.

She lay on her bed for several minutes until she finally could believe what had happened and then she began to cry against her pillow, cry hysterically. The door opened behind her and her mother came in silently and sat beside her. She put her hand on Courtney's head.

"Get out of here!" Courtney shouted into the pillow. "Get out of here!"

"Courtney, you don't blame me—"

"No! No, I don't blame you!"

"I know what Janet meant to you, but no one could have helped—"

"Don't talk to me about her! You have no right to! You're a parent, Goddammit, and it was parents—oh, let me alone and don't you dare to mention her name! You're none of you worth one of her! You destroyed her, all of you, and you'll never admit it! Get out of my room!"

Her mother left, shutting the door quietly behind her. She went into the kitchen.

"Marie, don't bother about Courtney's breakfast. She's very upset this morning, and I don't want her disturbed."

Then Sondra went to the phone and called Courtney's father.

Early that afternoon, when Courtney finally came into the living room, she found her mother and father sitting there, waiting for her.

"Do you want a drink, Courtney?" her father asked quietly.

"Yes, I think so," Courtney said. She turned to her mother. "Mummy, I'm sorry about what I said to you this morning. It didn't have anything to do with you, you understand that."

"Yes," her mother said softly. "I understand that. Not completely, I don't suppose I can. But I understand a little."

Her father handed her a drink, and made one for Sondra and himself. Robbie was always there in a crisis.

In the week that followed, Courtney saw no one but her parents. Somehow she felt that she shared the guilt for Janet's death; there must have been something she could have done. She had no desire to see anyone of Janet's generation. She did not want to be reminded. Both Anthony and Charles called, but Marie said that Courtney was not in.

Her parents understood, and determined to give her a new life, in the only way they knew—by making more money. Sondra began to make rounds, which she loathed, but she could no longer afford to wait for producers and directors of the fall plays to call her. Courtney needed more security than Sondra could give her with TV work, and Sondra could not let her pride stand in the way of Courtney's welfare.

Courtney did not expect her mother to get a part. She no longer allowed herself to believe that her world could be made better. As the weeks passed without success, Courtney sat in her room and was not surprised.

The weather grew crisp as fall came upon New York. Courtney's windows were closed against the September air, and her room was filled with cigarette smoke as her mother swept in.

"Courtney darling!" Sondra announced. "I got a part!"

Courtney looked up. "No reservations? Are you really certain of it?"

"Yes," her mother said, excited as a child. "We're starting rehearsal in a week! Isn't it marvelous?" Her mother sat on the bed and took Courtney's hand.

"Everything is really working out for us, darling. I called the real-estate woman and told her to start looking for our apartment, and I called your father. He's coming over this evening to celebrate with us." She looked at Courtney. "You must wear that lovely new cocktail dress, and you must come out of hiding. Really, darling, this moping around the house is no good for you. I know what a blow this has been for you, but you really must see someone. One of those attractive young men. Your father is taking us to dinner at Sardi's and you must ask someone to go with you."

"Mummy, I really don't want to. I'll just go with you and Daddy."

"No," her mother said with finality. "You simply must get yourself an amusing date. That's all there is to it."

"All right," Courtney said wearily.

"I'm so glad, darling. That makes everything just right. Now, you get on the phone and call one of those boys you've been avoiding."

As her mother left the room, Courtney looked out at the early September afternoon and lit a cigarette. Her mother was right as usual. She had been in hiding. She had been in hiding from a world that was suddenly too brutal and harsh for her. A world that had destroyed Janet, and yet didn't even care. She rose and went to the window. There were many things that Janet's death had asked her to face, which she had not faced. For so long her life had run a parallel to Janet's. Janet's death left her a legacy, a promise which she must fulfill. It was strange, the way she felt about it. Somehow she had to go on where Janet had failed and had given up, almost as though Janet had pointed the way for her. She had no right to withdraw from life now. She had almost an obligation to go on, to make something of the life Janet had fled and which, for so long, Courtney had fled.

"Miss Courtney—"

Courtney turned, startled. "Yes, Marie. What is it?" she said crossly.

"Mr. Neville again. Shall I tell him you're not in?"

"No," Courtney said suddenly. "No, I'll answer it this time."

"Hello, angel," said the low, familiar voice. "You've been avoiding me so."

"Hello, Anthony."

"Are you coming out of retirement, darling? I so want to see you. I knew how upset you must be—"

"Let's not talk about it."

"Could you see me this evening, angel?"

Suddenly Courtney was a little afraid. She was afraid that if she saw Anthony again, they would make love again, the old power that they held over one another would take over again. She didn't know if she would be strong enough. Then she knew what she would do. She would see Anthony but make a date with someone else, someone convenient like Charles, to have dinner with her parents. She would guard against herself. She would not make love again like that, she would wait until it was decent and sanctioned.

"I have a dinner date, darling," she said. "But I'll be able to see you for cocktails."

"Perhaps I can persuade you to break your date. It's been three weeks, you know, a wretchedly long time."

"I know," she said.

"I'll meet you at the Plaza, then, in the bar."

"All right, Anthony. At five."

"Goodbye, angel."

"Goodbye, Anthony."

Charles would be at work now, Courtney thought as she hung up. Well, even if he weren't free, she could go to dinner with her parents. She looked up the number. She would be safe from herself with Charles; there was a strength and decency to him.

"Charles Cunningham, please."

"Thank you. Who is calling?"

"Courtney Farrell."

"Hello, Courtney?" That familiar, self-assured voice.

"Hello, Charles."

"I suppose you know I've been trying to get you ever since I heard about Janet's death."

"Yes," she said. She ran her tongue between her lips. Why did everyone have to talk about it? "I wondered, Charles, if you could have dinner with the parents and me this evening. Mummy just got this part, and we must celebrate—"

"Well, I have a date, Courtney, but I can cancel it. It's just with a couple of Harvard Law friends, and they won't mind. I'd really love to see you; I've been worrying about you."

How strange, Courtney thought.

"Shall I meet you at your apartment?" he asked.

"No," Courtney said. "I have an appointment before, so why don't you meet us at the restaurant? At Sardi's, at seven."

"Wonderful, darling."

"Goodbye, Charles."

Well, that was done. Now, Courtney thought, it was all up to her. She would meet the test now, and if she came through it, she knew she would be able to trust herself.

As Courtney came into the bar, she saw Anthony sitting at a table against the wall. He was staring into space, deep in thoughts of his own, and did not see her. How striking he was, she thought, what a really beautiful young man, standing apart from the other people in the room, making them look somehow prosaic as he stared into his own world. She could not feel harsh toward him, seeing him again, watching him as he did not realize he was being watched. The decision that she had made, the resolves, the clarity of view that she had had away from him blurred as she saw him again.

"Hello, Anthony," she smiled.

"Darling." He stood up and pushed the table out. She sat beside him. "What will you have to drink?"

"A martini."

He looked at her.

"Won't you have some wine with me?"

"All right," she smiled. "I'll have some wine with you."

He gave the order to the waiter. When the waiter had gone, he turned to her. "I've missed you, angel," he said. "You know that."

She studied his face.

"Yes," she said.

He put his hand over hers on the table.

"And now, everything can be as it was before," he said.

"Yes," she said.

He watched her a moment in silence.

"What a waste that was," he said finally, voicing what was in both their minds. "Not a tragedy, poor Janet—she never could know tragedy, only a sad and futile waste. I watched it coming, we all did. But there was nothing we could do."

"No," she said. "There never is anything anyone else can do. Everyone must save themselves, no one can help them."

"You have a dinner date," he said in his low, quiet voice. "But after dinner, you'll come back to Tony?"

She looked at him, startled.

"No," she said, almost without thinking. "No, never again. I have to have a different life now, as though to make Janet's senseless sacrifice have some meaning. Do you understand? Do you believe me?"

He stared into space.

"Yes," he said. "I knew that. I knew when I talked to you on the phone. I knew before that, after Janet's death, when you didn't call me. You didn't turn to me, but I knew you wanted to turn to someone. You knew I wasn't capable of helping you. You turned to yourself. I began to realize it then. When you sat down beside me, I was certain of it."

There was a silence. The quiet days before reality, the days of the enchanted garden, of the castle of sand, were gone, and they both knew it. The days before reality, on the threshold of reality.

"Anthony—"

He turned to her, his glass of wine poised above the table.

"I wonder where it went," she said.

He set down his glass.

"I don't know."

"Our castle of sand. Battered by the waves of reality. It finally dissolved, didn't it?"

"I know," he said, rubbing the glass with his finger. "It happened while we weren't looking."

"There wouldn't have been anything we could have done to save it, even if we had known what was happening."

"That's the hell of sand castles," he smiled. "They are always doomed. That's part of their beauty—their impermanence."

"Anthony darling. Darling." She took his hand.

"Don't ever try to recreate it just as it was. You'll never be able to and neither will I. Realize that."

"I do," she said.

He ran his hand along her cheek.

"It isn't a tragedy, angel. People like you, and me, and Janet—we're not capable of tragedy. This was no epic play, with heroic characters and vast emotions. This was not a tragedy. It was a child's game that came to an end."

"But I feel a little sad," she said. "Now that it's here, I realize that I didn't want it to end."

"In a sense it doesn't have to. You and I will end, of course. But the beauty of it never lay in the characters. It was the enchantment that made it precious."

He ran his thumb musingly across the back of her hand.

"You never have to lose the enchantment," he said. "You needn't bother to remember *me*, I was unimportant. But do this for me, never let the enchantment go out of your life."

"I'll try not to," she said. "But it is so hard to keep the enchantment, the belief, after what's happened."

As he looked at her, his face was mature, as she had never seen it in tenderness.

"If I've given you the gift of enchantment," he said, "I'll have given someone something precious for the first time in my life." He took a sip of his wine. "God knows," he said with a slow smile, "it's not much. It's up to someone else to give you love. If I had it, I would have given it to you. But I couldn't. This is the most I can give you. Keep it for me."

"It's so hard," she said again. "Everything turns into ugliness, everything seems so harsh and real. The dead leaves fall into the swimming pool, and all I want to do is escape them." She turned to him. "I don't want to leave you."

"You haven't any choice, darling. You've outgrown this. I can't, you see. I can't go on, any more than Janet could. But you can." She rose. "Have a good life, angel," he said.

She smiled. "How foolish you are."

"You're going now?" he said.

"Yes," she said. "I don't want to, but I am going. Like the little boy in that story you told me," she smiled.

"That's as it should be," he said softly.

He watched her walk into the silent, crystal autumn evening that lay beyond the glass doors. He fingered his drink. Winter was coming; it would soon be time for him to go south, to his island. How quickly the summer had gone.

About the author

About the book

Read on

Insights,
Interviews
& More . . .

Looking Back on Pamela Moore

by Robert Nedelkoff

An earlier version of this article appeared in the Baffler *magazine in 1997*

IN THE SUMMER OF 1956, the hottest thing going in American (as well as western European) fiction was the slim oeuvre of a twenty-one-year-old Frenchwoman named Françoise Sagan. Her first book, *Bonjour Tristesse*, written at the age of eighteen, had caused a sensation in her native land in 1954 and had soon been translated into English, subsequently rocketing up the American and British bestseller lists the next year and settling in at number one. The title became such a catchphrase that not even Hollywood could bring itself to change the title of the 1958 film version, starring Jean Seberg, to *Hello Sorrow*.

It fell to Rinehart and Company, the publisher of Norman Mailer's first two books, to find the American Sagan. She turned out to be an obligatory adolescent—her book, in fact, was released three weeks before her nineteenth birthday. She was precocious in other ways as well, having begun college a month shy of sixteen and starting her senior year when her book came out. Her academic majors, rather than the expected English or creative writing, were ancient and medieval history (with an emphasis on military history) and, for her minors, Roman law and Greek—with straight A's. She had acted in summer stock and, as the daughter of a magazine editor, could be expected to handle publicity with aplomb. Her alma mater, Barnard College, struck just the right note of cutting-edge elitism. Best of all, her book was set in the world of the rich, spoiled haute monde—what had been called "café society" in the 1930s and had only just acquired the handle "jet set." Her name was Pamela Moore, and her book was *Chocolates for Breakfast*.

Pamela was born on September 22, 1937, in New York, the daughter of two writers. Her parents, expressing what may have been an only partially facetious disappointment in the fact that the child was a girl, sent out a notice that read, "We wanted an editor, but we got a novelist." Her father, Don Moore, was thirty-two at the time. He was the son of an Iowa newspaper publisher; in 1925, he had graduated second in his class at Dartmouth College. In the late 1920s, he edited Edgar Rice Burroughs and other pulp writers at *Argosy All-Story Weekly*, then signed on with Hearst's King Features Syndicate as writer for a new comic strip drawn by Alex Raymond (who'd just finished doing a G-man strip written by Dashiell Hammett). The strip was *Flash Gordon*, and Moore wrote it, as well as *Jungle Jim*, until 1954, occasionally making trips to Hollywood to work on the serial versions of the two strips.

Sometime in the 1930s, Don Moore married a young woman named Isabel Walsh. She already had a daughter, ▶

Elaine, who took her stepfather's name. Isabel was a writer as well, specializing in sensationalist stories and advice-filled articles for women's magazines, among them *Redbook* and *Cosmopolitan*. She also wrote three novels in the early 1940s for Rinehart, her daughter's future publisher, with titles like *The Other Woman* and *I'll Never Let You Go*. Just after World War II, Don and Isabel Moore split up. (In later years, Isabel devoted herself to supervising the show-horse riding career of her daughter Elaine, who won a number of championships in the 1940s before retiring to raise a family and run a horse farm in Cooperstown, New York.) Pamela shuttled back and forth between parents during this time: her mother's, in New York, where Isabel edited *Photoplay* for some years; her father's, mostly in Hollywood, where he supplemented his King Features earnings by working as a story editor for RKO and Warner Bros. Both of Pamela's parents moved in a world defined by columnists: Walter Winchell and Dorothy Kilgallen on one coast, and Hedda Hopper and Louella Parsons on the other. It was a world where childhood had to be cultivated like an orchid in a greenhouse, if it were to happen at all. For Pamela Moore the situation was a tragic one: childhood succeeded maturity rather than preceding it. One of the most poignant aspects of her first novel is the curious perspective of age with which the narrator describes her protagonist: "Years later, when Courtney heard that music . . ." or "As a grown woman, Courtney would realize . . ." When Pamela wrote these words she was seventeen; the character ages from fifteen to sixteen in the course of the book. Through the fictive and narrative personas of *Chocolates*, its author essentially pleads, over and over: *I don't understand how one endures these things now, but someday, when I'm older and wiser . . .*

Rinehart, as noted, snapped up *Chocolates for Breakfast* and, following a careful publicity campaign, unleashed it on the world in September 1956. It attracted attention at once, and no wonder: The first chapter depicts Janet Parker, heroine Courtney Farrell's best friend, "lying with her clothes off" (as the book's second paragraph pointedly informs the reader) in their prep-school dorm, while arguing over whether Courtney is stumbling into a lesbian relationship with her English teacher. Before many pages have passed, Courtney is attempting to lose her virginity to a pretty-boy acquaintance of her fading movie-star mother at the Garden of Allah in Hollywood—the onetime home of F. Scott Fitzgerald, as the author notes. True, Pamela does prudently postpone the deflowering until Courtney has safely reached sixteen, but the book's impact was still enormous, given the moral climate of 1956.

"[N]ot very long ago, it would have been regarded as shocking to find girls in their teens *reading* the kind of books they're now writing," observed Robert Clurman in the *New York Times Book Review*'s literary-news column—and that was before publication. *Newsweek*'s reviewer presciently observed: "[Moore] may well be also a part of a trend among publishers to start a new cycle of youth problem novels, as told by the young—a kind of literary parallel to the more overt delinquencies of the switch-blade hoodlums."

The novel went through two printings before publication and scraped onto the bottom of some hardcover bestseller lists for a few weeks in September and October 1956. The comparisons to Françoise Sagan continued, though William Hogan of the *San Francisco Chronicle* noted that the book "dabbles in sex, if not so blatantly" as the French writer's. He also remarked: "It would appear that Miss Moore had hoped . . . to become the female J. D. Salinger." This was one of the very first instances of a comparison made countless times since for a number of writers.

In the weeks prior to the appearance of her book, Pamela had, in fortuitously Salingerian fashion, traveled to Paris for her senior year of study and made herself unavailable for interviews with the American press. Instead, she busied herself studying the strategy and tactics of European warfare in a tour of battlefields, which struck the journalists of that time as an entertaining eccentricity in a young woman. But after publication, she juggled her studies with being, in her words, "caught between the American public and journalists who wanted to know about my love life, and my college friends studying creative writing who condemned me as 'commercial.' "

Publishers were deluged by manuscripts by young women ▶

seeking to imitate her, as she had been thought to be imitating Sagan (though Fitzgerald's *This Side of Paradise* was more likely the model she had in mind). Even in the 1980s, she was as much a star as her best-known counterparts. And all over the country young mothers and fathers began naming their daughters Courtney. (It seems worthwhile to note here that Pamela Moore's one permanent contribution to American culture was in the area of nomenclature. In all the baby-name books published before 1960 that I've seen, Courtney appears exclusively as a male name of French or Norman origin; prior to 1956, it was a common Christian name for men in England and the southern United States. But every female Courtney that this writer has known or heard of, in fact, was born in 1958 or afterward—that is, during or immediately after the period that *Chocolates* began to sell in paperback. In high school and college I encountered a number of Courtneys born between 1958 and 1960; thereafter, for four years—a time when the book was out of print—the name seemed to drop off in frequency, then reappeared, with a vengeance, in 1964 when a new printing of *Chocolates* arrived. The name has maintained its popularity since then, as Courteney Cox, Kourtney Kardashian, and Courtney Love can all attest. In fact, Courtney Love has stated in interviews that her mother named her specifically after the heroine of *Chocolates*, and that she read the book while staying in the same room as Courtney Farrell had at the Garden of Allah. *The Guinness Book of Names* includes a survey showing that through the 1990s Courtney has consistently ranked among the twenty names most frequently given to female infants in America.)

Pamela Moore was still in Paris ("to find my identity," she later wrote in her *Contemporary Authors* entry) when Bantam issued *Chocolates* in paperback in July 1957. That edition sold nearly six hundred thousand copies by the end of the year and, had Pamela returned to America at that point, might have consolidated her celebrity. Another thing that might have completed her fame would have been a movie version of the book, but no such film was made, perhaps because the studio moguls were wary of her unsentimental view of Hollywood. Pamela's reasons for going to Europe were clear: like the heroine of her book, she wanted to be taken seriously, not only as a writer but as a person. In Europe, *Chocolates* not only made the bestseller lists but was favorably reviewed in both Italy and France, whose pundits warmed unexpectedly to a novel in which Pamela had added scathing attacks on American society. In America, the public wanted to know about Pamela's boyfriends and eating habits; "in Paris," she observed, "they wanted to know my politics and metaphysics."

Her timing was fortuitous; the first stirrings of the Beat movement—in the form of "Howl," *On the Road*, and contraband chapters of *Naked Lunch*—were already before the public, and the "alternative" culture that continues to beguile aging columnists and sell running shoes was in its nascent stages. In Europe, where all subsequent translations of her book were based on the French *nouvelle édition*, Pamela Moore was perceived as part of this culture. She spent 1957 and the first months of 1958 explaining herself in the press and on radio and television in France and Italy. She was even listed in a multivolume literary encyclopedia published by the prestigious Milan house Mondadori in 1961. The entry includes a photograph of her posing in a coffeehouse that was probably in Paris but could have just as easily passed for Greenwich Village, complete with guitarist, mazes of cigarette smoke, flattened paperbacks, and black-clad denizens.

In the spring of 1958 she returned to America. But she was not interested in resuming her career as a celebrity. She got married instead. Her husband, Adam Kanarek, was of Polish-Jewish origin and had very little in common with the residents of Beverly Hills, the Westchester horse set, or the habitués of the 21 Club and the Stork Club. The couple settled down in New York, where he enrolled in law school.

By early 1959, Pamela, with her husband's encouragement, had resumed writing. She completed her second novel quickly; the use of a diary in the book's final pages suggests one source for her facility as a stylist. It was submitted to American publishers and rejected—unsurprisingly, since in terms of theme, style, and characterization, it was very different from *Chocolates*, and none but the most understanding publisher or editor is keen on such a step from a writer, especially when the earlier book has been the bonanza that Pamela's was. Instead, it was issued by her French ▶

publisher, Julliard, as *Les Pigeons de Saint Marc* in 1960 to favorable reviews. Similarly her third book, *East Side Story*, was issued by the London-based publisher Longmans in 1961; however, the book received a one-paragraph notice in the *Times Literary Supplement* and scarce notice elsewhere.

Still, she was a writer, so she kept on writing. In 1962, *L'Exil de Suzy-Coeur* appeared, only in France, and she traveled there with her husband and gave some interviews to *Paris Match* and *Le Figaro Littéraire*. Soon after this came what must have been hopeful news: Simon and Schuster accepted her fifth book, *The Horsy Set.* At the very end of the year she became pregnant. Things were going well, and given that Pamela Moore appears to have been suffering from bipolar disorder (her description of Courtney Farrell's mood swings in *Chocolates* is precise enough that a psychiatrist reading the book today might find it difficult to refrain from a long-distance diagnosis), it would have been preferable for things to stay that way, given the absence of meaningful therapy for such a condition in that era.

But things did not continue to go well. *The Horsy Set*, a story set in the wealthy, decadent world of show-horse racing in which her sister was such a prominent figure, received no notice in the *New York Times*, nor in any of the major news magazines or literary and cultural weeklies. What few reviews it received appeared in daily papers in those cities on the Gulf and Atlantic coastlines where show horses were big news, presumably to let the locals know that they might figure as characters in a book. Hardcover sales were minimal. Dell issued a paperback edition at the end of 1963, in what must have been a large printing—it shows up in secondhand stores about as often as *Chocolates*. But that one printing remained in stock for nearly five years. (Also in 1963, Doubleday reprinted it, bound with a war novel by another writer, as part of a book-club series called Stories for Men.) Pamela's bid for recognition as a serious writer had failed utterly; the publication of her fourth novel as *The Exile of Suzy-Q* in April 1964 by the second-rate house Paperback Library served only to underline this fact. The birth of a son, Kevin, and her husband's admission to the bar were all the compensation for this misfortune that she received.

She kept writing. Her sixth novel was tentatively titled "Kathy on the Rocks." Its protagonist was a washed-up writer, contemplating her failure. Pamela's model, F. Scott Fitzgerald, had taken sixteen years to travel the path from *This Side of Paradise* to "The Crack-Up"; she had covered the distance in less than half that time. Through the early months of 1964, as *Chocolates* was reissued and as stray readers in news shops and drugstores discovered she had other books, she continued to work. One of the characters in her new novel, according to Detective Robert Gosselin of the NYPD, "talked about marital difficulties and suicidal tendencies . . . there was a reference to that guy Hemingway and how he died."

On Sunday, June 7, 1964, she reached the end of the line.

It was late afternoon. Her husband was out of the apartment. Her nine-month-old baby was asleep in the bedroom. She sat in the living room, at her desk, and wrote in her diary. "If you put it all together," Detective Gosselin told the press the following day, "the last four pages, under the date June 7, indicate that she was having trouble with her writing and intended to destroy herself." He said that the pages describe the rifle barrel feeling "cold and alien" in her mouth, and continued: "She wanted the last four pages, the suicide note, added to the novel she was working on."

Pamela Moore finished writing, inserted a .22 caliber rifle into her mouth, and pulled the trigger. Her husband found her on the living-room floor. She was three months short of twenty-seven.

"Kathy on the Rocks" was never published. In September, Dell issued Moore's second novel under the title *Diana*; both it and *Suzy-Q* were out of print by the following year. Bantam reprinted *Chocolates* thrice more; it went out of print in America for the last time sometime in 1968, about when Dell pulped its last copies of *The Horsy Set* and not long after what would have been Pamela Moore's thirtieth birthday. In England and Europe, her books stayed in print until a little after the turn of the decade.

Since then, her work has never been reprinted. Apart from a 1982 reference that drew my attention to her, the *Contemporary Authors* sketch (last updated in 1968), and an entry in *Who's* ▶

Looking Back on Pamela Moore *(continued)*

Who of American Women for 1965–66 (apparently compiled before her death), her name appears in almost no books or reference materials. She has been the subject of no articles since the newspaper stories immediately following her suicide. Nor does she figure in any academic discussions of feminist literature, despite the fact that some of her work clearly prefigures the great awakening of feminism in the late 1960s and 1970s.

Don Moore, her father, was rediscovered when the movie version of *Flash Gordon* came out in 1980, and he colorfully recounted his years in Hollywood for movie and science-fiction magazines that year. He didn't discuss Pamela. He died in Florida in 1986.

Isabel Moore continued to write for a time. In 1965, under the pseudonym Grace Walker, she published a biography of her surviving daughter, the full title of which is: *Elaine Moore Moffat, Blue Ribbon Horsewoman: The Complete Life Story of a Champion Rider Who Learned to Cope with Life by Dealing with Horses*. Four years later, she published *Women of the Green Café*, a paperback novel about lesbians. In 1970, she published *That Summer in Connecticut*, a smoothly written but cliché-riddled account of a May–December romance that indicates the difficulty she must have had understanding her younger daughter, given the generational gulf that separated the women who came of age before the 1950s and those who matured just as the implications of Simone de Beauvoir's *The Second Sex* were beginning to resonate in America.

Had Pamela lived and continued writing, perhaps she would have ultimately proved incapable of serious literature and would have finished her career composing smart but schlocky bestsellers, stylish counterparts to those of Danielle Steel and Jackie Collins. But her work frequently manifests a fairly sophisticated awareness of her society and its workings, whether satirically or melodramatically expressed, that is absent from the other two writers. This awareness gives lasting value to *Chocolates* and, to some extent, *The Horsy Set*. Pamela's writing may have been polished, but still it was the work of a woman who either could not or, to some extent, was not allowed to mature as a writer; a woman desperately in need of the kind of social changes that the feminist movement brought into being over the years that followed. From a purely clinical perspective, and given *Chocolates*'s description of bipolar depression and how *The Horsy Set*, in its most frantic pages, epitomizes a classic "mixed state," it is important to remember that those years also saw the introduction of the first, and rather ineffective, medications for depression. Pamela Moore's chronicles of an America that is still with us in some ways, and in others as distant as the world of Jane Austen, deserve serious critical examination. ∾

In the Next Room

by Kevin Kanarek

ONE CLOUDY AFTERNOON in the summer of 1964, Pamela Moore adds several pages to her diary. The script is neat and lucid; the hand of someone who has made a decision and wishes to set it forth clearly.

She has kept a diary ever since she was a fifteen-year-old student at boarding school. Her journal has often consisted of notes to herself, ideas, outlines and drafts of stories. Over the past year, however, she has recorded in detail the circumstances of her own life: pregnancy, a difficult birth, and a long stay in the hospital; her return to the small apartment in Brooklyn Heights, where she has struggled to regain her health, adjust to her new role as a mother, and resume her writing.

She sets down a detailed record of her arguments with her husband, Adam, and all the ways in which she feels abandoned by him. "There is my $6000 in the bank, but he won't give me a vacation or let me hire a baby nurse!"

Adam, she writes, dismisses her ideas and questions her seriousness. He tells her that it's too late to do what she aspires to. She's already beaten. "I'm 26 years old, I'm 26 years old. I keep repeating that to him so much that I feel sometimes I'm secretly 36 and lying to us both."

A year earlier, pregnant and unable to finish her fifth novel, she had agreed to let her husband direct her writing—not just in the business aspects and the critiques of her drafts, as he had been doing until then, but in everything. She recalls the elation, the eagerness with which she told him her Big Decision. "The final and irrevocable submission of my will and being to his," she calls it. "I can't write without him. We really are one."

June 7, 1964. In the diary, she writes that before leaving for work that morning, her husband yelled at her for overfeeding the baby. But she is hardly eating anything herself, she writes, because there is no one to care for her, to cook a meal or even take her out to a restaurant. "Yesterday, ice cream and a doughnut. Today, so far, just coffee."

In the diary, she promises herself that she will no longer argue with him, no longer cry. She returns to a conclusion that seems to her inescapable: artists cannot love, and that by loving Adam so deeply, she has betrayed her art.

The summer afternoon has suddenly grown cooler, Pamela notes. A thunderstorm gathers. "Pure literature," she writes of the dramatic shift in the weather, as if the clouds are setting the stage for what she is about to do. At the end, she writes: "this diary should be added on to the unfinished ['Kathy on the Rocks']." There is a .22 caliber rifle in the closet, which Adam keeps in their small apartment for protection. It was her birthday present to him four years ago. She uses it to shoot herself.

I was in the next room, nine months old to the day, when this happened. The newspapers say I was asleep. ▶

. . .

Pamela Moore was my mother, but I never really knew her. I've heard it said that for an infant, when someone leaves the room it's as if he or she has left forever. When that person reappears, it's nothing less than a miracle.

For me, my mother reappeared mostly through her books—copies on bookshelves, larger piles of the later titles that sold fewer and fewer. There was also the unpublished writing that filled a locked filing cabinet in my father's office and folders stacked in a small, unused room with peeling green paint in the ancient apartment on 110th Street in Manhattan where my paternal grandmother, whom we called Baba, lived and where Pamela had sometimes stayed, to write and be fed Baba's Polish home cooking.

When I was thirteen years old, I lived in that 110th Street apartment for about a year, after my father and stepmother divorced, and Baba took it upon herself to initiate me into Pamela's full history. Baba had survived the Holocaust by hiding for three years in the Polish countryside with my father and my aunt, who later took care of me after my mother died. The three of them had spent the last year of the war living in a hole in the ground under a barn.

Most people try to turn their backs on such horror; Baba savored it. When I asked, "How did my mother die?" the answer was "She didn't just die! She shot herself!" Baba's version of my mother's story was very tabloid, like the brittle newspaper clippings she gave me along with a copy of *Chocolates for Breakfast*. It was the hardcover edition with the line drawing of the girl on the cover, so, of course, I assumed that girl was Courtney, and Courtney was Pamela. And the black-and-white author photo, her immense eyes with dark circles around them—that also was Pamela. I'd like to think that even without all the dramatic buildup—*this is your mother's soul, take it and read it*—I still would have liked the book. But I loved the book. It is very odd to acquire at age thirteen an aloof yet sensitive and melancholic teenager for a mother. I have continued rereading *Chocolates* at the junctures of my life where I needed . . . not guidance, necessarily, but to be reminded of something that preceded memory.

Who killed Pamela Moore? Of course I wondered what had

actually led to my mother's death. Choose one or more of the following: early celebrity, followed by a career on the skids; a difficult childbirth with complications for months after, including a likely case of undiagnosed postpartum depression; a marriage that had begun as a salvation but was becoming a prison. Added to these immediate circumstances were preexisting conditions. Pamela had had a difficult childhood, including her parents' bitter divorce, a mild-mannered and absent father, and a ruthless mother who was not above seducing her daughter's high-school sweetheart, John (the likely model for Charles Cunningham in *Chocolates*). The novel that Pamela wrote at the age of seventeen includes an episode of severe cutting and a suicide, both of which are seen as having a cleansing, redemptive effect, chastising the grown-ups and reminding them of their responsibilities. It is a very young person's seductive view of suicide as a means of somehow making things right again, a view that Pamela may not have ever outgrown.

The years I spent with my father from ages six to eighteen gave me a vivid picture of all the ways he might have been an accessory to my mother's death. After a lifetime of trauma, his default emotion was rage, and he was often vicious to others without seeming to realize his effect. He had learned, perhaps in hiding during the war, that the best way to motivate and engage people was to threaten them with doom. His work as a lawyer had fortified an innate tendency to be cynical and overbearing. He would later make pronouncements such as: "Feminism is nothing but an epistemological construct which holds that Zelda was a better writer than F. Scott Fitzgerald."

There was the matter of Pamela's last diary, which included the suicide note—a big red bounded ledger that the police held on to for a while and that still bears the evidence-room stamp. My father was very undecided about letting me see that volume. He once showed it to me briefly, but he didn't tell me where it was hidden until a few months before his death. "I may decide to destroy it," he periodically reminded me, and when I asked why he would even say that, he responded, "Because I am the hero of those diaries!" There was anger, and also real pain, in his words.

It turned out he had never read that volume. A few days before his own death, he asked me what was in it. I said something ▶

15

about the logic of a sixteen-year-old girl who thinks that, because her prince is late in saving her, she must die.

My assumption had always been that Pamela learned from Adam not to trust in her own experience, but rather to impose on it some larger plan. I blamed my father, with his legalistic mind and didactic tendencies, for teaching her that ideas are all that matter, and that raw emotions and sensations are, as he would put it, "simply nonsense."

But then, in my late thirties, having lived for a while in France, I came upon the French edition of *Chocolates* and was amazed at what I found. The French text was very different from the English, and in these new passages I could see the first stirrings of a change I had felt so strongly in my mother's writing. By this time, I knew the basic chronology of her life and work, and I knew that the French edition was published several years before her marriage to my father, at a time when they had just met. So contrary to the theme of most of his stories about her, and most of what she wrote about him in later years, Adam did not sit solidly at the center of Pamela's entire cosmos. He had rivals for that role, and neither he nor I could understand her without understanding their influence.

I had vaguely known that, after the first publication of *Chocolates*, Pamela had fallen under the sway of filmmaker, screenwriter, and international man of intrigue Edouard de Laurot. She had met him on the ocean liner that took her from New York to Paris in August 1956, around the time that the media buildup began around *Chocolates*. For the next two years she followed him on an odyssey across Europe, investing all the profits from the international sales of her book into his projects, supporting de Laurot on his "revolutionary missions," and purchasing a car—a Mercedes-Benz 180D—for his use.

During this time, Adam Kanarek, the man who would become my father, was back home in New York. He and Pamela had been introduced by a mutual friend, and they sometimes met in the libraries at Columbia University, where Adam had a job in the Slavonic department. During Pamela's European travels, she and Adam wrote each other with increasing frequency. Adam was cast in the role of loyal, steadfast friend, submitting Pamela's papers to Barnard College and lobbying her professors to give her the credits she would need to graduate.

Although she was nearly eight years younger than he, in her letters to Adam, Pamela often took to lecturing him on the importance of engagement in history. One must not allow one's fate to be determined by circumstances, she wrote, nor by lack of faith or courage. Adam sometimes responded that, having witnessed in Poland both the Nazi occupation and the Soviet liberation, he was suspicious of all ideologies and their calls to action.

(In addition to my father's letters and anecdotes, I had the complete typescript of Pamela's second novel, "Prophets without Honor," which was largely based on her experiences with de Laurot. Her agent, Sterling Lord, sold this book to Knopf in 1959. The villain, named André de Sevigny, is a bona fide military spy and a traitor, rather than a fabulist filmmaker. Like de Laurot, de Sevigny is of mysterious trans-European origins. There is a dangerous edge to his charm, as he and the heroine, Susan, engage in a kind of power play reminiscent of Anthony Neville and Courtney in *Chocolates*, only much darker. Once the full book was submitted to Knopf, however, it was rejected—in spite of the publisher having paid a hefty advance. Pamela continued to rework the story in various forms, including the unfinished novel she was working on at the end of her life, "Kathy on the Rocks," with its themes of "Europe versus America" and innocence betrayed.)

But what had really happened during that two-year hiatus? To find out, I began meeting with people who had known de Laurot, and they described a charismatic, fascinating, and often destructive genius of boundless energy who was always engaged in some highly important and secret mission. His son told me how his father had taught him to build pipe bombs for an explosion sequence on one of his films, and how he would disappear for years at a time. The widower of one of de Laurot's later companions told me that de Laurot had tested her usefulness early in their collaboration by instructing her to raise $10,000 for his next film. When she showed up a week later with the cash, he asked her, "How did you get this?" "We robbed a bank," she replied. According to the story I was told, this caught de Laurot ▶

off guard, but he must have decided that this girl was a keeper, because they remained lovers and then friends for many years, collaborating on screenplays with Abel Ferrara.

De Laurot also collaborated with the filmmaker Jonas Mekas on the magazine *Film Culture* and on Mekas's first film, *Guns of the Trees.* This was in the late 1950s, before Mekas went on to make dozens of acclaimed films and eventually founded Anthology Film Archives. When I met with Mekas in August 2012, he recalled de Laurot's imperious style, and how de Laurot had begun to direct the actors and the camera crew until Mekas kicked him off the set. He also recalled de Laurot's letter to him, when he first met Pamela on the ocean liner. She was interested in cinema, de Laurot wrote, and would be useful to their projects. Mekas then gave me a large envelope stuffed with my mother's letters, which de Laurot had entrusted to him for safekeeping nearly fifty years before.

With these letters, I have pieced together some of the story behind her two-year disappearance beginning in 1956, which the press took to be a charming eccentricity of a young writer— very Salingeresque, perhaps. My first discovery was that Pamela's relationship with de Laurot began long before she was a celebrity. Perhaps de Laurot had chosen her in part for her naïveté and usefulness to him, but her wealth and fame could not yet have been a factor. Her first letter to him, written after she had gotten off the boat where they had first met, was dated June 14, 1956. "I have been progressing in my elementary education, as you outlined it, so perhaps when I see you again, I shall have become more conversant."

Though a very charismatic man—the center of attention in any room, by many accounts—de Laurot always kept his activities shrouded in secrecy. Pamela wrote that she would do anything to support his projects, and that her greatest fear was to be unworthy of helping him.

Why did you go to Zurich? Only to earn money, or to work on a film? I am not interrogating you, but I was distressed to think that you might have been sent from Paris solely by need of money. It is now only a dream, but it is my most fervent wish that I might make enough money so that you could be freed for more significant work . . . I want to do so much, Edouard . . . I think, with the joy that one might have in contemplating a revolution, of how much you might do if you were not beset with the problem of mere sustenance.

With the income from her book sales and film rights, Pamela purchased a car for him. No cadre of the revolution should have to cross the continent in an unreliable or uncomfortable car—the stakes were simply too high, and his comfort and sense of style were essential to his ability to command. Pamela dwelled on the details of the car, and the kind of coat that she would send de Laurot, in her letters that Jonas Mekas handed me more than fifty years later.

These letters make plain her love for de Laurot, which she tried to contain with a soldierly resolve. She would put her talents at his command and "bear him a novel," as a wife would bear a man his child. She pined for him in nondescript towns along the Czechoslovakian and Polish borders while he made forays beyond the Iron Curtain.

She described in one letter her outline for "Prophets without Honor." Although the book was delivered to Knopf once she was married to my father, the outline on the basis of which Sterling Lord sold it had been written while she was still with de Laurot. I searched in the archives and found it: the heroine in the outline is a novelist, not the fashion model she would later become. In one scene she is on her way to meet André at a Paris café:

But when she sees him, the last refuge of her independence, the belief in her writing ability will be destroyed, and she will no longer be able to justify to herself her refusal to submit wholly to his intellectual domination. She stares from her hotel room out over the roofs of the Latin quarter: she is struck with horror at the vision of herself become the tool of this passionate, overpowering man. In this crisis, she even asks herself whether her abdication will make her lose his love, because he scorns and casts aside those that are weak. ▶

In the Next Room *(continued)*

In the outline, a dark hero. In the submitted manuscript, a craven villain. But the same man can be discerned in these very different renderings, the man who first captivated her on the ship sailing across the Atlantic in June 1956.

His appearance was bizarre, so flagrantly so that this seemed his intention. He wore his hair in a nineteenth-century manner only slightly modified with the dark, thick locks long and full, brushed back from his high, square, furrowed forehead . . . "Come with me," he repeated, the playfulness gone from his carefully-modulated voice. "You will find it more amusing than avoiding me."

After two years, Pamela was exhausted and broke. She returned to New York and confided in my father enough detail about de Laurot's past for him to begin showing her how much of it must have been fabrication. De Laurot then came to New York and summoned her to a meeting, to which my father showed up instead. This dramatic showdown on a highway overpass featured prominently in the final version of "Prophets without Honor." But most of her money was already gone; she owed more income tax to the IRS than she was ever able to pay off in her lifetime, and although *Chocolates* continued to sell briskly and generate royalties, her career had suffered a derailment and never got back on track.

In the wake of de Laurot, Adam Kanarek rose to the occasion and rescued and protected my mother—but in such a way, it seems to me, that ensured she would never be really free. Some vital force in her had already diminished. Or perhaps she allowed herself to be saved only on condition that she might sacrifice herself again. The arrow fits the wound exactly.

In trying to understand what happened to Pamela, I have to also consider the role of her mother, Isabel Moore. Clearly the model for the has-been actress Sondra Farrell, Courtney's mother in *Chocolates for Breakfast*, Isabel had even more of a malevolent streak than the fictional character. A successful writer of pulp fiction and editor of *Photoplay* magazine, Isabel, like Sondra, lived at the Garden of Allah in Hollywood in the late 1940s, although it was actually Pamela's half-sister, Elaine, who resided with her there, not Pamela herself. Paralleling a scene in *Chocolates*, where Sondra fails to warn Courtney of their impending eviction from the hotel, Isabel abruptly departed from an Arizona spa, where Pamela awoke to find her mother gone. Isabel had left nothing behind but the unpaid bill and her fifteen-year-old daughter as collateral. Pamela had to fend for herself until several months later, when Isabel settled the bill and sent for her.

When Pamela was nineteen, Isabel visited her in Paris. Pamela was already deeply involved with de Laurot but kept him and their activities a secret. In a letter to Adam, still back in New York, Isabel tantalized him with news about her daughter, while being coy and even flirtatious with her daughter's would-be suitor. The letter also gives a remarkable picture of Isabel's relationship with Pamela:

[S]he became quite petulant and demanding when I couldn't have dinner with her. You will like the fact that when she did complain, I burst out, "For heaven's sake, Pamela, I'm not—" and stopped, appalled. Pamela had the good humor to chuckle and to say, "That's very good, Mummy. You were about to say, 'I'm not your mother—' " And I said, "Yes, I've disciplined myself to the point where, I guess, the new arrangement is so without my having to pretend it's so."

In the same letter, Isabel told another story, one that a different mother might not have taken quite so casually:

I prefer not to think too much about her personal relationships, Adam. I think they were summed up pretty well by her when, in discussing Rimbaud, she said, "he had to destroy himself in order to prove that the things he represented should be destroyed—" and I said, "Is that how you feel," and her answer was, "Of course."

In the letters that Pamela wrote to de Laurot, she endeavored to show him how well she understood the importance of secrecy ▶

and her utter loyalty to their cause. But I suspect she also had her own reasons for keeping her mother at a distance—a mother who could refuse to be nurturing in any way, who placed her self-advancement ahead of any other person in her life, family included, yet respected no boundary between her daughter's psyche and her own.

In a letter postmarked June 24, 1964, Isabel Moore wrote to Adam Kanarek:

> It is now two weeks since Pamela's tragic death, and I have not heard from you regarding any of the questions I put to you in my previous letter . . . Meanwhile, I have been contacted, through my agent, by two publishing houses who wish me to do a biography of Pamela . . . I'm sure you as well as I wish to do full justice to her memory. Therefore it seems we should stop being immature and get together to make her death a memorial to the living rather than the tragic waste it is now.

Ultimately, she wrote the book by herself, entitled "Forgive Me My Darling," and sold it to World Publishing. Advance ads for it began appearing, until Adam and Pamela's father, Don Moore, convinced Isabel and her publisher that they would block the book's publication by any means necessary. Uncharacteristically, in this case, Isabel backed down.

As Pamela wrote toward the end of *Chocolates for Breakfast*, after Janet's suicide: "There never is anything anyone else can do. Everyone must save himself, no one can help him."

In the end, it was Pamela Moore who killed Pamela Moore.

In a diary entry written shortly before the end of my mother's life, she contemplates a possible different pathway her life might have taken. This reverie was triggered by the name of her old high-school boyfriend, the one who had inspired the character of Charles Cunningham:

> March 31 1964: In the phone book I see "John W."
> "Cortland" the name that inspired Courtney. So he must

have returned, John W., to become a broker like everyone else. Does he still associate with the old people? Would I, if I were with him? To think that my life might have taken that turn! I would have stayed in the same milieu, with the problems, like alcoholism, that I understood at 16! No Faustian despairs? Would I have written *Chocolates*? Yes, I have no doubt. And then what, if not for college if John instead? Nursing an alcoholic at worst, and a non-intellectual one, writing would without any doubt have reasserted itself.

Here she was, two months before her death, looking back over the trajectory of her life and considering the choices she had made. What if she had married John? She would have been spared the humiliation and abuse to which Edouard subjected her, and the airless claustrophobia of safety with Adam, these two very different men, who had so much in common: both of them far removed from the milieu of her own upbringing, both Polish refugees, survivors of World War II, dark and overbearing.

And then follows a refrain that crops up several times in her entries that last year, the invocation of "deviltry."

I bit off more than I could chew in this Europe . . . Please leave me alone and spare me all that heavy baggage of culture . . . As for deviltry—that is what I've done with Edouard and Adam. One was a con-man, the other gave up being a devil because he realized he was nothing on his own. The devil-principle is in me and must be realized in me.

I don't fully understand her meaning, and I do not wish to overstep whatever right a son has to question the archives and writings of his mother, looking for answers. Pamela is no longer here to explain herself, and I can only go so far in trying to decode her thoughts, or to infer a sequence of events and reasons from what is essentially a cry of pain, a call for help. ᵔᵔ

The Three Texts of *Chocolates for Breakfast*
Excerpts from the Original Manuscript and the French *Nouvelle Édition*

IN THE MANUSCRIPT that Pamela Moore submitted to Rinehart early in 1956, dozens of pages were crossed out and did not appear in the published book. By the time the first American edition came out in September 1956, Moore had already left the United States for France.

The first French edition was published by Julliard soon after, in November 1956. It was a straight translation of the book published in America. This French edition had already begun to ship when Moore came to René Julliard with dozens of typewritten pages that she wanted him to include in the book. As Moore would later tell the story, Julliard at first refused, saying, "Pamela, even if you were my mistress, I couldn't do this."

Eventually, he agreed. Julliard released the second edition with the heading "New Edition, Revised by the Author" printed on the cover. This *nouvelle édition*, dated January 1957, includes a great deal of new material, including a preface about the kind of self-censorship (*censure par anticipation*) that Moore believed she had imposed on herself in the United States.

But the restored material is different from the cut pages of the original manuscript. It is essentially a new text. A study of the original American manuscript, the French text, and Moore's notes, letters, and diaries from that time suggests that much of this French material was created after the original work, in collaboration with the filmmaker Edouard de Laurot. There are in fact three versions of the story: the book written by Moore, the book published by Rinehart, and the *nouvelle édition* that Julliard published afterward in French. This new edition was used as the basis for subsequent European translations.

Readers have sometimes remarked on the episodic nature of *Chocolates for Breakfast*. As Courtney moves from boarding school to Hollywood and then to New York City, the continuity with her previous situation isn't always apparent. But in the alternative versions of the story, there is a refrain: the memory of Miss Rosen, Courtney's kindly and intelligent boarding school teacher, comes back to Courtney at key moments throughout the book.

In the American manuscript, Courtney's attachment to Miss Rosen is visceral; her former teacher reappears as a kind of sense-memory of lost love and affection. In the French version, Miss Rosen embodies a political awareness and existentialist philosophy—one's destiny is created, not discovered—with which Courtney wrestles right up until she meets the Charles Cunningham character, who in the French edition is ▶

> 66 There are in fact three versions of the story: the book written by Moore, the book published by Rinehart, and the *nouvelle édition* that Julliard published afterward in French. 99

cast as a student revolutionary. The differences between these alternative versions of the same book can be quite striking.

La Nouvelle Édition: The French New Edition

The French book begins with a preface, in which Moore explains a process of self-censorship, which she calls a "a censorship by anticipation," that had caused her to leave out not only some of the more explicit sensual content but also what she now sees as the moral to her story: the conflict between American values and the human condition. "We turn away from this terrifying truth with what I would term a kind of collective bad faith (*mauvaise foi commune*)." She concludes by saying, "I felt obliged to try to arrive at the causes of this moral crisis that so afflicts the youth whom I describe in this book."

The passages that had been cut from the Rinehart edition in 1956 were vivid, direct, and often sensual. But the new material that Moore added to the French edition in 1957 is much more cerebral: discourses on politics and philosophy, delivered by Courtney, Miss Rosen, Anthony Neville, and Charles Cunningham. Moore may not have even had the original typescript pages with her in the Paris hotel room where, over the course of several weeks, she and de Laurot created the Julliard *nouvelle édition*.

For example, the conversation between Courtney and Miss Rosen now includes the following:

> "Just jargon!" the girl exclaimed angrily. "Even you, you spout the same jargon I hear all around me. You hide life between the pages of your psychology manual . . . We say 'relationship' when we mean 'love,' or 'communication' instead of 'meeting of minds.' It couldn't be that I love you because I see the truth in you. Of course not! It's a fixation due to transference of my mother-image—a fixation with lesbian overtones . . . We repeat phrases as we hear them, and we silence our hearts to better hear the anthem of our civilization."
>
> "It's true, Courtney. All my life, I've listened to that anthem. I sought my liberation in study, travel and

reflection . . . this jargon poisons our souls . . . it taints our food . . . It is a sterilizing mist sprayed upon the forests of America."

Soon after, Miss Rosen provides the lesson in existentialist philosophy that will serve as a kind of refrain further on in the book:

"I'm going to tell you something, Courtney, that you may not understand right away. You'll remember it in a few years, and maybe then you'll understand it. You will discover that truth and love are inseparable. One cannot know one without the other. Love flourishes not in innocence, but in purity. One cannot create love without destroying the Myth."

"You know this kind of love, then?"

"Yes, I do."

"How did you find it?"

"I didn't find it, I created it. I didn't discover myself, I created myself. I did not 'meet' my destiny, I forged it for myself. You must understand that, in order to understand what I represent, and why my Love is linked to Truth."

And here is Janet, stretching naked on her bed:

Courtney looked over at her roommate and admired her tanned and athletic body. Suddenly, this secret pleasure shocked her. She had always prided herself on repressing the latent sensuality that whispered between the walls of Scaisbrooke and troubled the protective silence of Puritanism.

Afterward comes Courtney's initiation of Janet—to revolutionary consciousness:

"Look," said Courtney, stretching her hand toward the New England countryside that unfolded before them. Janet ▶

leaned out . . . she saw the neatly trimmed walkways of Scaisbrooke and the asphalt driveway that disappeared into the foliage. Here and there, a Colonial house, freshly repainted, stood out from the shadows . . . "You can see the lush, well-tended countryside of an Empire, with its Metropolis over there, beyond the hills—The Empire State, as they say." She turned abruptly to her friend. "Is it my fault, Jan, that I see there a land where only fraud and wretchedness can thrive?"

There are times when this 1950s French Courtney sounds almost hip, like a teenager who's just discovered Beat poetry. In Hollywood, when Barry asks her if she likes it there, Courtney replies:

"I don't like this town. It's under the command of the Guardians of Myth. Here, by their order, the Myth is conceived, the idols are carved and the canticles are written."
　　Barry's eyes widened. She shrugged her shoulders and continued.
　　"I see you don't understand me. I'm not surprised. You just understand everyday things." She added in a theatrical tone: "The Hollywood sun doesn't make anything grow, doesn't change any season to show the passage of time. It tans the bodies of lotus eaters who never grow old, because they were never young. There's no winter or spring, no past and no future. The people are prisoners of this timeless irreality."
　　"Pete," says Barry, "another Martini. You want another glass?"
　　"Yes, a Daiquiri."
　　"And a Daiquiri for the young lady."

Anthony Neville and Charles Cunningham both win Courtney's approval by their renunciation of American values. As a European, Anthony has an easier time of it, complaining of American women and their puritanical ideas about sex.

"Puritanism is not a refusal to make love, it is a way of making love. It is cocktails that dull awareness, darkness that hides young bodies, the closed eyes . . . and silence that denies pleasure."

But even Charles Cunningham, the straight-arrow law student who put himself through school, chimes in with his own social criticism, sounding in French like a student revolutionary straight from the Left Bank of Paris. When Courtney repeats what Anthony has told her, that childhood is not an age but a world, Charles contradicts her:

"It is not a world but a state of mind. Retaining that state of mind is what protects the adults around us from destroying their childhood and accepting responsibility for their society. It is our national state of mind. That is why our youth does not know what Revolution is."

And at the end of the book, Anthony has given Courtney much more than enchantment; he has allowed her to fulfill the prophecy Miss Rosen gave her at the beginning:

"You have given me something much more precious, something you'll never know. A long time before I met you, someone told me that I'd learn some day what I'm telling you now. I would have never understood it if you had not given me my childhood. She told me that love does not exist in innocence, but in growth . . ."
"You have found this love?"
"No, I cannot find it. I must create it. I shall create it as I shape my destiny, and try to expose the Myth that destroyed Janet."

Armed with this new knowledge, Courtney sets forth to save the world, as Anthony retreats to his island and the summer comes to a close.

The Three Texts of *Chocolates for Breakfast* (continued)

The Preface to the *Nouvelle Édition*

Quelle est la raison d'être d'une préface? Apologie? Explication? Commentaire? Indice de faiblesse ou de mauvaise foi— si elle est écrite par l'auteur—, éloge de complaisance parfois, si elle est due à quelqu'un d'autre. Je n'ai jamais compris l'utilité des préfaces, j'ai peu de goût pour en écrire une. Une note pourtant s'impose ici.

La première édition française de mon livre a été traduite de la version américaine que je n'ai jamais considérée comme complète. Je me trouvais à cette époque-là aux Etats-Unis et il ne me semblait pas possible d'y faire paraître mon livre dans sa version intégrale. L'occasion de publier cette dernière me fut offerte lorsque j'ai rencontré à Paris mon éditeur français.

Voici donc l'édition non expurgée. Est-ce à dire que la version américaine avait subi des altérations arbitraires? Certes non. Il s'agissait plutôt d'une contrainte que je m'étais à moi-même imposée et que je voudrais pouvoir nommer : une censure par anticipation. Cette même contrainte existe dans l'esprit de beaucoup d'écrivains américains qui sont conscients de préférences du public à propos

What is the purpose of a preface? Apology? Explanation? Commentary? Indication of weakness or of bad faith—if it is written by the author—or obligatory praise, perhaps, if the work of another. I never understood the purpose of prefaces, and I have little desire to write one. A note, nonetheless, is called for here.

The first French edition of my book was translated from the American version, which I never considered to be complete. I was in the United States at the time and it didn't seem possible to me to bring out my book in its integral version. The possibility of publishing the latter was offered to me when I met my French editor in Paris.

Here then is the unexpurgated version. Is that to say that the American version was subject to arbitrary alterations? Certainly not. It was rather a constraint that I imposed upon myself and that I would like to be able to name: a censorship by anticipation. This same constraint exists in the mind of many American writers who are conscious of the preferences of the audience *duquel ils écrivent et qui connaissent bien aussi l'idée que se font de notre public ceux qui le servent.*

Il est difficile chez nous de servir à chacun ses quatre vérités, surtout lorsqu'il s'agit de ce conflit essentiel qui existe entre les principes de notre mode de vie et les exigences de la condition humaine. Ce conflit est latent dans tous les cœurs de notre pays, et il tourmente beaucoup d'entre nous. Nous nous détournons de cette vérité terrifiante avec ce que j'appellerai une sorte de mauvaise foi commune. C'est ce qui m'a poussé à m'exprimer avec certaines réticences au cours de mon travail initial. Mais après y avoir réfléchi, j'ai senti qu'il me fallait tenter de parvenir jusqu'aux causes de cette crise morale dont souffre tant la jeunesse que je décris ici.

about whom they are writing, and who also understand quite well how that audience is viewed by those that serve it.

It is difficult for us to offer each reader the unvarnished truth, especially when it concerns the essential conflict that exists between the principles of our way of life and the demands of the human condition. This conflict lies latent in all the hearts in our country and torments many of us. We turn away from this terrifying truth with what I would term a kind of collective bad faith. This is what led me to express myself with some reticence in the course of my initial work. But after having reflected on it, I felt obliged to try to arrive at the causes of this moral crisis that so afflicts the youth whom I describe in this book.

P. M.

Or as one contemporary critic wrote, after comparing the original with the new version: "Julliard, give us back the untutored freshness of the original work!"

The indictments of American capitalist society that Pamela Moore added to the French edition in 1956 turned out to be very good for business. *Chocolates for Breakfast* did well in France, remaining in print well into the 1970s. Moore's popularity in France also extended to her later books, which were better received abroad than in the United States. The French *nouvelle* ▶

édition also used as the basis for other translations, including the Italian edition published by Mondadori, which sold hundreds of thousands of copies and remained in print as late as 2005.

Edited or Censored Passages in the American Manuscript

But to return to the original manuscript, which Pamela had submitted to Rinehart in early 1956, the cutting of dozens of manuscript pages from the American published version may have been the decision of Moore herself; her agent, Monica McCall; or her editor at Rinehart, Sandy Richardson. Many of these passages underscore the sensual connection between Courtney and Miss Rosen. For example:

> Miss Rosen flinched. She got up and put her hand on Courtney's shoulder. Courtney felt the touch through her whole body, and the sensation was an agreeable one. Often at night she thought about Miss Rosen touching her, and being with her all the time, not just for a few hours in the evening. She would like to have that warm feeling more of the time instead of the loneliness. (Original manuscript, p. 17)

Unlike the lofty, sometimes stilted language of the French *nouvelle édition*, the passages cut from the conversation between Janet and Courtney about Miss Rosen sound much like the conversation of two teenagers discussing a taboo subject:

> "I don't dig this *thing* you two have," [Janet] went on. "You know, I was up in Alberts and Clarke's room before lunch, and they were talking about you and Miss Rosen. I'd watch out if I were you."
>
> "What do you mean, 'Watch out'?"
>
> "What I mean is, she seems queer as hell to me. Now don't flip, I mean it. I know she's engaged and all that, but she's not sleeping with the guy or anything, and funny things happen to people in boarding school. She's got this fixation on you, and she wants to make you a little Miss Rosen, and she loves the fact that you worship her."

"So what? You think of everything in terms of sex. I have a crush on her, everyone knows that, and like any teacher she loves to work with an intelligent student and feel that she's developing a person." (p. 4)

And the deleted portion of the teachers' conversation on the same topic sounds plausibly the way teachers might talk about it:

> The staff members began to get concerned about Courtney, and one afternoon in the staff parlor, where they could smoke, they talked about her . . .
> Miss Rosen was not there . . .
> . . . "Well, if we may speak frankly," said Mrs. Reese, "the relationship that Farrell had with Miss Rosen was— well, *unnatural*. Not that Miss Rosen had anything to do with that," she added hastily. (p. 34)

Here is Courtney watching Barry, her first lover, as he sleeps:

> She constructed his body beneath the blanket, lean and pale with an almost girlish grace. Then she felt almost embarrassed, with the sensual self-consciousness that she had known at Scaisbrooke when Miss Rosen leaned over her. (p. 55)

From her death in 1964 until the late 1990s, Pamela Moore was mentioned only in passing—and often in lists of lesbian fiction. In a 1965 article entitled "Feminine Equivalents of Greek Love in Modern Fiction," Marion Zimmer Bradley, who later wrote the bestselling *The Mists of Avalon*, compared *Chocolates for Breakfast* favorably with several novels about the obsessive love of a young girl for an older woman. Courtney, she wrote, "is taken up by a friendly, kindly teacher; but just as Courtney is coming out of her shell, the teacher realizes the nature of this attachment and rebuffs her . . . [T]his rejection of her overwhelming need for love touches off the sexual promiscuity and dissipation which characterize Courtney's later adolescent years." In *Contingent Loves: Simone de Beauvoir and Sexuality* (2000), Melanie ▶

Hawthorne surveyed French novels that feature an erotic bond between schoolgirls and older female teachers, and she cited *Chocolates for Breakfast* among the English language counterparts to this genre.

It would seem that these and other characterizations of *Chocolates for Breakfast* as lesbian fiction were based on little more than the schoolgirl crush depicted in the book's first chapter. But the relationship becomes more complex in light of the passages deleted from the manuscript. One can view these cuts as censorship, or self-censorship, or perhaps the editing process of paring a book down to a more suggestive, essential form. If the work is done artfully, the missing material might be sensed though not seen. It's as if a face were cropped from a photograph in such a way that certain viewers still perceive it to be there—a ghost image of a desire deferred, of original love and loss. ⌀

K. K.

Janet threw the banana peel across the room into the wastebasket. She picked up a mirror and began to pluck her eyebrows. Janet was sixteen, spontaneous, gay, attractive if usually too heavily made up, and loathed by women of any age. At Scaisbrooke, where lipstick and fur coats were prohibited, she made a fetish of looking unattractive, in a wrinkled uniform and shoes barely clean enough to pass morning inspection. She had just come from New York and a round of sub-deb parties and nightclubs, however, and she plucked her eyebrows by inadvertence.

"I don't dig this *thing* that you two have," she went on. "You know, I was up in Alberts and Clarke's room before lunch, and they were talking about you and Miss Rosen. ~~I'd watch out if I were you.~~"

"What do you mean, 'watch out'?"

"What I mean is, she seems queer as hell to me. Now don't flip, I mean it. I know she's engaged and all that, but she's not sleeping with the guy or anything, and funny things happen to people in boarding school. She's got this fixation on you, and she wants to make you a little Miss Rosen, and she loves the fact that you worship her."

"So what? You think of everything in terms of sex. I have a crush on her, everyone knows that, and like any teacher she loves to work with an intelligent student and feel that she's developing a person."

"~~Oh, here we go, Sweetie.~~ I've been meaning to talk to you for a long time about ~~this~~ her. I've gotta stretch first, though. Arm yourself with another banana or something."

-17-

"and I have to fix her lousy drinks because she doesn't like to feel she's drinking alone, and all that. I'm <u>awfully</u> sick of it!"

"Now, although I've never met your mother," Miss Rosen said, "I know that she's a very immature woman, but you have to put up with that and try to help her. She's also a very lonely woman, and you're really all that she's got ⊣ particularly now that she's divorced again."

"You're so damned holy," Courtney said bitterly. "I mean, you're just like my father. You say all these things and it's easy for you because you don't have to live them. This is all a lot of crap."

Miss Rosen flinched. She got up and put her hand on Courtney's shoulder. Courtney felt her touch through her whole body, and the sensation was an agreeable one. Often at night she thought about Miss Rosen touching her, and being with her all the time, not just for a few hours in the evening. She would like to have that warm feeling more of the time instead of the loneliness.

"You don't have to talk that way with me," the woman said gently. "You can relax when you're here. You don't need to strike out in self-defense, through a fear of getting close to me."

Courtney stared moodily ahead. She knew that if she looked up at Miss Rosen while her hand was on Courtney's shoulder, she would get that funny feeling that she sometimes had when she was taking a bath or about to put on her pajamas, as though a whole crowd of people were looking at her body.

"You told me once," she said searching, "that you loved me."

They laughed and split a banana and when Janet left for study hall Courtney stared at the ceiling again and fell asleep, although she wasn't tired.

The staff members began to get concerned about Courtney, and one afternoon in the staff parlor, where they could smoke, they talked about her.

"Her marks have dropped almost ten points this term," said her class advisor, Mlle. de Labry. "She'll pull them up in the finals because she's done well enough through the rest of the semester, but I don't like to see a good student's daily marks fall. It shows something is wrong."

Miss Rosen was not there, so Mrs. Reese said,

"Do you suppose it could have anything to do with Miss Rosen's telling her not to see her any more?"

"Possibly," said her medieval history teacher who was a friend of Miss Rosen's. "How did that come about, anyway?"

"Well, if we may speak frankly," said Mrs. Reese, "the relationship that Farrell had with Miss Rosen was - well, unnatural. Not that Miss Rosen had anything to do with that," she added hastily. "The girl's mother spoke to me about that when she was here in the spring. 'Courtney has always been a sensitive and withdrawn child,' she told me - as though that weren't clear."

"Parents always assume that we don't know their children," Mlle. de Labry remarked. "I could tell that the first time she recited in class. Her French was far above the average but she was hesitant until the third week or so, and wanted to

- 35 -

Academy coming up. I thought it strange, though."

"Yes, I have noticed her taking naps a great deal," said Mrs. Forrest. "Now, I would expect that of that roommate of hers, but Courtney is such an active girl."

"Oh, dear, that Parker," said the hockey mistress. "Always getting gym excuses. Lazy child."

"Sits in her room and writes letters to all those boys who try to call her, pretending to be her father or something," sighed Mrs. Forrest.

"Yes, Parker is a problem," sighed Mrs. Reese, "breaking so many rules and not helping Farrell any. But I don't think that she'll be with us next year."

"Oh, really? I'm almost relieved to hear that," said Mrs. Forrest.

"No," Mrs. Reese answered, "Parker has been a problem to us since she entered this year. She was expelled from her last three schools, you know. But I am afraid that Farrell is developing into quite another sort of problem."

outside upset her and weighed a little on her mind.

"Since you have charge of this child," he had said,
"I shall tell you what I have found by talking to her. Courtney
has marked suicidal tendencies, and these periods of depression
bring them out. Her sleeping and her daydreaming are indications
of this desire to escape."

He had seen the worried expression on the old woman's
face, and added,

"I don't mean that she will try to commit suicide. I
only mean that she must not be left alone in these periods of
depression, because solitude will aggravate her self-destruction.
Probably she will be better when she is at home, where she feels
that she is loved."

Of course, he did not know, as Mrs. Forrest knew, that
she felt less loved at home than in Scaisbrooke, and less important, but Mrs. Forrest did not go into that. Her responsibility
ended when Courtney left Scaisbrooke; then she was her mother's
problem. She only had to watch Courtney while she was at school.
She had better not try to talk to Janet about her roommate,
because Janet had such a deep hatred of all the older generation,
particularly those who represented authority, that she would tell
Courtney and they would both laugh at an old woman's fears. But
she would have to tell Courtney's mother. That woman should be
made aware of this, whether she tried to help her child or
continued in the wild life that Mrs. Forrest assumed everyone
in Hollywood must lead.

-58-

and possibly her own, had followed the former. Unable to receive unadulterated love and security from her parents, Courtney had found a substitute. Had she insisted on being a child, she would not have survived her childhood. By becoming an adult, she had made herself indispensable to her parents, particularly her mother. She was needed; this gave her life justification. She would seek the same need in men. Never having known love, she did not feel that she could be loved; she knew that she could be needed. It was this need that she sensed in Barry Cabot; although she could not know it then, this was the attraction this weak and boyish young man held for her.

Few people understood the substitution that she had made as a child. To them, her self-sufficiency and her strength seemed to indicate that she had no home, that she had no need of a home but was somehow a self-sufficient unit. Home, to Courtney, did not mean a familiar place with books and mementos of her childhood about the room and a circle of friends of long-standing nearby. Her home was a portable unit, a thing she carried within herself. Her home was a place where she was needed, where she did not feel extraneous. She did not depend upon externals; of necessity the idea of home was not associated with any physical property.

When she was a child, home was wherever Mummy was - on location, in Hollywood, in New York. Now that she no longer saw the world as emanating from her mother, Courtney's home was anyplace where she did not feel that she was imposing on anyone. It was thus that she maintained a comparative tranquillity in a life which forbade identification with anything outside herself. Courtney was a constant visitor who must regularly

each other. They allowed themselves the luxury of refusing
to be adult, and for the first time in both their lives they
found a real happiness, living in their intricate castle of
sand.

The Three Texts of *Chocolates for Breakfast* (continued)

£ 300 294

"I don't want to leave you," ~~she said.~~

"You haven't any choice, Darling. You've outgrown this. can't, you see. I can't go on, any more than Janet could. t you can." She rose. "Have a good life, Angel," he said.

She smiled. "How foolish you are."

"You're going now," he said.

"Yes," she said. "I don't want to, but I am going. Like the little boy in that story you told me," she smiled.

"That's as it should be," he said softly.

~~There was a lingering sadness in his face as~~ he watched her walk into the silent, crystal autumn evening that lay beyond the glass doors. He fingered his drink. Winter was coming; it would soon be time for him to go south, to his island. ~~It was time to be moving on again.~~ How quickly the summer gone.

~~Courtney walked into Sardi's and saw Charles at the~~ ble. He rose and held out her chair for her.

"I'm sorry I'm a little late," she said. "I guess the parents are having a drink at Mummy's; they'll be here soon."

"Will you have a martini with me?" he said.

"Yes," she smiled.

When the waiter brought their drinks, Charles said, "What shall we drink to, darling?"

"To enchantment," she said.

"Enchantment?"

"Yes," she said. "You'll think that's awfully young of me," she smiled, "but that's what I want to drink to."

THE END

Don't miss the next book by your favorite author. Sign up now for AuthorTracker by visiting www.AuthorTracker.com.